www.skulduggerypleasant.co.uk

Also by Derek Landy:

DEREK LANDY

Skulduggery Pleasant
PLAYING WITH FIRE

HarperCollins *Children's Books*

First published in hardback in Great Britain by HarperCollins *Children's Books* 2008
HarperCollins *Children's Books* is a division of
HarperCollins*Publishers* Ltd
77-85 Fulham Palace Road, Hammersmith, London W6 8JB

The HarperCollins *Children's Books* website address is
www.harpercollinschildrensbooks.co.uk

Skulduggery Pleasant rests his weary bones on the web at
www.skulduggerypleasant.co.uk

And has a bebo page at www.bebo.com/Profile.jsp?MemberId=3605555366

Or join the Skulduggery Pleasant Appreciation Society on Facebook at
www.facebook.com/group.php?gid=4195977322

1

Copyright © Derek Landy 2008

Derek Landy asserts the moral right to be identified
as the author of this work

Illuminated letters © Tom Percival, 2008
Skulduggery Pleasant™ Derek Landy
SP logo™ HarperCollins*Publishers*

ISBN-13 978-0-00-725704-1
ISBN-10 0-00-725704-X

Printed and bound in Australia by Griffin Press

This book is dedicated to my family — because otherwise I'd never hear the end of it...

Nadine: warm, kind and considerate. I am all of these things.

Audrey: the greatest thrill of your life is probably the fact that I'm your brother.

Ivan: meaningless words such as "brilliant", "amazing" and "inspirational" have been used to describe me, but not nearly enough.

If any of you thought that there'd be anything sincere or heartfelt in your dedications, allow me a moment to quietly laugh at you...

Because the heartfelt sincerity is reserved for my nana.

Chic, this book is also dedicated to you, for all the love and support you've shown me over the years. I love you much more than any of your other grandchildren do, I swear.

1

HANGING AROUND

Valkyrie Cain hit the parapet and tumbled, unable to stop herself, and with a panicked gasp she disappeared off the edge.

The church tower stood high and proud, looking out over Dublin City. The night breeze was brisk and carried snatches of laughter from the street below. It was a long way down.

A man in a tattered coat walked up to the edge and peered over. He smirked.

"This is insulting," he said. "Don't they know how dangerous I am? I am very, very dangerous. I'm a killer. I'm a trained killing *machine*. And still, they send *you*. A *child*."

Valkyrie felt her grip on the ledge loosen. She ignored the goading of the man standing above her, and looked around for something else to grab on to. She looked everywhere but down. Down was where the street was, where the long drop and the sudden stop was. She didn't want to look down. She didn't want anything to do with *down* right now.

"What age are you?" the man continued. "Thirteen? What kind of responsible adult sends a thirteen-year-old child to stop me? What kind of thinking is that?"

Valkyrie swung herself gently towards the tower, planting her feet against a small buttress. The fear started to work through her and she felt herself freeze up. She closed her eyes against the oncoming wave of paralysis.

The man was Vaurien Scapegrace, currently wanted in five countries for various counts of attempted murder. He hunkered down at the edge and smiled happily.

"I am turning murder into an art form. When I – when I *kill*, I'm actually painting a big, big picture, using blood and, and... messiness. You know?"

Below Valkyrie, the city twinkled.

"I'm an artist," Scapegrace continued. "Some people don't appreciate that. Some people don't recognise true talent when they see it. And that's fine. I'm not bitter. My time will come."

"Serpine tried to bring the Faceless Ones back," Valkyrie managed to say. Her fingers were burning and the muscles in her legs were screaming at her. "We stopped him. We'll stop you, too."

He laughed. "What, you think I want the old gods to walk the earth once again? Is that it? You think Nefarian Serpine was my leader? I'm not one of those nutbag disciples, all right? I'm my own man."

Valkyrie had one chance, but she needed to be calm to take advantage of it. Her powers, limited though they were, were Elemental – the manipulation of earth, air, fire and water. But at this stage of her training they didn't work when she was panicking.

"So if you don't want the Faceless Ones to return," she said, "what *do* you want? Why are you doing this?"

He shook his head. "You wouldn't understand. It's grown-up stuff. I just want a little appreciation for who I am, that's all. That's not much to ask, is it? But of course, you wouldn't know. You're just a kid." He shrugged. "Oh, well. Time to die." He reached down to shove her.

"Have you killed anyone?" she asked quickly.

"What? Did you miss what I said, about turning murder into an art form?"

"But you haven't actually *killed* anyone yet, have you? I read your file."

He glowered. "Technically, yeah, all right, maybe I haven't, but tonight's the night. You're going to be my first."

She readied herself, controlled her breathing. "Find the space where everything connects," she murmured.

Scapegrace frowned. "What?"

Valkyrie kicked upwards, taking her right hand from the outcrop and feeling the air against her palm. She pushed at it like she'd been taught, and it shimmered and hit Scapegrace, throwing him off his feet. Valkyrie clutched at the edge of the parapet, her legs swinging in open air. She grunted and pulled herself up, then flung her left arm across the edge and hauled herself the rest of the way. She got to her feet, her arms and legs trembling with the strain, and moved away from the edge. The wind whipped her dark hair across her face.

Scapegrace was already getting up and Valkyrie saw anger mottle his face. She clicked her fingers, generating a spark that she caught in her hand. She tried to focus, tried to build it into a flame, but Scapegrace was coming at her like a freight train.

Valkyrie jumped and thrust out both feet. Her boots

slammed into his chest and he hit the ground again and went sprawling. He turned to her just as she lashed a kick into his jaw. His body twisted and he tumbled back, came up to his feet then lost his balance, fell again. He spat blood and glared.

"You little brat," he snarled. "You uppity, sneaky little *brat*. You don't know who you're messing with, do you? I am going to be the greatest killer the world has ever known." He stood up slowly, wiping his sleeve across his burst lip. "When I'm finished with you I'm going to deliver your mutilated, bloody corpse to your masters, as a warning. They sent you up against me, alone. Next time they're going to have to send a battalion."

Valkyrie smiled, and Scapegrace's anger flared. "*What the hell is so funny?*"

"First of all," she said, her confidence growing, "they're not my *masters*. I don't have a *master*. Second, they don't need a battalion to take you down. And third – and this really is the most important point – whoever said I came alone?"

Scapegrace frowned, turned, saw someone walking up behind him, a skeleton in a black suit, and he tried to attack, but a gloved fist hit his face, a foot hit his shin and an elbow slammed into his chest. He fell in an awkward heap.

Skulduggery Pleasant turned to Valkyrie. "You all right?"

"I'll kill you both!" Scapegrace howled.

"Hush," Skulduggery said.

Scapegrace launched himself forward and Skulduggery moved into him, grabbed his outstretched arm and spun him around, then abruptly cut him off by slamming a forearm into his throat. Scapegrace flipped in midair, landed painfully. Skulduggery turned to Valkyrie again.

"I'm OK," she said. "Really."

Scapegrace had his hands to his face. "I think you broke my nose!" They ignored him.

"He talks a lot," Valkyrie said, "but I don't think he knows what all the words mean."

Scapegrace leaped up. "I am the Killer Supreme! I make murder into an art form!"

Skulduggery hit him again and Scapegrace did a little twirl before falling.

"Vaurien Scapegrace," he said, "by the power endowed unto me under the Sanctuary Rule of Justice, I am placing you under arrest for the attempted murder of Alexander Remit and Sofia Toil in Oregon, Cothurnus Ode and Armiger Fop in Sydney, Gregory Castallan and Bartholomew—"

Scapegrace tried one last desperate attack that Skulduggery cut short by punching him very hard on the nose. The Killer Supreme wobbled, collapsed and started crying.

2

KILLER ON THE LOOSE

The car was a 1954 Bentley R-Type Continental. It sliced through the quiet Dublin night like a black shark, gleaming and powerful. It was a beautiful car. Valkyrie had grown to love it almost as much as Skulduggery did.

They turned on to O'Connell Street, passed the Spire and the Pearse Monument. Scapegrace sat in the back and complained that the shackles were too tight. It was four in the morning. Valkyrie fought a yawn.

This time last year she would have been in bed, snuggled up

and dreaming about... well, whatever it was she dreamed about back then. Things were a lot different now, and she was lucky if she could get a few hours sleep a night. If she wasn't going up against crazies like Scapegrace, she was practising magic, and if she wasn't practising magic, she was training to fight with either Skulduggery or Tanith Low. These days, her life was a lot more exciting, a lot more fun, and a lot more dangerous. In fact, one of the major downsides to her new life was that she rarely had sweet dreams any more. When she slept, it was the nightmares that came to her. They waited patiently, and they were always eager to play.

But that was the cost, she reasoned. The cost of living a life of adventure and excitement.

The owners of the Waxworks Museum had closed it down after the events of the previous year, and set up a new and improved version of the Sanctuary of the Elders in another part of the city. The new building stood quietly beside its neighbours, humble and drab, its front doors closed and locked and sealed. But Valkyrie and Skulduggery had never used the front doors anyway.

They parked in the loading area at the back and took Scapegrace in through the rear door. The corridors were dimly lit, and they walked past the lonely historical figures and cinematic icons that had been left to collect dust. Valkyrie traced her hand along the wall to find the switch, and the door slid open beside her. She led the way through and down the steps, her mind flashing back to the summer of the previous year, when she had stepped into the Sanctuary's foyer to find it littered with dead bodies...

Today, however, there were no corpses in sight. Two Cleavers stood guard against the far wall, dressed all in grey, their scythes strapped to their backs, visored helmets pointing straight ahead. The Cleavers acted as the Sanctuary's law enforcers and its army. Silent and lethal, they still gave Valkyrie the creeps.

The double doors to their left opened and the new Grand Mage, Thurid Guild, came out to them. He looked to be in his sixties, with thinning grey hair, a lined face and cold eyes.

"You found him then," Guild said. "Before or after he managed to kill someone?"

"Before," Skulduggery said. Guild grunted and gestured to the Cleavers. They stepped forward and Scapegrace shrank away from them. They took him firmly by the arms and he didn't resist. He even stopped whining about his broken nose as they led him away.

Valkyrie looked back at Guild. He wasn't a friendly man by any means, but he seemed especially uncomfortable around her, like he wasn't yet sure if he should take her seriously. He tended to speak directly to Skulduggery, and only glanced at Valkyrie when she asked a question.

"A situation has arisen which requires your attention," said Guild. "This way."

Skulduggery fell into step beside the Grand Mage, but Valkyrie stayed two paces behind. Guild had taken over as head of the Council of Elders, but he still had to select the two sorcerers who would rule with him. It was a long and arduous process apparently, but Valkyrie suspected she knew who would be Guild's first choice. He was a man who respected power, after all, and there were few more powerful in this world than Mr Bliss.

They walked into a room with a long table, and Mr Bliss rose – bald, tall and broad shouldered, his eyes a piercing blue.

"I have received some disturbing news," Bliss said, getting straight to the point as usual. "It seems that Baron Vengeous has been freed from the confinement facility in Russia."

Skulduggery was silent for a moment. When he spoke, he spoke slowly. "How did he get out?"

"Violently, from the reports we've been getting," Guild said.

"Nine Cleavers were killed, along with approximately one third of the prisoners. His cell, like all the cells, was securely bound. Nobody should have been able to use magic in any of them."

Valkyrie raised an eyebrow and Skulduggery answered her unspoken question. "Baron Vengeous was one of Mevolent's infamous Three Generals. Dangerously fanatical, extremely intelligent, and very, very powerful. I saw him *look* at a colleague of mine and my colleague... ruptured."

"Ruptured?"

Skulduggery nodded. "All over the place." He turned to Guild. "Do we know who freed him?"

The Grand Mage shook his head. "According to the Russians, one wall of his cell was cracked. Still solid, but cracked, like something had hit it. That's the only clue we have at the moment."

"The prison's location is a closely guarded secret," Bliss said. "It is well hidden and well protected. Whoever is behind this had inside knowledge."

Guild made a face. "That's the Russians' problem, not ours. The only thing we have to concern ourselves with is stopping Vengeous."

"You think he'll come here then?" Valkyrie asked.

Guild looked at her and she saw his fist clench. He probably didn't even realise he was doing it, but it signalled to Valkyrie loud and clear that he still didn't like her.

"Vengeous will come home, yes. He has a history here." He looked at Skulduggery. "We have already sent our people to airports and docks around the country, in the hope of preventing him from entering. But you know better than anyone how difficult the Baron is to... contain."

"Indeed," Skulduggery murmured.

"I think we can assume," Guild continued, "that if Baron Vengeous is not already here, then he will be arriving shortly. You arrested him eighty years ago. I'm relying on you to do it again."

"I'll do my best."

"Do better, Detective."

Skulduggery observed Guild for a moment before answering. "Of course, Grand Mage."

Guild dismissed them with a curt nod, and as they were walking back through the corridors, Valkyrie spoke.

"Guild doesn't like me."

"That's true."

"He doesn't like you either."

"That *is* mystifying."

"So what about Vengeous? Is he bad news?"

"The worst. I don't think he's ever forgotten the time I threw a bundle of dynamite at him. It didn't kill him obviously, but it definitely ruined his day."

"Is he all scarred now?"

"Magic gets rid of most *physical* scars, but I like to think that I scarred him emotionally."

"How about on the Evil Villain Scale? Ten being Serpine, one being Scapegrace?"

"The Baron, unfortunately, turns it all the way up to eleven."

"Seriously? Because, you know, that's one more evil."

"It is indeed."

"So we're in trouble then."

"Oh, yes," said Skulduggery darkly.

3

VENGEOUS

The first thing Baron Vengeous did when he set foot on Irish soil was murder someone. He would have preferred to arrive without incident, to have stepped off the boat and disappeared into the city, but his hand had been forced. He had been recognised.

The sorcerer had seen him, picked him out in the crowd as he disembarked. Vengeous had walked away from the crowd, led the sorcerer somewhere quiet, out of the way. It was an easy kill. He had taken the sorcerer by surprise. A brief struggle and Vengeous' arm had wrapped around the man's throat. He hadn't even needed to use his magic.

Once he had disposed of the body, Vengeous walked deeper into Dublin City, relishing the freedom that was his again after so long.

He was tall and his chest was broad, his tightly-cropped beard the same gun-metal grey as his hair. His clothes were dark, the jacket buttons polished to a gleam, and his boots clacked on the streetlit pavements. Dublin had changed dramatically since he'd been here last. The world had changed dramatically.

He heard the quiet footsteps behind him. He stopped but he didn't turn. The man in black had to walk around him, into his line of sight.

"Baron," the man said in greeting.

"You're late."

"I'm here, which is the main thing."

Vengeous looked into the man's eyes. "I do not tolerate insubordination, Mr Dusk. Perhaps you have forgotten."

"Times have changed," Dusk responded evenly. "The war is over."

"Not for us."

A taxi passed, and the sweeping headlights illuminated Dusk's pale face and black hair. "Sanguine isn't with you," he noted.

Vengeous resumed walking, Dusk by his side. "He will join us soon, have no fear."

"Are you sure you can trust him? I appreciate that he freed you from prison, but it took him eighty years to do it."

Were Dusk any other man, this remark would have been the height of hypocrisy, as he himself had not lifted one finger to help Vengeous either. But Dusk was not any other man. Dusk was scarcely a man, *and as such, loyalty was not in his nature. A certain level of obedience perhaps, but not loyalty. Because of this, Vengeous harboured no resentment towards him.*

The resentment he harboured towards Sanguine *on the other hand...*

Dusk's breathing suddenly became strained. He reached into his coat and fumbled with a syringe, then jabbed the needle into his forearm. He depressed the plunger, forcing the colourless liquid into his bloodstream, and moments later he was breathing regularly again.

"I'm glad to see you're still in control," Vengeous said.

Dusk put the syringe away. "I wouldn't be much good to you if I wasn't, would I? What do you need me to do?"

"There will be some obstacles to our work, some enemies we will no doubt face. The Skeleton Detective for example. Apparently he has an apprentice now – a dark-haired girl. You will wait for them outside the Sanctuary, tonight, and you will follow them, and when she is alone, you will fetch her for me."

"Of course."

"Alive, Dusk.*"*

There was a hesitation. "Of course," Dusk repeated.

4

THE BEAUTY, THE BEAST

They left the Sanctuary and drove across town, until they came to a street lined with ugly tenement buildings. Skulduggery parked the Bentley, wrapped his scarf around his jaw and pulled his hat down low, and got out.

"I notice you haven't mentioned how I was thrown off a tower tonight," Valkyrie said as they crossed the road.

"Does it need mentioning?" Skulduggery queried.

"Scapegrace threw me off a tower. If *that* doesn't require mentioning then what does?"

"I knew you could handle it."

"It was a *tower*." Valkyrie led the way into one of the tenement buildings.

"You've been thrown off higher," Skulduggery said.

"Yes, but you were always there to catch me."

"So you've learned a valuable lesson – there will be times when I'm not there to catch you."

"See, that sounds to me like a lesson I could have been *told*."

"Nonsense. This way, you'll never forget."

Skulduggery removed his disguise as they climbed the stairs. Just as they reached the second floor, Valkyrie stopped and turned to him.

"Was it a test?" she asked. "I mean, I know I'm still new at this, I'm still the rookie. Did you hang back to test me, to see if I'd be able to handle it alone?"

"Well, kind of," he said. "Actually, no, nothing like that. My shoelace was untied. That's why I was late. That's why you were alone."

"I could have been killed because you were tying your *shoelace*?"

"An untied shoelace can be dangerous," Skulduggery said. "I could have tripped."

She stared at him. A moment dragged by.

"I'm joking," he said at last.

She relaxed. "Really?"

"Absolutely. I would never have tripped. I'm far too graceful."

He moved past her and she glowered then followed him to the third floor. They walked to the middle door and a slight man with large round spectacles and a bow tie opened it and let them in.

The library was a vast labyrinth of tall bookcases, one that Valkyrie had managed to get herself lost in no fewer than eleven times. It seemed to amuse Skulduggery no end whenever she found herself at a dead end, or even better, back where she had started, so she let him lead the way.

China Sorrows passed in front of them, wearing a dark trouser suit with her black hair tied off her face. She stopped and smiled when she saw them. The most exquisitely beautiful woman Valkyrie had ever seen, China had a habit of making people fall in love with her at first glance.

"Skulduggery," she said. "Valkyrie. So good to see you both. What brings the Sanctuary's esteemed investigators back to my door? I'm assuming it *is* Sanctuary business?"

"You assume correctly," Skulduggery said. "And I'm sure you already know why we're here."

Her smile turned coy. "Let me think... a certain recently-liberated Baron? You want to know if I've heard any particularly juicy rumours?"

"Have you?" Valkyrie asked.

China hesitated, looked around and gave them another smile. "Let us talk privately," she said, leading them out of the library and across the hall, into her luxurious apartment. Once Skulduggery had closed the door she took a seat.

"Tell me, Valkyrie," she said, "how much do you know about Baron Vengeous?"

Valkyrie sat on the couch, but Skulduggery remained standing. "Not a whole lot," she said. "He's dangerous. I know that much."

"Oh yes," China agreed, her blue eyes twinkling in the lamplight. "Very dangerous. He is a fanatical follower of the Faceless Ones, and there is nothing more dangerous than a zealot. Along with Nefarian Serpine and Lord Vile, Vengeous was one of Mevolent's most trusted generals. He was assigned to their most secret operations. Have you ever heard of the Grotesquery, my dear?" Valkyrie shook her head.

"Before he was caught, Baron Vengeous was given the task of resurrecting a Faceless One from the remains found in a long-forgotten tomb."

Valkyrie frowned. "Is that even possible? Bringing one of them back to life after all this time?"

It was Skulduggery who answered her. "Bringing a Faceless One back *whole* proved to be beyond his abilities, so Vengeous combined the remains with parts and organs from other creatures, forming a hybrid, what he called a Grotesquery. But even then an ingredient was missing."

China took over. "Two ingredients actually. First, he needed a Necromancer's power to revive it and then, once it was alive, he needed something to keep it that way.

"When Lord Vile died, Vengeous thought he could harness Vile's power. Vile was a Necromancer, a practitioner of death magic – shadow magic. It is the Necromancer way to place most of their power in an object, or a weapon or, in this case, his armour."

"So if Vengeous wore that armour," Valkyrie said, "he'd have all Vile's power..."

"But he couldn't find the armour," Skulduggery said. "Lord Vile died alone, and his armour was lost."

"What about the other missing ingredient? Did he find out what that was?"

China answered. "From what I have heard, yes. He did."

"So what is it?"

"He knows. We don't."

"Ah."

"Fortunately for us, and the world at large, Skulduggery was around to foil this plot before Vengeous could find the armour and retrieve this mysterious missing ingredient. He tracked the Baron to a known enemy hideaway and brought him to justice, in what became one of the most talked-about battles of the entire war. Skulduggery was badly injured in that fight, if I remember correctly."

Valkyrie looked at Skulduggery and he folded his arms.

"This is a history lesson," he said. "Why are we going over this?"

"Because," China said with a smile, "I have heard that this final missing ingredient – whatever it is – has at last been recovered, or at least located, by the Baron's associates."

Skulduggery's head tilted. "Who *are* these associates?"

"I'm afraid not even I know that."

"So if Vengeous now has the missing ingredient," Valkyrie said uneasily, "can he revive the, uh, the Grow Thing?"

"Grotesquery," China corrected.

"And no," Skulduggery said, "it's impossible. He'd need Vile's armour, which he doesn't have."

"But if he *did*, and he revived this thing, what would it do? Would we be able to stop it?"

Skulduggery hesitated for a split second. "The threat the Grotesquery would pose is a little bigger than that. Theoretically, it would be able to summon the Faceless Ones back to this world by opening a portal through realities."

"A portal?" Valkyrie said, a little doubtfully.

"Yes, but the Grotesquery would have to be at full strength to do it and that's not going to happen."

"Why not?"

"A heart had to be provided for it, but the only one suitable was the heart of a Cu Gealach."

"I'm sorry?"

"Cú na Gealaí Duibhe," China said, "to give it its full Irish title. They *do* still teach you Gaelige in school, yes?"

"Yes, it means... it's Black Hound of something, right?"

"Almost. Hound of the Black Moon. Terrible creatures. They're virtually extinct now, but they were ruthless, savage things."

"Ruthless, savage things," Skulduggery said, "that were only ruthlessly savage for one night every few years, at a lunar eclipse. So no matter how much power Vengeous pumps into that thing, the Grotesquery will not be strong enough to open a portal until the Earth, moon and sun line up, which won't be for another—"

"Two nights," China said.

Skulduggery sagged and his head drooped. "Well, that's just *dandy*," he muttered.

Later, on the motorway back to Haggard, Valkyrie turned to Skulduggery. "So," she said, "a legendary battle, eh?"

Skulduggery turned his head to her. "I'm sorry?"

"The battle between you and Vengeous, the legendary one. What happened?"

"We had a fight."

"But why is it one of the most talked-about battles of the war?"

"I don't know," he said. "Maybe people had nothing else to talk about."

"China said you were badly injured. Is that why you don't like him? Because you were injured?"

"I don't like him because he's evil."

"So it's got nothing to do with him injuring you?"

"It's because he's evil," Skulduggery said grumpily.

They stayed on the motorway for another five minutes, then took the slip road. The roads became narrower and curved between darkened fields and lone houses, and then orange streetlights appeared on either side and they were driving into

Haggard. They reached the pier, and the Bentley stopped.

"Tomorrow's going to be a big day," Valkyrie said.

Skulduggery shrugged. "Maybe. Maybe not. If we can keep Vengeous out of the country, we've got nothing to worry about."

"And if we can't?"

"Then we have a whole lot to worry about, and I'm going to need you rested and alert."

"Sir, yes sir," she said, raising a mocking eyebrow. She opened the door and got out, and moments later the Bentley's tail lights disappeared into the darkness.

Valkyrie stood beside the pier for a moment, watching the dark sea churn at the rocks and play with the small boats moored nearby. She liked watching the sea. Its power made her feel safe.

Back when Valkyrie Cain's name had been Stephanie Edgley, she didn't know much about life outside of Haggard. It was a small town, tucked into the east coast of Ireland, and things there were always so quiet and peaceful and so, so *dull*.

That all changed when Nefarian Serpine murdered her uncle. Gordon was a bestselling novelist, a writer of horror and fantasy, but he was also a man who knew the Big Secret. He knew about the subculture of sorcerers and mages, about the quiet little wars they had fought. He knew about the Faceless

Ones – the terrible dark gods, exiled from this world – and the people who wanted them to return.

In the days that followed, she had met the Skeleton Detective and learned that she had a bloodline that could be traced back to the world's first sorcerers, the Ancients. She was also faced with taking a new name. Everyone, Skulduggery had told her, has three names – the name they are born with, the name they are given, and the name they take. The name they are born with, their true name, lies buried deep in their subconscious. The name they are given, usually by their parents, is the only name most people will ever know. But this is a name that can be used against them, so sorcerers must take a third name to protect themselves.

And so Stephanie Edgley became Valkyrie Cain, and she started on the road to becoming an Elemental – she started to learn magic.

Valkyrie sneaked behind her house, stood directly beneath her window and concentrated. Until a few weeks ago, she had needed a ladder to climb up to her room, but every lesson with Skulduggery gave her more control over her powers.

She took her time, felt the calmness flow through her. She flexed her fingers, feeling the air touch her skin, feeling the fault lines between the spaces. She felt how they connected, and recognised how each would affect the other once the right amount of pressure was applied...

She splayed her hands beneath her and the air rippled and she shot upwards, just managing to grab the windowsill. She still missed it occasionally, but she was getting better. She opened the window and, grunting with exertion, pulled herself through. Moving as quietly as she could, she closed the window behind her and turned on the light.

She ignored the girl who sat up in her bed, the girl who was an exact replica of herself. She went to the door, put her ear to it and listened. Satisfied that her parents were sound asleep, Valkyrie shrugged off her coat as her replica stood up.

"Your arm," it said. "It's bruised."

"Had a little run-in with a bad guy," Valkyrie answered, keeping her voice low. "How was your day?"

"School was OK. I did all the homework, except the last maths question. I didn't know how to do that. Your mum made lasagne for dinner."

Valkyrie kicked off her boots. "Nothing strange happened?"

"No. A very normal day."

"Good."

"Are you ready to resume your life?"

"I am."

The reflection nodded, went to the full-length mirror and stepped through, then turned and waited. Valkyrie touched the glass and a day's worth of memory flooded into her mind as the reflection changed, the clothes Valkyrie was wearing appearing on it, and then it was nothing more then a reflected image in a mirror.

She sifted through the new memories, arranging them beside the memories she'd formed on her own. There had been a careers class in school. The teacher had tried to get them to declare what they wanted to be when they left school, or at least what they'd like to study in college. Nobody had any idea of course. The reflection had stayed quiet too.

Valkyrie thought about this. She didn't really *need* a regular career after all. She was set to inherit Gordon's estate and all his royalties when she turned eighteen anyway, so she'd never be short of money. Besides, what kind of career would interest her outside of magic? If she'd been in that class, she knew what she would have answered. *Detective.* That would have garnered a few sniggers around the room, but she wouldn't have minded.

The main difference between her and her friends was not the magic, she knew, and nor was it the adventure. It was the fact that she knew what she wanted to do with her life, and she was already doing it.

Valkyrie undressed, pulled on her Dublin football jersey and climbed into bed. Twenty seconds later she was asleep.

5

THE TERROR OF LONDON

A dark shape flitted high above the streets of London, moving from rooftop to rooftop, spinning and twisting and cavorting in the air. He wore no shoes and his footsteps were light, his tread no more than a whisper, snatched away by the night breeze. He sang to himself as he moved, and giggled, a high-pitched giggle. He was dressed in black, with a battered top hat that stayed perched on his misshapen head no matter what acrobatic feat he performed. His suit was torn, old and musty, and his long-fingered hands were tipped with long, hardened nails.

He landed on one leg on the edge of a rooftop and stayed there, his lanky body curled. He looked down on to Charing Cross Road, at the people passing below him, at the cars zipping by. His cracked lips pursed, his small eyes moving, he browsed the selection on offer, making a choice.

"Jack."

He turned quickly to see the young woman walking towards him. Her long coat was closed and the breeze played with her tousled blonde hair, teasing it across her face. And such a pretty face. Jack hadn't seen as pretty a face in many a year. His lips parted, showed small yellow teeth, and he gave her his best smile.

"Tanith," he said in a voice that was high and strained, in an accent that was a cross between East London and... something else, something unknowable. "You're lookin' ravishin'."

"And you're looking revolting."

"You are too kind, I'm sure. What brings you to my neck of the woods?"

Tanith Low shook her head. "It's not your neck of the woods any longer, Jack. Things have changed. You shouldn't have come back."

"Where was I gonna go? Old Folks' Home? Retirement Village? I'm a creature of the night, love. I'm Springheeled Jack, ain't I? I belong out here."

"You belong in a cell."

He laughed. "Me? In captivity? For what possible crime?"

"You mean, apart from murder?"

He turned his head so he was looking at her out of the corner of one eye. "That still illegal then?"

"Yes, it is."

She opened her coat, revealing the sword against her leg. "You're under arrest."

He laughed, did a flip in the air, landed on his right foot and grinned at her. "Now *this* is new. You were always pokin' your nose where it wasn't wanted, always dealin' out what you thought was justice, but you never *arrested* anyone. You a proper copper now, that it? You one of the constabulary?"

"Give up, Jack."

"Bloody hell, you are. Consider me impressed."

He dipped his head, looked at her with those small eyes of his. "What was it you used to say, before things got all rough and tumble? 'Come and have a go—"

"If you think you're hard enough."

He grinned. "Do you?"

She withdrew her sword from its scabbard. It caught a beam of moonlight and held it, and she looked back at him without expression. "I'll let you decide that."

And Springheeled Jack *sprang.*

He flipped over her and she turned, ducking the swipe of hard nails, moving again as he landed, narrowly avoiding the return swipe and twisting to face him as he came at her.

He batted the sword to one side and his right foot went to her thigh, his toenails digging in, and he clambered up, kneeling on her shoulder. She grabbed his wrist to avoid the nails. She stumbled, unable to support his weight, but he jumped before she hit the rooftop, landed gracefully as she rolled to a crouch and then he dived at her again.

They went tumbling. He heard the sword clatter from her grip, and felt her foot on his belly as she kicked. He did a flip and landed, but her fist was right there, smacked him square in the face. He took a few steps back, bright lights dancing before his eyes. She kicked his knee, and he howled in pain, then there was a grip on his wrist and a sudden wrenching. He pushed her away, his vision clearing.

"You should be leavin' me alone!" he spat. "I'm unique, me! They don't even have a name for what I am! I should be on the Endangered Species list! You should be protectin' me!"

"You know how they protect Endangered Species, Jack? They put them in a special enclosure, where no one can harm them."

His face twisted. "*Enclosure*'s a fancy word for a cell, innit? And you're not takin' me anywhere *near* a bloody cell."

And then it drifted up to them, the sound of a baby crying. Jack's expression softened and he smiled again.

"Don't even think about that," Tanith warned.

His smile turned to a grin then a leer.

"Race you," he said.

Jack ran to the edge of the building and then there was nothing beneath his feet but air, and the next rooftop swooped to meet him. He landed and ran on without missing a step. He glanced over his shoulder, saw Tanith Low trying to keep up. She was good, that girl, but this was something Jack was made for. He was the prince of London City. It let him go where it let no one else. He knew it like he knew his own face.

The baby's cry came again and he changed direction, heading away from the busier areas, tracking it over the streets and the alleyways. His powerful legs propelled him through the darkness and he spun and dug his feet into brick. He ran sideways, the length of the building. He saw Tanith moving on a parallel course, jumping from rooftop to rooftop, trying to intercept him before he reached his goal.

One last cry from the baby and Jack zeroed in on an open window, high above street level. He made a series of small jumps, building his momentum. He saw Tanith out of the corner of his eye, sprinting to catch up. *Too slow*, he thought to himself. He leaped from one side of the street to the other and dived straight in, clearing the window and going for the crib.

But the crib held only blankets, and the room was dark and unfurnished, not like a baby's room at all, and why had the window been open? It wasn't warm enough to have the window open—

The baby's cry, much louder, was coming from a small device that sat near the window.

It was a trap. She had tricked him.

He moved to the window, but she had walked up the side of the building and was climbing through.

"Out there," she said, "in the open air, I didn't have a hope of catching you. But in here, in a confined space? You're all mine, ugly."

Jack panicked, went to the door, but it wouldn't budge; there was a sheen to it he could see, even in the darkness, and he knew it would withstand whatever he had to throw at it. He whirled. The only way out was the window- the window that Tanith Low now guarded. She laid her sword on the ground, and took off her coat. Her tunic was sleeveless and her arms were strong. She rolled her neck, loosening up her shoulders, and nodded to him.

"Now," she said, "finally. Come and have a go if you think you're hard enough."

Jack roared and went for her and she kicked him. He swiped and she ducked, and smacked him across the jaw. He tried to flip over her, but the ceiling was too low and he bellyflopped into it, felt his breath leave him and crashed to the floor. After that, all that registered was a whole lot of fists and elbows and knees, and a wall that kept running into his face.

Jack collapsed. He breathed hard and groaned in pain. He stared up at the ceiling. He could see the cracks, even in the dark. Tanith stepped into view, looking down at him.

"You ready for your nice warm cell now?"

Jack whimpered.

6

FIREBALLS IN THE PARK

Valkyrie woke early. She took a pebble from her bedside table and sat on the floor, cross-legged. The pebble was flat and smooth in her hand. She focused on it like Skulduggery had taught her. She focused until she could feel the air on her skin, and she focused on how it all connected. Slowly, the pebble began to rise off her palm, held aloft by the air itself. A part of her still thrilled to see this, but she kept that part of her subdued. To use magic, she couldn't afford to let anything ruin her calm.

And then that voice, drifting up the stairs like the whine of a dentist's drill, and the pebble fell back into her hand. Muttering to herself, Valkyrie stood up and walked into the bathroom, her practice done for the day. She took a shower then pulled on her school uniform before heading down to the kitchen.

Her mother was there, and sitting beside her was Valkyrie's shrill, sharp-featured aunt, Beryl.

"Morning," Valkyrie said as she passed them, going straight for the cupboard.

"Hi, love," her mother said.

"Good morning, Stephanie," Beryl said primly.

"Beryl," Valkyrie said in greeting.

"How is school going for you?"

Valkyrie poured some cereal into her bowl and added milk. She didn't bother sitting. "It's OK."

"Are you studying hard? My girls are always studying. They get it from my side of the family, I have to say. It's a valuable work ethic I've instilled in them."

Valkyrie murmured and scooped a spoonful of cereal into her mouth, doubting the validity of just about everything Beryl had just said. Her aunt didn't like her and Valkyrie didn't like her aunt. Her aunt didn't like her because Valkyrie had inherited her late uncle's estate, and Valkyrie didn't like her aunt, or her aunt's husband Fergus, because they were dislikeable people.

Her father came in, dressed in smart trousers, vest and a tie around his bare neck. He winked at Valkyrie then noticed his sister-in-law.

"Beryl," he said, utterly failing to hide his dismay.

"Desmond, good morning."

"Beryl, what are you doing here? It's not even 8 o'clock. You know I don't like seeing you before I've had my first cup of coffee."

Beryl laughed that hideous fake laugh of hers. "Oh Desmond, you're such a messer! I'm just here to talk to Melissa, that's all. We've got a lot to organise for tomorrow night."

"Oh, dear God, the family reunion thing."

"It'll be wonderful!"

"But you'll be there," her dad said, puzzled, and Valkyrie nearly choked on her cereal.

Her mum looked up at him. "You forgot your shirt."

"Oh, yes, the reason I'm here. I don't have a clean one."

"Behind the door."

He turned, saw the crisp white shirt hanging on the coat hook and rubbed his hands together. He took it off the hook and put it on, sliding the collar up beneath the tie as he buttoned it.

He didn't like wearing ties – he owned a construction company so he'd always thought he'd be in workboots and jeans. But every now and then he had to dress up and pretend – as he put it – to be civilised.

"So Steph," he said, "looking forward to a great day in school?"

"Oh yes," she said with mock enthusiasm.

"What do you think you'll learn today?"

"I can't begin to guess. Maybe how to subtract."

He waved his hand dismissively. "Subtraction's overrated. It's like adding, only backwards. You're not ever going to need it."

"Desmond!" Beryl said sternly. "You shouldn't take that attitude. Stephanie is at an easily-influenced age, and she needs to be taught that everything she learns in school is valuable. Joking around is all well and good, but some things just have to be taken seriously. How can you ever expect Stephanie to be responsible when all you ever do is set a bad example?"

"I don't know," he answered. "Luck, I suppose."

Beryl sighed in exasperation and looked like she was about to give them a lecture. Valkyrie and her father both pounced on the same opportunity before Beryl could utter another word.

"I'm going to school," Valkyrie said quickly, shovelling

the last spoonful of cereal into her mouth.

"I'm going to work," her dad said, only a millisecond behind.

Valkyrie slipped her bowl into the dishwasher and made for the door.

"But Desmond, you haven't had any breakfast," Valkyrie's mother said with a frown.

"I'll get something on the way," her father said, following her out. They got to the hallway and Valkyrie turned for the stairs as her dad picked his keys up off the small table. They looked at each other and nodded their silent goodbyes. Then they both smiled, and he walked out and she went to her room.

Not for the first time, she wondered how her father would react if he knew that the family legends were true, that they *were* descended from the Ancients, that his grandfather and his late brother had been right. But she didn't tell him. If he knew the truth, he'd try and stop her from going out every day, try to protect her from people like Serpine, and Vengeous, and whoever else wanted to kill her. Or worse, maybe he'd want to get involved. She didn't think she'd be able to cope with her father putting himself in danger. She wanted her family to be normal. Normal was good. Normal was safe.

She closed the door then took off her school jumper and

dropped it on the bed. She touched her mirror and a moment later her reflection stepped out. She had forgotten about the logo rule *once* and the reflection had gone to school with the school crest on the wrong side and the school motto written backwards. Valkyrie hadn't made that mistake again. She waited until her reflection had pulled on the jumper then handed it her schoolbag.

"Have fun," she said, and the reflection nodded and hurried out of the room.

Not for the first time, Valkyrie grinned to herself. She'd hardly been to school since Skulduggery had worked his magic on that mirror, yet she was up to date on all the classes, all the gossip, all the day-to-day workings of an ordinary, everyday, run-of-the-mill thirteen year old. Without having to actually set foot through a classroom door.

Sure, there were times when she wished she'd been there to experience something firsthand instead of reliving it through the reflection's eyes. It wasn't the same merely having the memories of, say, a joke being told, instead of actually having been around for the real thing. Just another price to pay, she reckoned.

Moving quietly, Valkyrie took off the rest of her uniform, hid it under her bed and dressed in the black clothes that had been made especially for her. She'd grown a bit since Ghastly

Bespoke had designed them, but they still fitted, and for that she was thankful. They had saved her life on more then one occasion, and it wasn't as if she could ask Ghastly to make her any more. In a fight with the White Cleaver he had used the earth power as a last-ditch defence and turned himself to stone. She hadn't known him that well, but she missed him and she knew that Skulduggery did too.

She slipped into her coat and opened the window. She breathed deep and slow. Checking to make sure she wasn't being watched, she climbed out on to the sill and paused there for a moment, focusing her mind. Then she slipped off the edge, displacing the air beneath her to slow her descent. It wasn't graceful, and her landing was still a little too hard, but it was a lot better than it had been.

She hurried down the road to the pier. When she was younger she used to join her friends there. They used to sprint for the edge and leap as far as they could over the rocks right below them, splashing down into the sparkling water. Yes, it was dangerous, and yes, poor J. J. Pearl once shattered his knee on those rocks, but the danger gave the exercise a certain extra kick. These days, J. J. walked with a slight limp and she'd long since drifted apart from her childhood friends. She missed swimming though. She didn't get to do a whole lot of that now.

The Bentley was waiting for her, parked beside a rusty old Fiat. It stood out by a mile – but then it stood out by a mile wherever it went.

"Good morning," Skulduggery said when she got in. "Well rested, are you?"

"I had two hours' sleep," she said.

"Well, no one said being a great detective leading an action-packed life was easy."

"*You* said it was easy."

"I said it was easy for *me*," he corrected. "Was that your lovely aunt's car I saw outside your house?"

"Yeah, it was," said Valkyrie, and told him about her brief run-in with Beryl.

"Family reunion?" Skulduggery said when she had finished. "Are you going?"

"And, what, leave you to stop the bad guys without me? No way. I'll send the reflection in my place, thank you very much."

"A reunion might be fun."

"Right. Fun. Because I have so much fun with that side of the family. I wouldn't mind so much if it was Mum's side – I have a laugh with them. Dad's side is just... weird, you know?"

"I do. Gordon spoke of them often. Never forget, however, that you're weird too."

She glared at him. "I'm not weird like that. I'm good weird. I'm cool weird."

"Yes," he said doubtfully. "Yes, you are."

"Shut up. But anyway, all of Dad's cousins will be there, with their families, people I hardly know and, of course, Beryl and Fergus and the Toxic Twins, and it's pretty much going to be horrible, so there's no way in hell that I'm going."

"Well, that's good enough for me."

Skulduggery started the engine and Valkyrie sat low in her seat as he pulled out on to the road and started driving.

"So have you found out anything about Vengeous?"

"One of our people at the docks hasn't reported in yet," Skulduggery said. He was wearing his usual disguise – wide-brimmed hat, overlarge sunglasses, fuzzy wig and a scarf wrapped around the lower half of his face. "It might be nothing, but..."

"But Vengeous might already be here?"

"Well, yes."

"That's bad."

"It's not good."

They were driving down Main Street and Valkyrie glanced out as they passed the bus stop. Five bored-looking teens stood in school uniform.

"My reflection's not there," she said with a frown.

"Maybe it got delayed."

She shook her head. "It left before me."

The Bentley slowed. "What do you want to do?"

"It's probably nothing. It could have cut across the Green... although it should still have made it here by now. But no, it's probably nothing."

Skulduggery pulled over to the side of the road and tilted his head at her. "You use that reflection a lot more than is recommended," he said. "You ought to expect some unusual behaviour every now and then."

"I know..."

"But you want to go and look for it, don't you?"

"I juat want to check that everything's all right. I'll get out here, go through the Green."

"I'll turn around, head back to the pier, meet up with you there."

Valkyrie nodded, made sure no one was looking and then got out of the car and ran between two buildings. She climbed the fence and dropped to the grass on the other side. The green was actually a small park, an oasis of trees and flowerbeds and a fountain, tucked behind Main Street. It was the site of many a game of football when Valkyrie was younger.

She could have been overreacting. Her reflection had probably met some people Valkyrie knew. In fact, Valkyrie herself could be the one to ruin things, by running straight into a situation that the reflection was handling with its usual efficiency. And then she heard her own scream.

Valkyrie left the main path, running towards the small clump of trees. Beyond the trees, near the fountain, there were two figures struggling. It was her reflection, trying to break free from a man in black.

"Hey!" Valkyrie shouted.

The man in black looked up. He was pale and oddly beautiful, and way too calm. "There you are," he said. "I was almost fooled. Almost. But this one doesn't feel fear. And I can *smell* fear." He thrust the reflection from him, and it stumbled to its knees.

"Get to school," Valkyrie told it. The reflection nodded, picked up the fallen schoolbag and ran past her through the trees, not even glancing back at the attacker.

Valkyrie glared. "Who are you? How did you find out where I live?"

"I followed you," he said. "I lost you when you came into town, so I decided to wait around until you showed up again. I even made some new friends."

Now she saw them, a young couple, walking towards her.

She knew them. She didn't know their names, but she'd seen them around, holding hands, laughing. They weren't laughing now. They were pale, as pale as the man in black. They looked sick and there were bloodstains on their clothes. They watched her with dark, dead eyes. Valkyrie looked at the man in black, remembered the graceful way he had moved. "You're a vampire," she breathed.

"And you are Valkyrie Cain and you're coming with us."

She couldn't fight them. There was no way she was even close to being ready.

So she ran.

The young couple were after her, sprinting, feet thudding on the grass. She kept ahead of them. She didn't even have to look back, she could hear how close they were. But she couldn't hear *him.* The man in black was running at her side, moving without effort. She tried to duck away, but he reached out a lazy hand, his fingers closing around her arm, and stopped suddenly. She jerked to a painful halt.

She swung a punch but he moved slightly and her fist connected with nothing but air. She tried to kick and he took a step, the expression on his face never going beyond bored, and he grabbed Valkyrie's arm and twisted it behind her back and her knees hit the ground.

"The Baron wants you alive," he said. "Bear in mind, he did not specify *unharmed*. Do not try to hit me again."

"How about me?" Skulduggery said as he ran up behind him. "Can *I* hit you?"

The man in black released Valkyrie and turned, too late to stop Skulduggery's fist from smacking into his jaw. He staggered and Skulduggery splayed his hand. The air rushed into the vampire and sent him backwards, head over heels. Instead of sprawling on to the grass, however, his body moved with an inhuman agility and he twisted sideways and landed on his feet.

"Detective," he murmured.

"Dusk," Skulduggery said. "It's been a while. Still evil?"

The man called Dusk smiled. "When the mood takes me." He gestured to the young couple. "Allow me to introduce you to my friends. I like to call them Minion One and Minion Two. You can decide among yourselves which one is which."

The young couple attacked. Skulduggery dodged their clumsy grabs and threw them into each other's way. Dusk blurred and in an eye-blink he was beside Valkyrie, pulling her to her feet.

Skulduggery lunged at Dusk and they went down, and Skulduggery lost his hat and scarf. Valkyrie stumbled back. Minion One, the male, snarled and came at her. He looked even worse close up. His eyes were dull and red-rimmed, and she could see the bite on his neck beneath his shirt collar. It wasn't the dainty twin pin-pricks she'd seen in the movies- his neck had been savagely torn open. She could smell the dried blood on his skin. It smelled of copper.

For a moment she panicked. His hands were gripping her collar, forcing her back, and he was strong. His girlfriend, Minion Two, was right behind him, eager to inflict some damage of her own. Valkyrie made herself relax, remembering the drills she'd run with Skulduggery and Tanith, conditioning her body to relax when every part of her wanted to scream.

She allowed herself to be pushed back. Her left hand gripped Minion One's wrist and her right hand came up between his arms to his face. She planted her left foot and dug in and twisted her hips into him, and Minion One collided with her and went over.

Minion Two snarled and punched and Valkyrie's world rocked. She deflected the grab that followed, tried a lock that didn't work then stomped on Minion Two's knee and shoved her away.

She saw Skulduggery and Dusk. Now that he could no longer be taken by surprise, Dusk's supernatural grace and athleticism were keeping him away from Skulduggery's strikes.

He swept out of range of the punches and kicks, and every hold Skulduggery tried, Dusk eased out of before it was even completed.

He kicked Skulduggery and moved backwards, and as he did so something fell from his pocket. He glanced at it and moved to retrieve it, but Skulduggery held out his hand and it flew into his grip.It was a syringe, filled with a colourless liquid.

Dusk shrugged. "You can keep it," he said. "I've got plenty more."

The Minions were regrouping. Valkyrie clicked her fingers, but failed to ignite a spark. She tried again, and this time she felt the heat of the friction. She focused, curled her hand, and let the energy pour from the centre of her body into her arm, into her palm. Then she took the spark and made it into a flame.

"Stay back," she warned. The Minions didn't answer. She didn't even know if they were *capable* of answering.

The flame expanded into a ball of fire in her hand and she hurled it right at them. And then Skulduggery was shouting something and running forwards, his arms sweeping up, and a rush of wind hit the fireball and knocked it off course even as the flames extinguished. Then he was at Valkyrie's side, holding her arm, walking backwards with her as the Minions stalked them.

"They've been infected," he said, "but they're not lost. Not yet. We don't want to kill them."

Dusk strolled after them. "It's not their fault I chose them after all."

Skulduggery glanced at her. "It takes two nights for an Infected to become a vampire. Until then, they're innocent victims."

"But in two nights," Dusk added, "this will all be over."

Skulduggery took out his gun, aimed it straight at Dusk. The Minions stopped and snarled. Dusk's smile never left his face. "This is your chance to leave," Skulduggery said.

"Why would we do that? *You're* the ones backing away. *You* can't kill my friends. *You* are losing this little altercation."

Skulduggery thumbed back the revolver's hammer. "I said we don't *want* to kill them. I didn't say we *won't.*"

"If you fire that gun," Dusk said, "you will have the whole town running to see what's going on and you've dropped your disguise."

"That's the only reason I'm not putting you out of our misery right here and now."

Dusk considered his options then shrugged. "Minions," he said, "we're leaving." The infected couple snarled their displeasure, but did as they were told. They joined Dusk as he backed away.

Skulduggery didn't lower the gun. "Tell Vengeous I expected more from him. Going after my colleague to get to me is the sort of thing Serpine tried. Tell him if he wants me then be a man and come and get me."

"The Baron is an honourable man."

"The Baron is a coward."

Dusk smiled, but didn't respond. Valkyrie stood by Skulduggery's side, and they watched Dusk and his Minions fade into the cover of the trees.

7

UNWELCOME VISITORS

The Hibernian Cinema stood like an old man, stoop-shouldered and grey-faced, squeezed in on either side by taller, broader and healthier buildings. Its façade was a decaying remnant of a forgotten time, and most of the vowels were missing from its name. Fifty years ago, this cinema had thrived, its Dublin audiences flocking to it every weekend. Skulduggery himself had first visited the Hibernian to see *High Society*, and he'd had a crush on Grace Kelly ever since.

He parked the Bentley in the lane at the back, and Valkyrie

followed him in. The carpeted surroundings absorbed their footfalls. They passed framed posters for obscure movies starring dead actors. No paying customer had been in this building for decades.

The cinema was quiet, as usual, and empty. They walked down the steps between the rows of seats. The screen had a heavy red curtain in front of it, musty with age. As they approached, the curtain parted and the screen lit up, showing an old black-and-white film. The film showed a brick wall and an open door. The soundtrack was of a city at night. Valkyrie followed Skulduggery up on to the small stage and they walked to the door, their shadows falling on to the image. Then they walked through the screen.

They took the stairs that lay on the other side and gradually the artificial light swept the gloom away. They reached the top floor, where all signs of the old cinema had been replaced by gleaming corridors and laboratories. The owner of the Hibernian had spent a lot of time renovating the building, developing it into the magic-science facility he'd always dreamed about. Because of the delicate nature of the work done in all the various sections – the medical bay, the brand-new Morgue, the Theoretical Magic (R&D) Department – there were no windows, and the temperature was carefully controlled.

Although he had the run of the entire building, shared only with his two assistants, the owner still chose to work in the smallest, darkest laboratory, and that was where they found him.

Professor Kenspeckle Grouse looked around when Skulduggery said his name. "You again," he said in a voice that was not overflowing with warmth and hospitality. "What do you want?" Kenspeckle was a small, elderly man with a mass of white hair and very little patience.

"We have something for you, Professor," Skulduggery said, showing him the syringe that had fallen from Dusk's pocket. "We were wondering if you'd have time to analyse it."

"Oh, as if I'm not kept busy enough as it is," Kenspeckle said gruffly. "Valkyrie, I haven't seen you in weeks. Staying out of trouble?"

"Not really," Valkyrie admitted.

"Nor did I expect you to," he said with an exasperated sigh. For all his crotchety behaviour and ill manners, the elderly scientist seemed to have a soft spot for Valkyrie. "So what has he dragged you into this time?"

"I haven't dragged her into anything," Skulduggery said defensively.

Valkyrie smiled. "Fights, kidnap attempts, more fights. Business as usual, you know how it is." Skulduggery's phone rang and he stepped away to answer it.

Now that Skulduggery was out of earshot, Kenspeckle let his voice soften in tone. "How is the shoulder from last month?"

"Much better," she answered. "I was barely left with a bruise."

Kenspeckle nodded. "I used a new mixture. The ingredients are a little harder to find, but for my favourite patients I like to make sure the healing process is as painless as possible."

"I'm on that list?" Valkyrie asked, her smile growing wider.

Kenspeckle snorted. "You *are* the list." Valkyrie laughed.

"Your partner certainly isn't," Kenspeckle continued, returning his attention to Skulduggery as his phone call ended. "Let me see that syringe." Skulduggery handed it over.

"Where did you get it?"

"It fell out of a vampire's pocket."

Kenspeckle held the syringe up to the light, examining the liquid within. "Fascinating creatures, vampires. Two completely separate layers of epidermis, the upper layer of which regenerates when the sun comes up. Human by day, gifted with slightly enhanced speed and strength, but essentially mortal. But at night..."

Valkyrie nodded. "I know what they're like at night."

"Hmm? Oh, that's right. You have firsthand knowledge,

don't you? How did you get that I wonder? Oh, yes." He glared at Skulduggery. "Someone with absolutely no sense of responsibility dragged you in front of a *vampire* and almost got you killed."

Skulduggery tilted his head. "Are you talking about me?" he asked innocently.

Kenspeckle scowled and went back to examining the syringe. "I've seen this before," he said, "but only once. It's a rare concoction of hemlock and wolfsbane. It would be used by a vampire to suppress his bestial nature at night."

"Makes sense," Skulduggery murmured. "Dusk is of no use to Vengeous if he loses control every time the sun goes down."

Kenspeckle loosened his tie and undid his top shirt button. "I had a run-in with a vampire in my youth, and I barely escaped with my life. That's why I carry this with me everywhere I go." He showed them a glass vial that hung around his neck.

"Is that holy water?" Valkyrie asked, a little doubtfully.

"Holy water? No, no, *no*, Valkyrie. It's *sea water*."

"Right," she said slowly.

"Holy water doesn't work," Kenspeckle explained, "and stakes through the heart won't kill them. Decapitation *is* effective, but then decapitation is effective against most things.

The one vampire legend that *does* have merit, however, is running water."

Valkyrie frowned. "OK, and that seems to be the one legend I've never heard of."

Skulduggery spoke up. "There's an old myth that vampires can't pass over running water, so they couldn't cross a bridge that spans a river, for instance. Now, while crossing bridges doesn't phase them in the slightest, the truth of the myth stems from salt water."

"Vampires have an extreme allergic reaction to the stuff," Kenspeckle said. "If ingested, it would swell a vampire's throat, blocking its air passage. Which is why I carry some with me at all times."

"But wouldn't they have to swallow it?" Valkyrie asked.

"Well, yes..."

"And how would you get a vampire to swallow the water before it killed you?" Kenspeckle blinked and didn't say anything.

"Never mind," Valkyrie said quickly. "I'm sure, you know, you'd find a way. Like, you could throw the water into its mouth when it's, uh, about to bite you."

Kenspeckle's shoulders slumped, and Valkyrie felt incredibly guilty that she had poked a hole in his plan. "Leave me," he said a little mournfully.

"I'm sorry..." Valkyrie began, but he held up his hand.

"No need to apologise. I am a *medical* genius, a *scientific* genius, but obviously not a *tactical* genius. And to think, for the last 180 years I was unafraid of vampires because I had a vial of salt water tied around my neck. What an idiot."

Kenspeckle shuffled off and Skulduggery patted Valkyrie on the shoulder. "Congratulations," he said. "You've just reinstated a 300-year old neurosis. Our work here is done."

Feeling absolutely terrible, Valkyrie followed him back the way they had come. They passed the two assistants in white labcoats, Stentor and Civet, wrestling in an empty room. Valkyrie had been here more times than she could count, and sights like this were not uncommon. The assistants waved, then got back to wrestling.

Valkyrie was the first one down the stairs, and she walked to the back of the screen and stepped through. She jumped from the stage, turned and waited for Skulduggery. She watched him pass through the image of the door, and a moment later the film flickered, the screen went blank and the gloom closed in. He left the stage and the curtains began to drift together behind him.

"Who was that on the phone?" she asked, trying to forget about what she had done to Kenspeckle.

"The Grand Mage," Skulduggery said, "checking in on us

once again. His eagerness to recover the Baron is making him quite... irritable."

"He's always irritable."

"Obviously he's decided to take it to new heights."

"I wish Meritorious was still alive. He was a good Grand Mage. Guild is... He's like a politician, like he's got people to please."

They left the cinema and walked into the bright sunshine, and Skulduggery didn't say anything until they got to the Bentley.

"We're supposed to meet Tanith at the library, so I'm going to drop you off there and meet up with you later, is that OK with you?"

"Where are you going?"

"Nowhere special. I just have some... things to do."

"Why did you pause?"

"I'm sorry?"

"You paused. You have some... things to do. Why did you pause?"

"No reason, I just—"

"You're up to something."

"No—"

"Then why'd you pause?"

"Get in the car." She got in. He got in.

"Seatbelt," he said.

"Why'd you pause?"

His head drooped. "Because I'm up to something."

"And why can't I come with you?"

"Because it's something sneaky."

"Do you promise to tell me later?"

"I do."

"Well, all right then." She clicked her seatbelt into place. "Let's go."

Valkyrie went into the tenement building and climbed the stairs, passing a man who didn't have a shadow. She got to the third floor just as China Sorrows crossed from the library to her apartment.

"Valkyrie," China said. "How nice to see you again so soon." The skirt she wore was a light green, and the jacket was of a green deeper than a thousand crushed emeralds. Her necklace was exquisite.

"That's beautiful," Valkyrie said, looking at it.

"Isn't it? This necklace has cost two very fine men their lives. At times, I wear it in tribute to their sacrifice. Other times, I wear it because it goes with this skirt. Would you like to come in?"

"Sure," Valkyrie said and followed China inside. She closed the door after her. She would never have admitted this, but Valkyrie adored China's apartment. The carpet was lush and intricate, the décor was elegant and restrained, and it looked out over Dublin in such a way that the city seemed prettier and more romantic than it had ever been.

"Any new developments?" China asked, picking up a stack of letters and rifling through them.

"Not especially. I was attacked earlier though."

"Oh?"

"By a vampire and his minions."

"Can't stand those things," China said. "Once they bite, the infected person has two nights of mindless slavery to endure, and if they're not treated, they become full vampires. Such a horrible condition. Did you happen to catch his name?"

"Dusk."

"Yes, I know Dusk. He has a habit of holding grudges. I had an associate who crossed him. It took years, but Dusk finally managed to track him down and the death he provided was not a quick one. There was a lot of blood and screaming and..."

She caught herself, and smiled. "I apologise. I must confess to being in a very bad mood of late. Because of this Grotesquery business, everything I've worked so hard for – my library, my collections, my influence – all of it could be wiped out in the blink of an indifferent eye."

"Along with the rest of the world," Valkyrie reminded her.

"Yes. That would be unfortunate also." China put the letters down. "Have you seen him yet? The Baron?"

"No. Not yet."

China sat on the luxurious yet tasteful sofa. "An unusual man. He likes to think of himself as straightforward. He is anything but. He shares the same elitist attitude as Nefarian Serpine, but where Serpine was independent and self-serving, the Baron carried out his duties with a selflessness, and a blind and unwavering faith. What Serpine began, Vengeous seeks to finish. To him, the return of the Faceless Ones is the only thing that has ever truly mattered."

"Sounds like you know him well."

"Oh, I do. Didn't Skulduggery tell you? I too used to worship the Faceless Ones."

Valkyrie felt her face drain. "What?"

China smiled. "Obviously he didn't tell you. Bliss and I were raised in a family that worshipped the dark gods. My brother rejected our family's teachings at an early age, but it took me some time to do the same. While I worshipped, however, I joined a small group of like-minded individuals, of which the

Baron was one. Remember when I told you that there is nothing more dangerous than a zealot? We were dangerous even by a zealot's standards."

"I... I didn't know that."

China shrugged. "I was young and foolish and arrogant. I've changed. I'm not foolish any more." She laughed. Valkyrie forced a smile.

"And now," China continued, "you're wondering, once again, if I can be trusted. After all, when Skulduggery first told you about me, what did he say?"

"He... he said not to trust you."

"Because I am not worthy of it, Valkyrie. I will endanger those close to me for my own advantage. I am not a nice person, my dear. I am not... one of the good guys."

"Then why does he still rely on you?"

"Because he himself has gone through change and he is no hypocrite. He will not condemn me for my past actions, so long as I don't revert to the person I once was. The war with Mevolent changed everyone who fought in it. We each saw things in ourselves that we would rather not admit to."

"What did Skulduggery see?"

"Rage. His family was murdered in front of him, and when he returned from death, his rage came with him. For most, anger that fierce can burn only for so long. Skulduggery, being Skulduggery, is the natural exception. His rage stayed."

"So what happened?"

"He disappeared. If you want my opinion, I think he saw what he was capable of and he knew he had a choice – to let that rage consume him, or to fight it. So he left. He was gone for five years. When he came back, the anger was still there, but there was something else – a realisation I think. A new purpose. He was able to joke again, which was a welcome return, for he is one of the very few men able to make me laugh. Soon after, we received word that Lord Vile had fallen, and then Skulduggery himself brought down the Baron, and Mevolent's plans began to unravel."

"Where did he go? For the five years?"

"I don't know. We all thought he was dead. Dead *again*, you know. But he came back just when we needed him. That's one thing you can count on him for – the nick-of-time rescue. He's quite good at it."

There was a knock on the door. They both stood, and from out in the corridor they heard a muffled voice and then a loud thump.

China looked at Valkyrie. "Go into the bedroom," she said quickly. "Do not argue with me. Go into the bedroom and close the door." Valkyrie did as she was told, but left the door open a crack – just enough to see through. She saw China pick up the telephone, and then the door to the apartment burst open and the slender man in the bow tie came flying through. He landed in a heap and didn't move.

A figure stepped in. He looked to be in his fifties, with grey hair and a tightly cropped beard. His clothes were dark and vaguely militaristic, and his boots were polished to a gleam. He had a cutlass in his belt.

"Hello China," he said. "It's good to see you again."

"Baron Vengeous," China said slowly and put the telephone down. "I dearly wish I could say the same. Why are you here?"

"You mean you don't know?"

"If you wish to return an overdue book, the library is across the hall. I think you will find the fine to be stern, yet reasonable."

"I'm here for you, China. Within a few hours I will have Lord Vile's armour and the final missing ingredient will be within my grasp. It's time to take off this mask you wear, to end this charade. You need to take your place."

"My place is right here."

"We both know that's not true. You could no more turn your back on the Faceless Ones than *I* could. I have seen your devotion."

"My devotion, as you call it, has waned."

Vengeous shook his head. "You have sworn your allegiance to the dark gods. You cannot simply change your mind."

"I'm afraid I can, and I have."

Through the crack in the door, Valkyrie could see the anger seeping into the Baron's face. "You are their servant," he said, his voice low and threatening. "If *you* will not uphold the vow you made on your own then *I* will do it for you. You *will* be there when the Faceless Ones return, even if it is just so you can be the first traitor they kill."

He reached for her, and China put her left hand flat on her belly and flicked her right, and every piece of furniture in the room flew at Vengeous.

Valkyrie stared, open-mouthed, as tables and chairs and bookcases crashed into Vengeous at a terrible speed. They clattered to the floor and he staggered and fell, blood running down his face. China tapped her belly twice and gestured with her right hand, sending everything – the furniture and Vengeous – skidding across the floor and slamming into the wall. Then another tap of her belly and another whip of her hand and the furniture moved away, clearing a space around the Baron.

"You do not threaten me in my own home," China said and sent the furniture hurtling back to him.

But Vengeous was quick and he lunged forward, eyes flashing yellow. The table that was coming directly for him suddenly exploded into a hundred thousand splinters and he dived through them, escaping the rest of the furniture that impacted on the wall behind him. He sent his hand into her chest and she pitched backwards. She hit the wall and fell to one knee.

Valkyrie gripped the door, about to fling it open, but China looked up at Vengeous and her eyes narrowed.

"As my words draw closed, the circle binds, secures you to your fate."

Vengeous reached for her, but hit something, an invisible wall. He tried to back off but he only got a couple of steps before he hit another barrier. He looked down, looked at the elaborate carpet and saw the circle hidden in the design.

"Clever girl..."

"You didn't think I would install some security measures?" China said.

"Very, very clever." His eyes flashed yellow.

"That's not going to work, my dear Baron. Symbols are my power. *Your* powers can't break that shield. You can't hurt me. But I can hurt you." Vengeous looked down at the carpet again, at the hidden intricacies, symbols woven into the very fabric around the circle, symbols that were now pulsing with blue energy. Blood started to run from his nose.

"China," he said, struggling to keep his voice even, "you don't want to do this."

"Who are you allied with?" she asked. "Who ordered you set free? Who is behind all this?"

He barked out a desperate laugh that was cut short by the pain. "You've chosen the wrong... side here, woman. I wish I could... I wish I could let you live to regret it..."

Vengeous dropped to the floor. "I wish I had the time... to make you beg... to make you plead with me. I would have... I would have made you *scream*..."

"Fine," China said, crossing to the phone. "I suppose I'll have to call in the professionals."

"China..." Vengeous gasped.

She turned. "Yes, dear Baron?"

"You didn't... you didn't really think it would be that easy, did you?"

Dusk walked through the door. A man followed. The stranger had blond hair and wore a brown suit, a white shirt and dark sunglasses. His cowboy boots were old and scuffed, and he was grinning. The carpet at his feet frayed and split, and he sank downwards, disappearing into the floor. China dived for the phone, but Dusk darted in and shoved her back.

Valkyrie stared as the stranger's hand burst up through the floor at Vengeous' feet, grabbed him and pulled him down. The floor sealed up behind him and the symbols pulsed one last time then returned to normal.

A moment later Vengeous and the stranger stepped through the wall beside China.

"Your hospitality used to be so much better," Vengeous said. His eyes flashed and China stumbled. Dusk picked her up.

"Don't let her touch anything," Vengeous told him. "She has symbols everywhere. Some are invisible. Some are even etched on to her body. Don't let her touch *anything*." Dusk grabbed both her wrists and wrenched her arms behind her.

Vengeous took out a handkerchief, used it to wipe away the rest of the blood. "I expected more from you, China. When you left us, I thought you'd be back. No one could do the things you'd done and then walk away. I didn't think it was possible."

She looked up at him, grimacing against the pain that was locking her arms straight behind her. "I found other interests. You can too. Stamp collecting, maybe." Dusk twisted her arms and she gasped. The man in the sunglasses laughed.

Vengeous put the handkerchief away. "I can still be merciful, even if my gods are *not*. The girl, China. Valkyrie Cain. Tell me where she is, and I will let you live."

"Skulduggery doesn't care about her," China said through gritted teeth. "She's a hobby, nothing more. You won't be able to get at him through her."

"My mercy is on a timetable. Tell me where I can find her or I shall torture you until you *beg* to tell me."

"OK," China said, "OK, I'll tell you." She nodded to the bedroom. "She's in there." Valkyrie went cold, but Vengeous just shook his head sadly.

"China, I don't like this side of you, these *jokes*."

"I've been spending too much time around Skulduggery. You remember *his* jokes, don't you, Baron? What else do you remember? You remember him arresting you?"

"I remember almost killing him."

"Almost wasn't enough," China said and actually managed a laugh. "He's coming for you, you know. I hope I'm there when he gets you." Dusk twisted and China cried out in pain.

"Tell me where the girl is," Vengeous said, "or I will have your arms broken."

"Here I am," Valkyrie said, kicking the door open as the fire flared in her hands.

8

BILLY-RAY SANGUINE

Her aim was off on the first fireball she threw and it missed Dusk. The second fireball, however, was on target, and it would have hit Baron Vengeous if he hadn't moved out of the way at the last moment. He was fast. Maybe even faster than Skulduggery.

"Cain," he snarled.

"Run!" China shouted and Valkyrie obeyed. She was out in the corridor before she glanced back, just in time to see China wave her hand. The door slammed shut, sealing the men in the apartment.

Valkyrie got to the stairs, heading down, when something grabbed her ankle and she nearly fell. She kept going, looking back in time to see a hand disappear back into the steps. She reached the second floor, banged off the wall and kept going down. The wall below her cracked and crumbled, and the man in the sunglasses lunged out. Valkyrie gripped the banister and jumped, using her momentum to lend force to the kick. Her boot slammed into his chest and he hit the wall hard and bounced off.

At the first floor she almost tripped over herself, the man right behind her. She jumped the last few steps and ran out on to the street. Cars were passing and people were walking. Too many innocent people that could be caught up in a battle they weren't ready for. She sprinted into the alley beside the tenement building. It was narrow and cut off from the sun. The other side led out on to a quieter road.

The man in the sunglasses was behind her, closing the gap between them to an arm's length. She barely kept out of reach.

Valkyrie dropped and the man's legs crashed into her and he went flying over, losing his sunglasses in the process. He hit the ground and sprawled, and when he snapped his head to her, she saw that he had two small black holes where his eyes should have been. She spun, ran back the way she had come, and glanced over her shoulder in time to see the man sink into the ground, straight down, like he was in an invisible elevator. With five paces left to the street, the ground in front of her exploded and a man surged upwards. She fell back, trying to wipe her eyes clear of gravel and dirt.

"I don't see what all the fuss is about," the man said. He was American and spoke with a strong Deep South drawl. "You're just a little girl."

Valkyrie clicked her fingers, but he smacked her hand down before she could conjure a flame then grabbed her. She felt something cold and sharp on her throat.

"Don't try that again," the man said. He held a straight razor with a wooden handle, and as her vision cleared she saw the initials B-R. S. engraved on it. She raised her eyes. Up ahead, parked at the side of the quiet street, was a black motorbike. Tanith's black motorbike.

An old woman with a lined face and bad teeth stepped into the alley. She stared at them, then turned and hurried away.

The man shook his head. "See, that's the problem with ordinary, regular folk. They see somethin' freaky, somethin' scary, they run the other way. Y'know what that means, don't you? It means no one's comin' to help you. It means you're all alone."

And then someone coughed right behind them. The man looked around and Tanith Low kicked him in the face. He stumbled and Valkyrie tore herself free, spinning around to keep him in sight as she backed off to the wall. He would have been handsome were it not for those awful black holes.

The man smiled. "And who might you be?"

"You first," Tanith said.

The man chuckled. "Very well. Billy-Ray Sanguine, master of all manner of unpleasant deaths and purveyor of cruel and unusual punishments, at your service."

"You're a hitman?"

"Not merely a hitman, darlin'. I am a hitman *deluxe*. I also do muscle-for-hire and a nice little sideline in mercenary activities. I'm very, very expensive and I'm very, very good. And you are?"

"The end of you," Tanith said.

Sanguine laughed. "Oh, I see. I often wondered what the end of me would look like. Never imagined it'd be somethin' quite so pretty."

Tanith reached into her coat and revealed her sword, still in its sheath. "Are you going to come along quietly, Mr Sanguine, or do I have to hurt you?"

Sanguine's face fell. "Oh come on! Look at the size of yours and look at the size of mine! I just got this little razor here! That's hardly fair!"

"But your blade against an unarmed girl, *that's* fair?"

He hesitated, stepping back as she neared. "Seemed fair to me," he said, "at the time. At this juncture, lookin' back, perhaps it *was* a bit one-sided. Twenty-twenty hindsight and all that."

She took off her coat and let it fall. The muscles moved beneath the skin of her arms. She slid the sword from its scabbard as she walked towards him.

"Ooh," he said. "Gettin' interestin' *now*."

Tanith lunged and Sanguine ducked, the sword whistling over his head. Tanith flicked her wrist and the blade zipped back towards him, but he jumped back out of range, giving a laugh.

"Now this is fun! Two grown people gettin' to know each other the old-fashioned way. Romance is in the air."

"You're not my type."

"You don't know what your type is, darlin'."

"I know you're not it. Mr Sanguine, I've got some shackles with your name on them."

"Shackles can't hold me, pretty lady. I'm immune to just about every binding spell I reckon you ever heard of, and a few more you haven't. That's what makes me special."

"That and your psychopathic tendencies."

"Oh, those don't make me special. They just make me *fun*."

This time it was Sanguine who moved first, feinting right to draw the sword away then skipping in, the razor slicing up through the air. Tanith lifted her elbow, hitting his forearm and making him miss, then she kicked out at his knee and slashed back with the sword. Sanguine had to dive out of the way. He rolled awkwardly and came up, rubbing his knee.

"That hurt," he said with a smile.

"I can make this easy on you."

"You gonna give me that sword of yours?"

"No, but if you tell me what Baron Vengeous is planning, I'll let you walk away from this."

He frowned. "But I drove here."

"This is a one-time offer, Mr Sanguine."

"And very considerate it is too. Unfortunately I am a professional, I got paid to do a job and I intend to do it – I have a reputation to protect after all. So how about this: you stand very still and allow me to kill you, and then I take the girl here and we go about our merry business. That sound good?"

"Afraid not."

"Darn. Ah, well, back to basics, I guess."

He smiled again and stood with his feet together. Valkyrie watched the surface beneath him start to crack and break, and when it was loose enough he sank straight into the ground and disappeared from view.

Tanith held the sword ready. The ground had closed up behind him, leaving only hundreds of little cracks to mark what had happened. Valkyrie kept very still. The seconds ticked by. Tanith was frowning, probably wondering if her opponent had simply run off. She glanced at Valkyrie, about to speak, then the wall behind her crumbled and Billy-Ray Sanguine dived at her.

Tanith, for her part, seemed incapable of being taken by surprise and simply stepped away, her sword casually slicing Sanguine's forearm. Covered in dirt, he howled in pain and the razor fell to the ground. He danced back, trying to stem the flow of blood. Valkyrie looked at the ground beside her feet.

"Don't you dare," Sanguine warned, glaring at her with those black holes, but she paid no heed. She stooped and picked up the straight razor and this infuriated him even further.

"What is it with you women?" he yelled, kicking at the air. "You come into our lives, you take everythin'! Throughout the years you got little pieces of me, of my very *soul*, and *now*? Now you got my damn straight razor! How am I supposed to kill people? How am I supposed to even *shave*?"

Behind Sanguine, Baron Vengeous strode in off the street and stood in the mouth of the alley. Valkyrie tensed.

"Get it done," Vengeous called out angrily.

"Yes sir," Sanguine responded then lowered his voice. "See that? You're getting' me in trouble with the boss. You better hand over the girl right this second." A side door opened, a door Valkyrie had never noticed before.

"Sorry," China said as she stepped out, "that's not about to happen." She had a fresh cut along her forehead, but was otherwise unharmed. A black jeep pulled up beside Vengeous and Dusk got out.

Valkyrie saw something, high above, a figure on the rooftop. For a moment she thought it was another of Vengeous' bad guys, and then the figure stepped off and dropped, and Mr Bliss landed beside them. He straightened up. Valkyrie saw the Baron scowl.

"Sanguine," he called out, "there are too many of them. We're leaving."

"Be right with you, Baron."

But Vengeous wasn't waiting. He got in the jeep and Dusk got back behind the wheel, and they drove off. Suddenly alone, Sanguine stopped glowering. He looked at his adversaries and licked his lips. He was still holding his injured arm, blood trickling between his fingers.

"What is Baron Vengeous planning?" asked Mr Bliss, his voice terrible and quiet.

"I don't know," Sanguine said. "No wait, I'm lyin'. I do know, I'm just not tellin'."

Valkyrie watched him draw his feet together and the ground beneath him started to crumble. "Stop him!" she cried.

Tanith lunged, but it was too late, and he sank down into the earth again.

"Damn," Tanith said, scowling. "Some 'hitman deluxe' *he* turned out to be. Nothing more than a sneaky little coward."

"I heard that!" They tensed, ready to fight, looking down at the piece of broken ground – and at Sanguine, who was poking his head up through the surface. They relaxed their stances.

"I am not a coward," Sanguine said hotly, looking up at them. "I have just been momentarily outclassed. It takes a man to admit when he is beaten."

"You must be very manly then," Valkyrie said, which drew a glare from the American.

"No one likes sarcasm, Miss Cain. I've merely delayed my exit to promise you something. You took my straight razor, li'l darlin'. That I view as an unforgivable offence. So when the time comes, when you have served your purpose, I swear to you I'm gonna kill you for *free*." And with that, Billy-Ray Sanguine disappeared into the ground. Then he popped his head back up.

"Or at least half price." And he was gone again.

9

THE HIDDEN ROOM

After Valkyrie hung up the phone, she used the library bathroom to clean the dirt from her face. She dried her hands and watched them shake. Her hands always shook after a fight, as the leftover adrenaline took the opportunity to charge randomly through her.

Tanith was waiting for her outside, and together they walked down the stairs. They were headed over to Gordon's house, to see if her late uncle's office held any books on the Grotesquery, and they were leaving Bliss to help China restore some order to her apartment. Valkyrie had never seen a brother and sister regard each other with as much wariness as they did.

"How did Skulduggery sound?" Tanith asked.

"Angry," Valkyrie replied, "and worried. He's only OK when I'm attacked by people he knows. He'd never even *heard* of this Sanguine guy."

"Still, at least we know how Vengeous got out of his cell."

Valkyrie nodded. "That little tunnelling trick *is* useful, all right. I just wish he wasn't using it to get *me*. I don't much like the idea of being a hostage. Doesn't sound like fun."

They emerged into the open air, and approached Tanith's motorbike.

"So how's training?" Tanith asked.

"Good. Well, mostly good. There are a few moves I've kind of... mislaid."

"Mislaid?"

"Forgotten."

Tanith smiled. "When this is over we'll run through it again. You'll get it, don't worry. How're the parents?"

Valkyrie shrugged. "Parents are fine."

"Have you been going to school much?"

"Ah, Skulduggery makes me go whenever we're not in the middle of a crisis. But that's the great thing about having the reflection – I don't have to deal with all that."

Tanith pulled on her helmet then flipped up the visor to give Valkyrie a strange look. "I wouldn't get too dependent on that reflection if I were you. You may absorb all its memories so it *feels* like you're going to school, but you're not. You're on the outside, looking in at an important part of your own life. You're thirteen, Val. You should be spending time with people your own age." She swung her leg over the bike.

Valkyrie raised an eyebrow as she pulled the spare helmet over her head. "People my own age don't fight monsters, Tanith. If they did, I'd be hanging out with them a lot more."

They were headed over to Gordon's house, to see if her late uncle's office held any books on the Grotesquery. Valkyrie got on the motorbike behind Tanith.

The first time Valkyrie had ridden on Tanith's bike she had started off holding the sides of Tanith's coat, but as they picked up speed, her hands had got closer and closer together, until finally her arms were wrapped tightly around Tanith's waist. Once she'd got over her initial fear – that they were roaring along open roads and one bad turn would flip them to a painful and skin-shredding demise – she'd started to enjoy the sensation. Now she loved travelling by bike. It was *fun*.

Tanith swerved through traffic and took bends at an alarming speed, and Valkyrie started to laugh beneath her helmet.

They turned off the road and took a trail, the ride getting decidedly bouncier. It was only Tanith's superior reflexes that saved them from hitting one of the trees that blurred past. They burst from the treeline and shot up a small hill, leaving the ground for a few seconds and landing smoothly on a narrow road, then zipped over a humpbacked bridge. Moments later they were passing through the massive gate that led to Gordon Edgley's house. Valkyrie *still* thought of it as her uncle's house. The fact that she had inherited it changed absolutely nothing.

Tanith braked and let the back wheel skid sideways a little, throwing up a small shower of pebbles. She cut off the engine and leaned the bike on to its kickstand. They got off and removed their helmets.

"Enjoy that?" Tanith said with a little grin.

Valkyrie grinned back, her eyes bright. "I keep telling Skulduggery he should get a bike."

"What does he say?"

"He says people who wear leathers, like you, should ride motorbikes. People who wear exquisite suits, like him, should drive Bentleys."

"He has a point." Tanith looked up at the house. "So are we going to go in?"

Valkyrie laughed, took the key from her pocket and opened

the front door. "I still find it hard to believe you're a fan."

They walked in. The hall was grand, with Gothic paintings on the walls. They passed through into the living room.

"Your uncle was the best writer *ever*," Tanith said. "Why *wouldn't* I be a fan?"

"You just, I don't know, you don't really strike me as being the type. It's like when your friend thinks that your dad is the coolest guy in the world, y'know? It just seems a little silly."

"Well, there was nothing silly about your uncle's writing. Did I tell you that one of his short stories was based on something that happened to *me*?"

"You told me. Many times."

"I never met him, but he must have heard about it somehow. Maybe Skulduggery heard it and he told Gordon."

Tanith stood in the centre of the living room, gazing around with a slightly wistful look on her face. "And this is where Gordon lived. This is where he wrote his masterpiece. You're a lucky girl, Val. What was it like, having an uncle like Gordon Edgley?"

"We're not getting into this conversation," Valkyrie said. "Not again." She went to the bookshelf, took down a book bound in black and handed it to Tanith. Tanith bit her lip.

And The Darkness Rained Upon Them was the last thing Gordon

Edgley had written. It was set to be published in a few months, but Valkyrie had let Tanith read the advance copy. Every time Tanith was at the house, she devoured another few chapters until it was time to go. She loved coming here, and seized every chance she had to drop by.

Without another word spoken, Tanith took the book to the sofa, curled up and resumed reading. Valkyrie tried not to laugh. She left the living room and climbed the stairs, crossing the landing to Gordon's study and closing the door after her.

Unlike the rest of the house, Gordon's study was a chaotic affair, a mass of straining shelves and piles of stacked manuscripts. She went to the bookshelf that covered the far wall, scanning the titles. This was where he had kept his research material. Very occasionally, Valkyrie would find books on magic in this room that she hadn't even been able to find in the library of China Sorrows.

Valkyrie traced her finger along the spines. If anyone had collected information on a being as bizarre and unique as the Grotesquery, it would have been Gordon. That was his kind of thing.

Her fingertip stopped on a thick, leather-bound book with no title on its spine. She'd seen it before but had never paid it much attention. She tried slipping it from the shelf but it wouldn't budge. Frowning, she gripped it and pulled. It came out halfway and stuck, and then the wall started to move.

"No way," Valkyrie breathed, as the bookshelf swung open before her, revealing a room as black as night.

A secret room. An actual real, secret room.

Not bothering to subdue the excited grin that spread across her face, Valkyrie stepped in. The room immediately lit up with candles.

Like the study, the secret room was lined with shelves, and on those shelves were objects both alien and familiar. Among those she could categorise were ornate musical boxes, intricate statuettes, silver daggers and golden goblets. Before her was a table, and on that table was a blue jewel, nestled in a golden claw centrepiece. A faint light within the jewel started to glow as she stepped closer, and a man faded up from nothing on the other side of the room.

Portly. Wearing brown slacks and a matching waistcoat over a shirt with the sleeves rolled up to his forearms. Sandy hair that perched on top of his head like a loose bale of straw, shot through with grey. He turned and his eyes widened when he saw her.

"Stephanie," he said, "what are you doing here?"

She stared. "Uncle Gordon?"

Her dead uncle put his hands on his hips and shook his head. "What are you doing sneaking around this house? I always said you were far too inquisitive for your own good. Admittedly, it's a trait we share, but I for one am not above the occasional bout of hypocrisy to get my point across."

Valkyrie just stood there, mouth open. "Is that... is that really you?"

He stopped, like he'd been caught out in a lie, and then he started waving his hands and bobbing his head from side to side. "This isn't me," he said, "this is all a dream..."

"Stop that."

"Go back the way you came," he continued, drawing out his words, "and try to wake up. Remember, this is all a dreeeammmm..."

"I'm serious, Gordon; quit it." He stopped bobbing his head and dropped his hands to his sides.

"Fine," he said. "Then get ready for a shock. Stephanie: the world isn't what you think it is. There is magic here, real magic, and it is—"

"I know about the magic," she interrupted. "Just tell me what's going on. How are you here?"

"You know about the magic? Who told you?"

"Are you going to answer my question?"

"I suppose. What was it again?"

"How are you here?"

"Oh, well, I'm not. Not really. This isn't me. I mean, I am me, but I'm not. See the blue jewel? It's very rare, it's called an Echo Stone and generally it's used—"

"I know about Echo Stones."

"You do?"

"People sleep with the stone close by for three nights to imprint it with their personality and memories."

"Oh. Yes, you're quite right," he said, and looked a little disappointed. "It's generally used by the dying, and then given to loved ones to help comfort them through their grief. For me, however, it was more like a writing aid."

"A writing aid?"

"I imprinted my consciousness on to the stone. Or rather, the *real* Gordon imprinted *me* on to the stone. He comes in whenever he's stuck on a plot point or when he needs a new perspective on a story, or when he just wants a conversation with someone who can actually challenge him intellectually. We have some pretty interesting talks, let me tell you."

"That's... that's so..."

"Narcissistic?"

"I was going to say weird, but OK, we'll go with yours. How long do we have before it runs out of power?"

Gordon, the Echo-Gordon, shook his head and gestured to the centrepiece which held the stone. "When the Echo Stone is in its cradle, it's constantly recharging. I could stay out here forever – providing there was someone around, of course. It'd be pretty boring if it was just me.

"I have to say, Stephanie, while I welcome the chance to talk to you, and I would give you a hug only I'd pass right through you and that would be strange, Gordon himself is going to be a mite annoyed that you found your way in here."

"Um, actually... I don't think he will be. Do you remember the last time you spoke with Gordon – the *other* Gordon, the *real* Gordon?"

His eyes narrowed. "Why? Stephanie, what's wrong?"

She hesitated. "My name is Valkyrie."

"Valerie?"

"Valkyrie. With a K. Valkyrie Cain. You left this house to me in your will."

He stared at her. "Oh. Oh, no."

"Yes."

"Oh, my God I'm... I knew, I mean, I knew I might be in danger once I had the Sceptre of the Ancients, but, but... Tell me the truth, OK? Just be totally, brutally honest, just tell me flat out... Am I dead?"

"Yes." He covered his face with his hands.

She waited for him to look up. When he didn't, she searched for words to fill the silence. "I understand that this must come as a shock..."

Finally, he raised his head. "How did I die?"

"Nefarian Serpine killed you," Valkyrie said, as gently as she could under the circumstances. "Well, killed *Gordon*. Killed *you*, I suppose..."

"Serpine killed me? Then he has the Sceptre! Quickly, Stephanie, we have no time to lose—"

"Don't worry, he's dead. Skulduggery killed him last year."

"Oh," Echo-Gordon said, his impetus interrupted. "I see. You know Skulduggery then?"

"He's been showing me the ropes."

"And the Sceptre?"

"It's not a threat to anyone any more."

"Did you solve the clues I left? The brooch and the caves?"

"Yes we did. That was very clever of you."

"The riddle was my idea," he said proudly. "Gordon, the real Gordon, just wanted to leave clear instructions in case anything bad happened to him, but I convinced him to do it all in a riddle. It gives the whole thing an extra flair, don't you think?" His lower lip quivered for a moment.

"Are you OK?" asked Valkyrie.

"Not really. I'm the memories of a dead man. I'm struggling to find the purpose of my existence. Was there uproar? When I died, I mean? Was there a national day of mourning?"

"Uh... not a day, I don't think..."

He frowned. "But I was a bestselling author. I mean, I was *loved*. What about a minute's silence, observed throughout the country?"

Valkyrie rubbed her arm. "A minute? I'm not sure if, you know, if it was an *official* minute, but I'm sure I noticed that people were... quieter than usual..."

"What about sales?"

"Oh, well, your last two books went straight back into the top ten."

"What about my last book? What's happening with that?"

"The release date is three months away."

"That'll sell well," he said, stroking his chin. "Now that I'm dead."

"There were loads of people at your funeral," Valkyrie said. "Crying, saying how great you were, how much you'll be missed."

Echo-Gordon digested this and nodded. "I *will* be missed.

And I *was* pretty great." His face suddenly turned sour. "Was Beryl there?"

Valkyrie laughed. "Yes she was, and she was doing her best to squeeze out some tears and get all the sympathy."

"Never liked that woman. I always thought Fergus could do better. Not much better, mind you, the man has the personality of a wet towel. But anyone would be better than Beryl. Oh, Gordon left them a boat in the will, didn't he? How did they like that?"

"Fergus went all quiet and Beryl started squeaking."

Echo-Gordon laughed and clapped his hands. "Oh, I wish I could have been there. That would have certainly been something to see. We have *some* family, eh?"

"You're telling me. In fact, there's a family reunion tomorrow night."

"Really? Oh that's wonderful! Will you bring me?"

"Uh... what? Gordon, you're dead."

"Just put the stone in your pocket, then leave me in an empty room so I can gaze out at all the Edgleys and laugh. Or maybe I'll pretend to be a ghost and haunt Beryl."

"That's incredibly mature of you, but I don't think I'll be going. Saving the world tomorrow night, so..."

"Ah, of course. But if you change your mind..."

She grinned. "I'll bring you, I promise. So, what is this room? What are all these things?"

All of a sudden his chest puffed out. "These, my dear niece, are objects of great magical and historical relevance. The items you see on the shelves around you are so rare, many a collector would kill to get their hands on them. And I mean that, quite seriously. There is a woman—"

"China Sorrows?"

"You've met her then. Yes, China. If she knew about the existence of this little horde, she would stop at nothing to get it. So it probably wouldn't be a good idea to mention it to her. You know, I was in love with her for quite some time."

"Everyone's in love with China."

"Ah yes, but my love was stronger and true. I think she knew that, and I think, in her own way, she loved me as much as I loved her. Or loved Gordon as much as he loved... no, as much as I loved... she loved Gordon as much as I loved her. Or something."

"Are... are you sure you're OK?"

"Just having a small existential crisis, nothing to worry about." He paused, seemed to reflect for a moment and then brightened. "So Skulduggery has taken you under his wing, has he? You'll be safe with him. He's one of the good guys."

"Yes, he is. I'm learning all kinds of magic and he's teaching me to fight... It's dangerous, but I'm having a great time."

"I used to help him out on a few cases you know. Nothing big, just a few mysteries every now and then. I wasn't really a throwing-punches kind of action hero, though. I was more into the research, tracking down things, people. So what are you working on now?"

"We're trying to track down this nutjob who escaped from prison, Baron Vengeous."

"Vengeous?" Echo-Gordon said. "He's out?"

"We think he wants to bring the Grotesquery to life."

Echo-Gordon's eyes bulged. "The Grotesquery? That is quite unfair! I've been meaning to write a book about that whole thing and now I'm dead!"

"That *is* very unfair," Valkyrie said, nodding in agreement. "So do you know anything about it?"

"A little, I suppose. I don't have any books about it, but I know that it was put together from bits and pieces of some quite impressive creatures. I didn't think it was possible to bring it to life though."

"We're trying to figure that out too."

Echo-Gordon shook his head in awe. "Astounding. Genuinely astounding. It's got a stinger apparently, from a Helaquin, and parts of a Shibbach were grafted on. From what

I've read, Baron Vengeous had to rearrange its insides entirely, give it a whole new set of internal organs. The heart he gave it, from a Cú na Gealaí Duibhe, is on the right side, and lower than usual, about here." He gestured to his own ribs.

"If it does come back, would destroying its heart be enough to kill it?"

"Oh, yes. Kill it stone dead."

"Then... that's how we kill it, right? Simple."

"Not quite. Because most of it is comprised of a Faceless One, it will heal quickly. The stronger it gets, the faster it will heal until it suffers no injuries at all. It would take an awful lot to damage the Grotesquery while it's at full strength, I'm afraid. Have you found it yet?"

"No, we don't even know where to start looking."

"You should ask the Torment."

"Who?"

"A few years ago, I heard a rumour that a man called the Torment might know where the Grotesquery is hidden."

"*The* Torment? Not, like, Joey Torment or Sam Torment? An actual *the*?"

"An actual *the*, yes. He's probably dead by now if he even existed at all. It was just a rumour. You should ask Eachan Meritorious if he knows him."

"Um, actually, Meritorious is dead. So is Morwenna Crow. Sagacious Tome, too, but he betrayed the others, so I'm not sorry *he's* dead."

"Oh, dear. Meritorious and Crow? That's a lot of people dead. Is there anyone who *isn't* dead?"

"Uh... Ghastly Bespoke is a statue."

"Well, that's something at least."

Valkyrie glanced at her watch. "I better go. Tanith's waiting downstairs."

"Tanith?"

"Tanith Low."

"Oh, I've heard of her. Never actually met her, but I've heard of her. You know my tale *The All-Night Horror Show*, from my short story collection? That was inspired by something I heard about her."

Valkyrie smiled. "I think she'd be delighted to know that."

Echo-Gordon gazed fondly at Valkyrie. "You're suited to all this, you know. I helped Skulduggery for a time until I realised I didn't like putting my life in danger. Sometimes I regret taking a step back. But you... I always knew you'd be cut out for this adventuring lark. It's why everything was left to you in the will."

"Thanks for that by the way. It's... amazing."

"Think nothing of it. How did Serpine die, anyway?"

"Painfully."

Echo-Gordon grinned. "Oh, good."

The Bentley pulled up outside Gordon's house just as Valkyrie was closing the door.

"Are you all right?" Skulduggery asked as soon as he got out.

"I told you on the phone, I'm OK. Tanith arrived just in time to save the day."

Skulduggery looked at Tanith. "Thank you."

"Val had it handled," Tanith said with a shrug.

"How did your top secret sneaky business go?" Valkyrie asked, eager to change the subject.

Skulduggery hesitated. "This is a sensitive subject."

"We're all friends here, aren't we? So where'd you go?"

"Well, I... I broke into the Sanctuary."

"I'm sorry, you *what*?"

"What you were saying earlier, about how Thurid Guild is like a politician with people to please. It got me thinking. So I broke into his private chambers. I had a hunch."

Tanith stared at him. "That's... that's pretty dangerous, Skulduggery. If the Cleavers had caught you..."

"I know. It would have been an interesting fight. But I had to risk it, really. I was curious."

"About what?" asked Valkyrie.

"There may be reason to believe that Thurid Guild was involved in Vengeous' escape."

"Involved how?" Valkyrie asked, her eyes narrowing. "Is he a traitor?"

"My illicit investigation is just beginning. It's too early to—"

"Just like Sagacious Tome," Valkyrie interrupted. "And China!"

Skulduggery tilted his head. "China's not a traitor."

"But she used to worship the Faceless Ones, didn't she?"

"Well, yes, but we've all done things we're not proud of."

"Even you?" Skulduggery looked at her, but didn't say anything.

"How could a traitor be elected as the new Grand Mage?" Tanith asked, and he shook his head.

"These are my suspicions, nothing more. I liberated some files belonging to the Grand Mage—"

"*Liberated?*"

"—and I'll need some time to go over them. Until then, Thurid Guild is innocent until proven guilty. That said, obviously we still don't trust him. That would be silly."

"Sure," Tanith said.

"Absolutely," Valkyrie said.

"All right then, have either of you managed to turn up anything that will help us?"

Valkyrie looked at Tanith, who suddenly looked down at her boots.

"I've been... reading."

"Research?" Skulduggery asked. Tanith went a little red and Skulduggery tilted his head.

"You've been reading Gordon's book again, haven't you?"

"It's a white-knuckle roller-coaster ride," she mumbled.

He sighed and looked to Valkyrie. "And you?"

Echo-Gordon had asked her not to tell anyone about him, at least until he had grown used to the idea that he was the only version of Gordon Edgley left on the planet. Valkyrie had reluctantly agreed.

"I found something in one of Uncle Gordon's notebooks," she lied. "Apparently someone called the Torment might know where Vengeous hid the Grotesquery."

"The Torment?"

"I don't know if he's real or not."

"He's real."

"Do you know him?"

"No," Skulduggery said. "But I know someone who does."

10

THE ARMOUR OF
LORD VILE

Billy-Ray Sanguine didn't like the Infected.

He looked at them as he passed, looked at their blank faces and dull eyes. Half of them dug, half of them cleared rocks and they never took a break. Dusk's command over them was absolute.

Sanguine left them to it. As he walked, he felt the knife in his belt. It was big and heavy and awkward. He much preferred his cut-throat razor, but that girl had taken it from him. He was looking forward to seeing her again.

The caves were big, and the lights they had rigged up barely made a dent in the darkness, through which Baron Vengeous now strode.

"The Infected have cleared the chambers to the east," Sanguine told him. "The armour ain't there. I've searched the caves to the west, didn't find anythin'. Tunnelled through a couple of collapsed passageways to the north, still nothin'. Looks like the armour, if it's here at all, is in one of the chambers to the south."

"It's here," Vengeous said with confidence. "Lord Vile died in these caves, I know it. What of my garments?"

In order to don the armour, Vengeous would need special garments to protect him from the Necromancer power within. It had been Sanguine's job to obtain these garments.

"They'll be ready by nightfall," Sanguine said, "as promised."

"They had better be."

Sanguine looked at him, but said nothing. The Baron was not a man to be trifled with, especially at a time like this. Someone else Sanguine didn't like was Dusk. He didn't like vampires as a rule, but he really disliked Dusk, especially the way he could sneak up without making a sound. Vengeous was the only person Sanguine had ever met who could hear Dusk approaching. Which was why, when Dusk spoke from right beside Sanguine, Sanguine jumped and Vengeous remained perfectly still.

"Baron," Dusk said. "We have found it."

Vengeous' eyes glittered in the lamplight. They followed Dusk deeper into the cave system. Water trickled down rock walls, made the ground slippery. They walked towards a pack of the Infected, who stood back to let Baron

Vengeous pass into this newly discovered chamber. Sanguine made his way to the front, and stood beside Dusk.

The lamps cast long shadows on the uneven walls. In the centre of the chamber was a large circular stone table and on that table lay the armour. It was dull, black and plain, without etchings or imprints. To Baron Vengeous, it must have been the most beautiful thing he had ever seen.

Lord Vile's armour.

11

THE TERRIFYING
BRAIN-SUCKER OF LONDON

Vaurien Scapegrace sat at the table across from Skulduggery. Tanith stood directly behind him and Valkyrie stood in the corner beside the door, her arms folded.

Skulduggery looked up from the folder he was reading. "Vaurien, you haven't been very co-operative with your interviewers, have you?"

"Don't know what any of them are talking about."

"You are a known associate of a man they call the Torment."

He shrugged. "News to me."

"What is?"

"That I know him."

"Know who?"

"What?"

"That you know the Torment?"

"Yeah."

"Then you *do* know him?"

"Yeah." Then quickly, "No."

"You don't know him?"

"I, no, I, no. Never heard of him."

"I hate to say this, Vaurien, but that's astoundingly unconvincing."

Scapegrace shook his head. "Who is he? I've never heard of him. Torment who?"

"Do you recognise the pretty lady behind you?"

Scapegrace tried to turn in his chair, but the shackles meant he could only crane his neck. He looked back to Skulduggery and shrugged. "Should I?"

"That there is Tanith Low. Perhaps you've heard of her. Tanith is a renowned interrogator, known the world over for her one hundred percent success rate in getting the information she needs." Valkyrie saw Tanith arch an eyebrow, but she said nothing.

"Oh, yeah?" Scapegrace said. He was looking a little worried. "And how does she manage that?"

"Well, to put it delicately, she has the power to suck out people's brains."

Scapegrace stared and Tanith had to clap her hand over her mouth to stop from laughing. Valkyrie struggled to keep the smile off her face, and really wished she was anywhere but in Scapegrace's line of sight.

"She can't do that," he said. "That's illegal!"

"I'm afraid it's not. It's a loophole she's been exploiting for years. She sucks out the brain and swallows it, thereby digesting and absorbing the knowledge."

"But that's horrible," Scapegrace said weakly.

"You've left us with little choice. Tanith, if you wouldn't mind?"

From her position behind Scapegrace, Tanith held up her hands in a *what-do-you-expect-me-to-do?* gesture. Her hands dropped when Scapegrace tried to look back at her and she became deadly serious. The moment he took his eyes off her again she went back to helpless gesturing.

Scapegrace righted himself in his chair and made his hands into fists, and screwed his eyes shut. "You're not going to suck out *my* brains!" he yelled.

Skulduggery sat back and didn't offer Tanith any advice. She pointed a finger at him, wagged it slightly and then turned her attention to Scapegrace. She sighed, walked up beside him and held her hands over his head. His eyes were still screwed shut.

Tanith changed her mind about the hands thing and leaned over, putting her mouth next to his ear. His body went rigid. Her lips parted, and the barest sound of skin leaving skin made Scapegrace scream and jerk back and topple over sideways. He crashed to the floor.

"I'll tell you!" he squealed. "I'll tell you everything I know! Just keep her off me, you hear? Keep her away from my brains!"

"Is the Torment still alive?" Skulduggery asked, standing over him.

"Yes!"

"When was the last time you had contact with him?"

"Two years ago, I swear!"

"What was the nature of the meeting?"

"I just wanted to talk to him!"

"What did you talk about?"

Scapegrace peeked up, made sure Tanith wasn't about to start with the brain-sucking. "Nothing. He walked away. He wouldn't talk. I don't think he likes me."

"Why doesn't he like you?"

"I don't know. Maybe it's my smell."

"What do you know about the Grotesquery?" Valkyrie asked.

"Nothing, not a thing, honest."

"Tanith," Skulduggery said wearily, "suck his brains."

"No! Wait! I don't know anything, but *he* does! During the war – the war with Mevolent. He was tracking Baron Vengeous."

"Why?" Skulduggery asked.

"He was going to kill him. During that whole thing, the war, he was on *your* side. *I* was on your side too."

"I never saw you fight."

"I was somewhere near the back," Scapegrace said weakly. "But the fact is, we were all fighting the same enemy – that counts for something, right?"

Skulduggery tilted his head. "The enemy of my enemy is not necessarily my friend."

"The Torment, he told me once that he'd been watching Vengeous and he'd been about to strike when, when *you* showed up. You fought, and you took Vengeous away, and the Torment decided it was time to retire. He's an old guy. He was around long before Mevolent even arrived on the scene. But he told me, while he'd been watching Vengeous, he'd seen where he'd stashed the Grotesquery."

"Where?"

"Well, he didn't tell *me* that. Said something about me being unable to keep a secret or something."

"Where is he?"

Scapegrace looked up, eyes wide. "You swear you'll keep her away from my brains?"

"You have my word."

"Roarhaven," Scapegrace said after a hesitation. Valkyrie had heard of Roarhaven. It was a town of sorcerers, a dark little town that didn't take kindly to strangers. "He's in Roarhaven."

Scapegrace sat in the back of the Bentley, wrists and ankles shackled and a gag over his mouth. He had got into the car with the shackles, but the gag had been a recent addition. Skulduggery had grown tired of his conversation.

They drove east out of the city, left the streets for the suburbs, then left the suburbs for the countryside. After half an hour of driving along the narrow winding roads, pulling over occasionally to let massive tractors rumble by, they came to a small town beside a dark lake that shimmered in the early afternoon sun.

The Bentley came to a stop in the shade of a large tree that stood on the outskirts of the town, and Valkyrie and Skulduggery got out. It was warm and strangely quiet.

"No birds are singing," Valkyrie said.

"Roarhaven's not the kind of town to inspire song," Skulduggery responded. "Unless it's the dirge variety."

She could see people on the street, but they passed each other without a word.

Skulduggery pulled Scapegrace out after them and removed the gag. "Where do we find the Torment?"

"Give me a moment, OK?" Scapegrace said, looking over at the town. "I haven't been back here in years. I'm home again, you know? This is a big personal thing for me."

Skulduggery sighed. "Either you start being useful or we stuff you in the trunk and go looking ourselves."

"There's no need to threaten me," Scapegrace said, annoyed. "You're in a hurry, I get it. That's no excuse for being rude to me in my own home town."

"Are you going to be useful?"

Scapegrace glowered. "Yes."

"Good."

"But can you at least take my shackles off?"

"No."

"Even around my ankles? This is my first time home in twenty years – I don't want everyone to think I'm some kind of criminal."

"You *are* some kind of criminal," Valkyrie said.

"Yeah, but..."

"The shackles stay on," Skulduggery said.

Scapegrace muttered, but did as he was told. His shackles clinking as he walked, taking baby steps so he wouldn't trip over himself, he led them into town, staying away from the main street and sticking to the narrow alleys between buildings.

"Where does he live?" asked Skulduggery.

"Right over there."

Scapegrace nodded to the building right in front of them.

Valkyrie frowned. "In a pub? The Torment lives in a pub?"

"Not just any pub," Scapegrace snapped. "*My* pub. Well, it *was* my pub before I lost it. I took it as a sign, you know? A sign to move on, to see what else the world had to offer. Sometimes I regret it, leaving all this behind, going where I didn't have family, didn't have friends. There have been times when I've been so, so lonely..."

"It must have been awful for you," Valkyrie said. "Of course, maybe if you didn't go around trying to kill people..."

"I am an artist," Scapegrace said proudly. "When I kill, I make messy art."

They ignored him and came to the side door. Skulduggery hunkered down to pick the lock.

"Tanith could open that just by touching it," Valkyrie chided.

Skulduggery turned his head to her slowly, and a moment later the lock clicked and opened. He returned the lock pick to his pocket. "I like the old fashioned way better."

"Only because you don't have a choice."

"I'm an Elemental," he reminded her. "Tanith is an Adept. I'd like to see *her* throw a fireball."

Scapegrace coughed nervously. "She's not going to be here, is she? That Tanith woman?"

"Don't worry," Valkyrie said, "your brain is safe. For now."

Skulduggery opened the door and peeked inside then gripped Scapegrace by the elbow and pulled him in. The pub corridor was dark and smelled of stale beer and wet towels. There were a few voices coming from the front.

"Where does he stay?" Skulduggery asked quietly.

"Underground," Scapegrace said. "I converted the cellar into a living space then he made his own additions." They moved to the rear of the building.

"Back then," Scapegrace continued, "I was full of ideas. I was going to renovate the whole front of the pub, and extend out to the west, maybe get in a music system, a little dancefloor. In the end, I decided not to. Too expensive, you know. And, like, there was the fact that nobody wanted to dance, so..."

Valkyrie kept an eye out behind them, to make sure no one was sneaking up.

"But those were good times," Scapegrace said, his voice tinged with regret. "All the old crowd used to come and meet in my pub – Lightning Dave, Hokum Pete, Hieronymus Deadfall. We used to drink and talk and laugh. Back in the day."

Skulduggery tilted his head. "Vaurien, if you're trying to kill us, there are quicker ways than telling us your life-story."

"Less painful too," added Valkyrie.

"I just thought you'd like to know," Scapegrace said indignantly. "I thought it might help if I told you the history of the place and my relationship to it."

"Any particular reason *why* you think this knowledge would be helpful?" Skulduggery asked.

"If you'll let me finish, I'll tell you."

"OK then. Finish."

"The reason they frequented *my* pub in particular was because, in a town that's full of sorcerers, there weren't a whole lot of places you could get together and feel special, you know? But I took care of that. So while out in front the pub catered to the rest of Roarhaven's mages, there was also a private section just for me and my friends, to sit and talk and plan."

"Is that so?" Skulduggery asked as Valkyrie opened the door.

"Yep," Scapegrace said with a nod. "A private section right here in the back."

They walked in. Two men sitting at the bar. Two more playing pool on a ratty old pool table. A surly bartender and, standing in the corner, a giant, his balding head touching the ceiling. They all stopped and and looked over. Valkyrie and Skulduggery froze.

Scapegrace grinned. "Hi, fellas."

12

BARFIGHT

A fly buzzed loudly. It tapped a grimy window that looked out on to a dead tree. The bartender came out from behind the bar and the two men got off their stools.

"Scapegrace," said the bartender, chewing the name as he said it. "You've got some nerve showing your ugly face in my pub."

"*Your* pub?" Scapegrace said with a scornful laugh. "You won this place off me in a poker game and you cheated."

"So did you," the bartender said. "I just cheated better. Why're you back?"

"Couldn't stay away, could I? This town holds so many fond memories for me. Actually Hieronymus, I was hoping your sister might be around – is she here?"

Hieronymus Deadfall looked like he might explode. "Don't even *mention* her, you hear me?"

Scapegrace shrugged. "What you gonna do about it?"

"I think there's been a misunderstanding," Skulduggery tried, but he was ignored.

Deadfall stepped forward, fists bunched at his sides. "How about I finish what we started twenty years ago, how about that?"

Scapegrace scoffed. "You want to kill me, is that it?"

"Oh, it's not just me, pally. Anyone else in here want to kill this piece of scum, step forward."

Everyone took one step forward. "So that's how it is, is it?" Scapegrace said, acting upset. "After all that talk of friendship, after all those years, all that we've been through... you all want to kill me?"

"Kill you," said one of the pool players, "horribly."

"I'd love to help you out, fellas," Scapegrace said, holding up his hands and showing them his shackles, "but as you can see, I'm a little tied up at the moment. Still, I suppose if you manage to kill these two fine people who walked in with me, you might get your wish."

Deadfall narrowed his eyes. "Kill a little girl? Yeah, I think we could just about manage *that* momentous task. And what about you, skinny man? Who the hell are you?"

"We're really not looking for trouble," Skulduggery said.

"Then it'll come as a nice surprise," said the man to Deadfall's left. Electricity crackled in his open hand. Lightning Dave no doubt.

"We're here on Sanctuary business," Skulduggery tried.

The man on Deadfall's right bristled, and Deadfall grinned. "Hear that, Pete? They're with the Sanctuary."

Hokum Pete snarled. "I *hate* the Sanctuary."

"Oh," Skulduggery said.

"We *all* hate the Sanctuary."

"Ah. Then we're not here on Sanctuary business. I was just joking."

"Then you're going to die laughing," Deadfall sneered, "unless you tell us who you are right this second."

Skulduggery observed him for a moment then removed his disguise and laid it on the pool table. Eyes widened. Mouths opened. Backward steps were taken.

"The Skeleton Detective," said one of the pool players.

"I'm not going up against the *skeleton*," said his friend. "No way."

"What's wrong with you?" Deadfall barked. "This is *my* pub, you understand me? This is *my* turf. I'm the only one you should be worrying about in here. It's a dead man – what's the big deal? We can take him. There's six of us, there's one of him. Oh, and a little girl. That too much for you, tough guys?" The pool players glanced at each other nervously, then shook their heads.

"Well, there you go," Deadfall said. "We're agreed. We kill these two then we kill our dear old friend Scapegrace."

"This is gonna be fun," Scapegrace said, shuffling over to a booth and sitting down. "So how are you going to do it?"

"It's been a while since Brobding got himself some exercise," Deadfall said and the giant stepped forward.

Valkyrie glanced at Skulduggery. "You can have that one," she whispered.

"I'm gonna kill you," Brobding the giant said in a rumbling bass line of a voice. "Want you to know, it's nothing personal."

"That's good to hear," Skulduggery told him. "In which case, I'm going to knock you down and hit you with the pool table, and I want you to know, it's nothing personal either." Brobding laughed. They all laughed.

Skulduggery stepped forward and splayed both his hands, and Brobding the giant hurtled off his feet and slammed into the far wall. Valkyrie snatched a pool cue off the table and broke it off the first pool player's face. He went tumbling into the corner and the second player ran at her.

Hokum Pete ran forward and threw a punch that Skulduggery didn't even bother to block. He moved in past it and shoved, and Hokum collided with Deadfall.

Lightning Dave's whole body crackled with electricity, standing his hair on end and filling the room with the smell of ozone. He charged and Skulduggery kicked a bar stool. It hit Lightning Dave's legs and he cursed and fell.

The second pool player was trying to get his hands around Valkyrie's throat. She kicked his shin and poked his eye, and he cried out. He swung wildly and her block couldn't stop it, and his fist hit the side of her head. Skulduggery kicked Lightning Dave while he was trying to get up, and then Deadfall was on him. Skulduggery grabbed him and twisted, and Deadfall shrieked in a surprisingly high voice as he was hip-thrown to the dirty, sticky floor.

The pool player picked Valkyrie up and slammed her on to the table. The breath rushed out of her. He raised her up again and once more slammed her down. She grabbed the 8-ball, and when he raised her up a third time she smacked the ball against his ear. He bellowed in pain and dropped.

Skulduggery slammed his fists into Hokum Pete, then

twisted his arm and sent him facefirst into the wall. Hokum Pete slumped to the ground. Deadfall roared as Skulduggery turned to him. The bar owner strained, the muscles in his neck knotting. His face turned red, his fists grew and distorted and turned into sledgehammers. Spittle flew as he laughed in triumph.

Across the room, Valkyrie faced off against the pool player. He was rubbing his ear and he moved with a limp. He was squinting at her with one eye. "I'm gonna murder you," he threatened unimpressively. She still had the 8-ball in her hand so she threw it. It struck the pool player right between the eyes and bounced away. The pool player stood there, a look of puzzlement on his face, then he fell to the floor and went to sleep.

Valkyrie watched Deadfall slam one of those sledgehammer fists into Skulduggery's side and Skulduggery stumbled back to the wall. Deadfall swung for his head but Skulduggery ducked, and the fist hit the wooden panelling and went through. Deadfall tried pulling it out but his fist wouldn't budge. Skulduggery hit him. Hit him again.

Deadfall twisted and turned and swung his other fist. It hit the wood panelling and stayed stuck. "Aw, no," Deadfall whimpered.

Skulduggery took careful aim and punched. Deadfall's head

rocked back and his body slumped against the wall. He would have fallen in a heap were his sledgehammer fists not keeping him upright.

"Skulduggery," Valkyrie warned. Brobding the giant was getting to his feet, and he looked angry.

"Once again," Skulduggery told him, "nothing personal."

Brobding growled and Skulduggery ran at him and jumped, his body spinning and his right foot snaking out. His kick caught Brobding right on the hinge of the jaw. Skulduggery landed and Brobding whirled and fell to one knee. Valkyrie stared at Skulduggery.

"What?" he asked.

"You kicked him," she said. "But you don't *do* those kind of kicks. *Tanith* does those kind of kicks."

"You're impressed, aren't you?" He put both hands flat against the side of the pool table and shrugged. "I'm probably your hero."

"Oh, shut up."

Brobding the giant looked around then the air rippled and the pool table shot across the room and crashed into him. The pool table tipped over on impact, the balls flying through the air, and Brobding was sent sprawling. He didn't get up.

"Well," Valkyrie admitted, "you *did* warn him."

"That I did," Skulduggery said, leaving through the door they had come in through. A moment later he returned, pushing Scapegrace ahead of him.

"Hey, steady on!" Scapegrace yelled. "These shackles don't make it easy to walk, you know!"

Valkyrie looked at him. "You didn't get very far, did you?"

Scapegrace looked around at all the still bodies. "Oh, good," he said unenthusiastically. "You beat them."

"Nice try."

He shrugged. "Forgot Deadfall owned the place, honest."

"The cellar," Skulduggery said.

"Behind the bar," Scapegrace grumbled. Valkyrie went to the bar and peered over, saw the trapdoor. She nodded at Skulduggery.

Skulduggery shackled Scapegrace to a pipe that ran along the wall to stop him from shuffling away. Valkyrie opened the trapdoor and Skulduggery went first, drawing his revolver. Valkyrie followed him down the wooden steps, closing the trapdoor behind them.

The cellar was dimly lit and cold. The steps took them down into a badly wallpapered corridor. The carpet was worn, like a trail in a forest. One doorway led off to their right and another, a little further up, led off to their left. A small painting hung at an odd angle. It was a painting of a boat in a harbour. It wasn't very good. At the end of the corridor was a living room. Music played. *The End of the World*, by the Carpenters. Holding the revolver in both hands, Skulduggery took the lead.

The first room had a single bed and a set of drawers. Skulduggery stepped in, crossed to the bed and checked under it. Satisfied that the room was empty, he rejoined Valkyrie in the corridor. The second room had a toilet, a sink and a bath. None of these three were particularly clean, and there was nowhere for anyone to hide. They moved on towards the living room.

There was a lamp, and it was on, but the bulb was fading. The closer they got, the more Valkyrie could see. She could see that the carpet didn't match the wallpaper, and the curtains, which must have been added for aesthetic reasons because there certainly weren't any windows down here, didn't match anything.

Skulduggery had his back to the corridor wall and was sliding soundlessly closer. Valkyrie did the same thing on the opposite wall, allowing herself a view of the room that Skulduggery couldn't get. She saw two old-fashioned heaters, neither of which was turned on. She saw another painting, this time of a ship on a stormy sea. There was an armchair underneath the painting and a small table beside the armchair.

No sign of the Torment though. They stopped moving and she shook her head at Skulduggery. He nodded, and stepped into the living room, sweeping his gun from one corner of the room to the other. He checked behind the armchair. Nothing.

Valkyrie followed him in. On the other side of the room were a radio, a portable TV with a cracked screen and the record player that was playing the Carpenters. She parted the curtains, which led to nothing more interesting than a wall, and turned to tell Skulduggery that Scapegrace must have somehow warned the Torment, when she saw the old man glaring at her from the ceiling.

He had long dirty hair and a long dirty beard. He dropped from the rafters on to Skulduggery and knocked him to the ground. The gun flew from Skulduggery's hand and the old man grabbed it. Valkyrie threw herself sideways as he fired. The bullet hit the record player and the song cut off. Skulduggery twisted and pushed at the air, but the old man was already running through the corridor. Skulduggery scrambled up then stepped sideways as the old man fired twice more. Skulduggery peeked out to make sure it was clear and then ran after him.

Valkyrie wasn't entirely certain that her armoured clothes could stop a bullet. And what about her head? For the first time, she wished her coat had come with a hood. She ran after

Skulduggery, just as he ducked into the bedroom. She got to the bedroom, raised an eyebrow at the opposite wall which had parted to reveal a stone corridor, and sprinted through the gap. She could just make out Skulduggery ahead of her, moving fast in the darkness. She saw light flare up, saw his silhouette hurling a fireball.

Valkyrie ran on, aware that the ground was now slanting upwards. Her legs were getting tired. Her footsteps on the stone ground were uncomfortably loud in her ears. She couldn't see anything now. It was pitch black. She focused on the energy inside her then clicked her fingers and caught the spark. The flame grew and flickered in her palm, and she held it at arm's length to light her way. She didn't like the fact that it made her an easy target, but neither did she like the idea of falling into a pit full of metal spikes or something equally nasty. And then she came to a junction.

"Oh, come on," she muttered, in between gasps for breath.

She could go straight on or turn either right or left. She had no idea which direction Skulduggery had taken. She tried to stop herself from imagining lethal traps, or getting lost in a maze of corridors and dying down here, in the darkness and the cold.

Valkyrie cursed. She had to turn back. She decided to head up and look around the town, try and find where these tunnels would surface. It was better than standing around being useless, she figured.

It was at this exact moment that she heard a rumbling.

The path to the cellar was closing up. The walls were shifting back together. Right, left or straight ahead. She chose straight ahead and she *ran*.

13

ROARHAVEN

he walls were moving in, faster and faster. Valkyrie glanced back as the junction closed up. If she tripped, if she stumbled, the walls on either side of her would shift together with that terrible rumbling noise and squash her into something less than paste.

Her lungs burned like they used to do when she was swimming off Haggard beach. She liked swimming. It was much better than being squashed. And then, a light ahead of her, a flickering flame in the hand of Skulduggery Pleasant.

"It would be a tad redundant," he called out over the

rumbling, "to encourage you to hurry up, wouldn't it?" She let the fire in her own hand go out and concentrated on sprinting.

"Whatever you do," he continued loudly, "do not fall over. Falling over, I think, would be the wrong move to make at this moment."

She was close, close to Skulduggery, close to that wide open space he was standing in. The walls ahead of her shook and rumbled and started to close and she dove through, hit the floor and rolled to her feet as the corridor closed behind her and the rumbling stopped. She fell to her knees and sucked in air.

"Well," Skulduggery said cheerfully. "That was close."

"Hate..." she gasped.

"Yes?"

"Hate... you..."

"Breathe some more air; the lack of oxygen is making you delirious." Valkyrie got to her feet, but stayed bent over while she controlled her breathing.

"We better be careful," he advised. "The Torment may be old, but he's fast, and he's agile, and he still has my gun."

"Where... are we?"

"One unsavoury aspect of Roarhaven's chequered past was an attempt, some years ago, to overthrow the Council of Elders and establish a new Sanctuary here. We're in what was supposed to be the main building."

Valkyrie saw a switch on the wall and thumbed it. A few lights flickered on overhead. Most of them stayed off. Skulduggery let the flame in his hand go out, and they followed the corridor, then turned right and kept going. They walked through small patches of light and larger patches of darkness. The floor was covered in dust. He turned his head slightly. She knew him well enough to know when something was wrong.

"What is it?" she asked.

"Keep walking," he said quietly. "We're not alone."

Valkyrie's mouth went dry. She tried to read the air, like Skulduggery was doing, but even on her best day she couldn't sense more than a few metres in any direction. She gave up and resisted the urge to look around. "Where is he?"

"It's not him. I don't know what they are, but there are dozens of them, relatively small, moving as a pack."

"They might be kittens," she said hopefully.

"They're stalking us."

"They might be shy."

"I don't think it's kittens, Valkyrie."

"Puppies then?" Something scuttled in the darkness beside them.

"Keep walking," Skulduggery said. There was scuttling behind them now.

"Eyes straight."

And then they broke from the shadows ahead, into the light: spiders, black and hairy and bloated, as big as rats, legs tipped with talons.

"OK," Skulduggery said. "I think we can stop walking now."

The spiders emerged from cracks in the wall, moving across the ceiling, clacking as they came. Valkyrie and Skulduggery stood back to back, watching them close in. They each had three eyes, wide and hungry and unblinking.

"When I count to three," Skulduggery said quietly, "we run, all right?"

"All right."

The spiders clacked as they moved, closing in, drawing in tighter, the clacking becoming a din.

"In fact," Skulduggery said, "forget about the count. Just run." Valkyrie bolted and the spiders attacked.

She jumped over the spiders in front, landing and kicking out as one of them got too close. It was heavy against her boot, but she didn't wait to see if she had done any damage. She ran on as Skulduggery hurled fireballs. They swerved off course when the corridor ahead became alive with hairy, bloated bodies then ran into a room with a large conference table in its centre, the scuttling mass behind them quickly growing in size.

A spider scuttled on to the tabletop and sprang at Valkyrie as she passed. It struck her back and clung on, trying to pierce her coat with its talons. Valkyrie yelled out and swung round, stumbling as she did so, rolling and feeling the spider beneath her. She came up and the spider was still holding on. It darted up to her shoulder, towards her face, and she saw fangs. She grabbed it, tore it from her and flung it away. Skulduggery hauled her back and then she was running again.

They ran for the double doors ahead, and Skulduggery snapped out his hand, the air rippled and the doors were ripped from their hinges. They sprinted through and kept going, into a room that must have been the foyer. Skulduggery threw a few more fireballs and Valkyrie got to the main door, slammed her shoulder into it and burst into the warm sunshine. The light hit her eyes and blinded her momentarily. She felt Skulduggery beside her, tugging on her sleeve, and she followed him. She could see fine now, she could see the dark lake ahead and blue sky above.

They stopped running. They heard the spiders, the *click-clack* of their talons, the frantic scuttling in the doorway, but the spiders were unwilling to leave the darkness for the daylight and eventually the scuttling went away. A few moments passed and Valkyrie breathed normally and noticed for the first time that Skulduggery was looking at something over her left shoulder.

"What?" she asked, but he didn't answer.

She turned. The Torment was standing there, his long grey hair tangled in his long beard, pointing Skulduggery's gun pointed right at her.

"Who are you," the Torment said in a voice that hadn't been used in years, "to come after *me*, to disturb *me*, after all these years?"

"We're here on Sanctuary business," Skulduggery said. "We're detectives."

"She's a child," the Torment said. "And you're a dead man."

"Technically speaking, you may well be right, but we are more than we appear. We believe you have information that may aid us in an investigation."

"You say that as if I am obligated to help you," the old man responded, the gun not wavering. "What do I care of your investigations? What do I care of detecting and Sanctuary business? I hate the Sanctuary and the Council of Elders, and I loathe all they stand for. We are sorcerers. We should not be *hiding* from the mortals, we should be *ruling* them."

"We need to find out how to stop the Grotesquery," Valkyrie

said. "If it opens the portal and lets the Faceless Ones back in, everyone suffers, not just—"

"The child is addressing me," the Torment said. "Make her stop." Valkyrie narrowed her eyes, but shut up.

Skulduggery tilted his head. "What she says is true. You had no love for Mevolent when he was alive, and I'm sure you have no wish to see the Faceless Ones return. If you help us, there might be something we can do to help you."

The Torment laughed. "Favours? You wish to trade favours?"

"If that will make you help us, yes."

The Torment frowned suddenly, and looked at Valkyrie. "You. Child. You have tainted blood in your veins. I can taste it from here." She said nothing.

"You're connected to them, aren't you? The Ancients? I despise the Ancients as much as I despise the Faceless Ones, you know. If either race were to return, they would rule it all."

"The Ancients were the good guys," Valkyrie said.

The Torment scowled. "Power is power. Sorcerers have the power to run the world – the only reason we don't is weakness of leadership. But if the Ancients were to return, do you really think they'd make the same mistake? Beings of such power have no place on this earth. I had hoped the last of your kind had died out."

"Sorry to disappoint."

The Torment looked back to Skulduggery. "This information, dead man, must be worth a lot to you. And this favour you are promising – this too would be equally substantial?"

"I suppose it would be."

The Torment smiled and it wasn't a pleasant sight. "What do you need?"

"We need to know where Baron Vengeous has been keeping the Grotesquery since his imprisonment, and we need to know how he plans to raise it."

"I have the information you seek."

"What do you want in return?"

"My needs are modest," the Torment said. "I would like you to kill the child."

14

SPRINGING JACK

ack couldn't spring. Even if he could, even if this cell, with its narrow bed and its toilet and its sink, was big enough, he still wouldn't have been able to spring. The cell was bound and dampened his powers.

Springheeled Jack sat on his bed and contemplated life without springing. He also contemplated life without killing, which was twisting him up inside, without his favourite foods, without dancing about on rooftops and without everything he loved. They'd throw away the key, he knew they would. The English Council, once they finally got the chance to put him away, wouldn't be lenient. His trial would be over in a flash and he'd be looking at hundreds of years in prison.

Jack lay down, resting his forearm over his eyes to block out that dreadful artificial light. No more open sky for him. No more stars. No more moon.

"You're uglier than I remember."

Jack catapulted off the bed. A man was standing in the cell, leaning against the wall and grinning.

"Sanguine," Jack said, his own mouth twisting. "Come 'ere to gloat, 'ave you? I'd like to say I'm surprised, but naw, that kinda behaviour is what I've come to expect from you."

"Jack, my old friend, your words, they sting."

"You're no friend of mine," Jack said.

Sanguine shrugged. "We may have had our differences over the years, but the way I see it, all that's behind us now. I'm here to help you. I'm here to get you out." He tapped the cracked wall. Loose chips crumbled and fell, trailing dust.

Jack frowned. "What gives?"

"I just want you to do a little favour for me, is all."

"Don't much like the idea of doin' *you* a favour."

"You'd prefer to sit in a cell for the rest of your life?" Jack didn't answer.

"Just a little favour. Somethin' you'd enjoy actually. I want you to cause some trouble."

"Why?"

"Never you mind. Think you'd be able to help me?"

"Depends. What kind of trouble?"

"Oh, nothin' much. Just want you to kill some folks."

Jack couldn't help it. He smiled. "Yeah?"

"Easy as pie for someone of your talents. You agree to do this, I take you with me right now and we scoot on outta here."

"Killin', eh?"

"An' lots of it."

"And that's all? Once I do it, we're even? Cos I know who you've worked for in the past, Tex, an' I ain't gonna start workin' for the Faceless Ones or nothin'."

"Did I mention the Faceless Ones? No, I did not."

"It's got nothin' to do with them?"

"Cross my heart and hope to die. So, you in?"

Jack put on his coat and picked up his battered top hat. "Let's go."

15

POINT BLANK

Bracing his left hand against the wall and gripping the chain with his right, Scapegrace heaved. The pipe was begging to give. He could feel it. He could hear it. Every other pipe in the place would have broken by now – he should know, he'd had them installed. Just his luck that the skeleton would shackle him to the only *secure* pipe in the building.

He gritted his teeth. His face was red from exertion and he really needed to start breathing again sometime soon. And then the pipe broke and Scapegrace went flying backwards, his *whoop* of triumph cut short when he hit his head on the floor. He lay there for a moment, free at last and trying not to cry, and then he got up, the shackle dangling from his wrist. There was nothing he could do about the shackles around his ankles, so he quickly shuffled to the door.

Making sure the skeleton and the girl weren't anywhere close, he stepped out. His steps were ridiculously short, and he probably looked like some sort of demented penguin as he made his way away from the pub. He'd find someone to help him, someone who could get these shackles off. After all, the *entire* population of Roarhaven couldn't want him dead, surely.

He came around a corner, near the Roarhaven Sanctuary, and froze. For a moment he was too stunned to even smile. But then the smile appeared and it brightened his day. The Torment was pointing a gun at Pleasant and Cain.

Chuckling, Scapegrace shuffled over. The skeleton's skull was as blank as ever, but the girl was looking at the Torment like she couldn't believe what he had just said. Nobody paid any attention to Scapegrace.

"You can't be serious," said Cain.

Scapegrace loved the way the Torment ignored her, and spoke only to the skeleton. "Kill the child," he was saying. "Shoot her, if you want. Set fire to her. Strangle her. I do not care." If Scapegrace had been able, he would have done a dance there and then.

"I'm not going to kill Valkyrie," Pleasant said.

"Dead man, what is one life compared to billions? And if the Faceless Ones return, billions *will* die. You know this."

"That may be so, but I'm not killing her."

"Those are my terms."

"There must be something else," Skulduggery said. "Something reasonable I can do."

"I'll make this easy for you."

The Torment tossed the skeleton's revolver back to him. The skeleton caught it and pointed it right between the Torment's eyes. Scapegrace lost his grin. Things had suddenly taken a turn for the worse.

"No one dies here," Pleasant said, "except maybe *you*. Where is the Grotesquery?"

"I am the Torment, dead man. Do you really think I fear death?"

For another few seconds, the gun didn't waver, but then Pleasant lowered his arm. Scapegrace could breathe again and the Torment nodded with satisfaction.

"You need my help," he said. "You have my terms. Kill the child."

"You can't just—"

"Time is running out."

"Listen to me, this is *insane*. She's done nothing—"

"*Tick*," the Torment said. "*Tock*."

The skeleton looked at the girl and Scapegrace saw the doubt in her eyes. She pointed at the Torment. "Beat him up. Beat him up or, or *something*. Shoot his foot."

The skeleton shook his head. "Threats won't work."

"*Empty* threats won't work, but if you *actually* shoot his foot—"

"Valkyrie, no. I've met people like him before. Everyone has a breaking point, but we don't have time." Pleasant turned back to the Torment. "How do I know you have the information I need?"

"Because I'm telling you I do," the Torment answered, "and you don't have the luxury to doubt me. By now, Baron Vengeous will have retrieved Lord Vile's armour. The time you have left is like sand clasped in a fist. It's sifting through your fingers, dead man. Will you kill the child?"

"He will not!" Cain said defiantly. "Tell him, Skulduggery!" Scapegrace's heart almost burst with joy when Pleasant remained silent.

Cain stared at the skeleton, and took one step away.

"Don't tell me you're actually *considering* this."

"Do you have your phone?"

"What?"

"You need to call your parents. You have to say goodbye."

A moment passed and Cain turned to run but Pleasant was too fast. He grabbed her wrist and twisted, and she fell to her knees in pain.

"Be brave," the skeleton said.

"Let go of me!" Cain shouted.

Pleasant looked at the Torment. "Give us a minute."

"A minute," the Torment said. "Nothing more."

Scapegrace watched as the skeleton pulled Cain to her feet, his hand still gripping her arm, and led her away. The words he spoke were quiet, and the girl shook her head and tried to pull away again. They got to the corner of the Roarhaven Sanctuary and finally the girl started nodding. She took out her phone.

"This is brilliant," Scapegrace said to the Torment.

The Torment turned his head to him and frowned. "Who are you?"

"I'm... sorry? It's *me*, it's Vaurien. Vaurien Scapegrace. I... built the cellar for you?"

"Oh," the Torment said. "*You.* Why are you back? I thought you were dead. It would have been nice if you were dead."

Although he had never known the Torment to make a joke, Scapegrace decided he was making a joke now, so he laughed.

"This is brilliant," he said again. "Making him kill Cain. I mean, it's just brilliant. It's *genius*. I'd never have thought of something like this."

"I know."

"Do you mind me asking, where do you get your ideas? Do they come to you in a dream or is it just, you know, instinct? I'm keeping a, like a journal, where I jot down all my ideas and my thoughts and—" The Torment looked at him again and Scapegrace shut up.

"You irritate me," the Torment said.

"Sorry."

The Torment went back to ignoring him. "Dead man," he said loudly. "Your minute is up."

Pleasant put his hands on Cain's shoulders. He spoke to her and went to hug her. She twisted and broke away, shoved him back. For a moment she was obscured from view, but when Pleasant moved again Scapegrace could see the tears in her eyes. Pleasant took her arm and they walked back.

"You will kill her?" the Torment asked.

Pleasant sagged. "Yes."

Scapegrace looked at Cain. She was standing silently, as

straight as she could, trying to be fearless despite the tears.

"Then by all means," the Torment said, "kill her."

Pleasant hesitated then took his gun from his jacket.

"I'm sorry, Valkyrie," Pleasant said softly.

"Don't talk to me," Cain said. "Just do what you have to do."

"That looks like protective clothing," the Torment commented. "Be sure to shoot into her flesh. You wouldn't want me to think you cheated after all."

Cain parted her tunic and Scapegrace smiled. He wished this entire thing was being recorded so he could play it back in the future, again and again. The moment when Skulduggery Pleasant killed Valkyrie Cain.

"Please forgive me," Pleasant said, then aimed the gun at the girl and pulled the trigger.

The gunshot hurt Scapegrace's ears. Cain's body jerked and her eyes widened. She stepped back then fell awkwardly to her knees, clutching the wound. Blood trickled from her fingers.

Valkyrie Cain fell forward, her face hitting the ground.

Pleasant looked down at her. "She was an innocent girl," he whispered.

"She had Ancient blood in her veins," the Torment responded, "and so was a fitting payment for the information you require. The Grotesquery is hidden in castle ruins, on the hill in Bancrook. Detective? Can you hear me?" Pleasant raised his head slowly.

"I wonder if you can get there before Vengeous," the Torment continued. "What do you think?"

"If you're lying..." Pleasant began.

"Why would I lie? I asked you to kill the child and you did. I keep my bargains."

Pleasant stood over Valkyrie Cain's dead body. After a moment he hunkered down and picked it up. "Scapegrace," he said. "Back to the car."

Scapegrace laughed. "What, do you think I'm nuts? I'm staying here."

"No. I'm taking you back."

Scapegrace grinned, and looked over at the Torment.

"Why are you looking at me?" the Torment asked.

Scapegrace's smile faded. "What?"

"There was nothing in our bargain concerning you."

"But I can't go back!" Scapegrace cried. "He'll put me in jail!"

"You seem to think I care."

"Scapegrace," Pleasant said, in a voice devoid of any human emotion. "Get back to the car. Start walking."

Scapegrace looked around desperately, but there was no

one to help him. Trying not to cry, he shuffled off.

"I wish to thank you, Detective," the Torment said. "I look around at this world, at what it's become, I look around at my fellow sorcerers as they huddle in shadows, and I realise now that I have been waiting. Do you see? I have been waiting for a reason to live again, to emerge from my dank and squalid cellar. I have a reason now. I have a purpose now. For years I have slumbered, but now I am awake. You have awoken me, Detective. And we shall meet again."

"Count on it," Pleasant responded. The Torment smiled then turned his back and walked away.

Scapegrace was betrayed. Let down. Abandoned. Pleasant walked beside him, carrying the dead girl in his arms. Scapegrace doubted he would survive the journey back to the Sanctuary. He had heard tales of the Skeleton Detective's fury, and there was no one else around for him to take it out on. Scapegrace couldn't reason with him, he couldn't bargain with him. There was no hope. No hope left.

They got to the car and Pleasant laid the girl's body carefully in the boot then looked back at the town. The Torment was gone from sight and the town looked empty now, as night fell.

"Well, we did it," Pleasant said, sounding relieved. Scapegrace frowned, but didn't say anything.

"This has been a good day so far, all things considered," Pleasant continued. "I have the location of the Grotesquery *and* I got to kill Valkyrie, which admittedly is something I've been wanting to do since I met her. She can be incredibly annoying. Had you noticed that?"

"Um."

"She hardly ever shut up. I pretended to be friends with her, but honestly, I just felt sorry for the poor girl. Not the brightest, you know?"

"You're such a goon," said a voice from behind, and Scapegrace whirled around and squealed as Valkyrie Cain walked up, hands in her pockets and a smile on her face.

16

THE SWITCH

Valkyrie knew it was a bluff, she just knew it, and Skulduggery confirmed it when he uttered the code words.

"Be brave."

He was gripping her arm tightly. Her knees were sore from where she had dropped. Her performance was pretty impressive, she had to admit. Hopefully, it was also pretty believable.

"Let go of me!" she shouted.

Skulduggery looked over at the Torment. Scapegrace was

standing beside him, enjoying every second of what he thought was going on.

"Give us a minute," Skulduggery said.

"A minute," the Torment replied. "Nothing more."

Valkyrie let Skulduggery pull her to her feet and led her away. "Keep shaking your head," he said softly.

"What are we going to do?" she asked. "The only way he tells us what we want to know is if you kill me."

"I'm not going to kill you."

"Oh, good."

"I'm going to kill your reflection."

"What? How?"

"Where is it right now?"

"Half-day in school, so it should be at home."

"Call it, tell it to step back inside the mirror."

To keep up the act, Valkyrie tried, and failed, to pull away. When Skulduggery pulled her back to him, she continued. "But if you do kill it, what will happen? Will it, like, actually *die*?"

"It doesn't live," Skulduggery reminded her, "so it can't die. It will, however, *appear* to be dead. I think if we return it to the mirror afterwards though, it should be fine."

"You *think*?"

"This hasn't been done before. No one has bothered, simply

because sorcerers can tell a reflection from a real person with ease. The only way this will work is if the Torment is as out of practice as we're hoping."

They reached the corner of the Roarhaven Sanctuary and Valkyrie took out her phone. Skulduggery stepped behind the corner and hunkered down out of sight. He started to dig a hole with his hands.

Valkyrie dialled her home phone and it was answered after two rings.

"Hello," her own voice said.

"Are you alone?" Valkyrie asked.

"Yes," the reflection answered. "Your parents are still at work. I'm sitting in your room, doing your homework."

"I need you to step into the mirror, OK? We're going to try something."

"All right."

"And leave a note for Mum. Tell her I'm spending the night at a friend's."

"What friend?"

"I don't know," Valkyrie said impatiently. "Pick one."

"But you don't have any friends."

Valkyrie glowered. "Tell her I'm sleeping over at Hannah Foley's."

"Hannah Foley doesn't like you."

"Just do it!" Valkyrie snapped, and hung up. Skulduggery was scooping out handfuls of earth, making a shallow hole about a metre in diameter.

She hesitated. "It'll be OK, won't it? Once we put it back in the mirror, it'll come back to life, right? I know it's not '*life*' life, but..."

"Valkyrie, me shooting the reflection is just the same as me tearing up a photograph of you. There is absolutely no difference."

She nodded. "OK. Yes, I know. OK."

He smoothed out the base of the hole and with his finger he drew a large circle in the dirt, and in that circle he drew an eye with a wavy line through it.

"Are they looking?" he asked.

Valkyrie held a hand to her face like she was crying, and glanced back. "No, they're talking. The Torment is looking annoyed."

Skulduggery stood and held out a hand. The air around him became damp, and droplets of moisture began to form. A rainbow appeared in this mist and cloud, and abruptly vanished when Skulduggery drew it all in tighter and let it fall, as rain, into the hole.

He said, "Surface speak, surface feel, surface think, surface real," and then his fingers curled. The puddle became a mini-whirlpool that erased the pattern at its base. Skulduggery calmed the water and nodded to Valkyrie.

She stood directly over the puddle and looked down, then dipped her toe in the water. The puddle rippled, obscuring her view. And then a hand broke the surface. They watched the reflection, clad in the same black clothes Valkyrie was wearing, as it slowly climbed up, out of the puddle. No, Valkyrie corrected herself, it wasn't climbing out of the *puddle*, for she could still see the bottom of the hole. Rather, the reflection was climbing out of the *surface* of the puddle, and changing from a two-dimensional image into a three-dimensional person before her eyes.

Skulduggery took its hand and helped it out the rest of the way, and it stood there and didn't speak. It wasn't even curious about why it had been summoned.

"We're going to kill you," Valkyrie told it.

It nodded. "All right."

"Can you cry?"

The reflection started weeping. The sudden change was startling.

"Dead man," the Torment called. "Your minute is up."

Skulduggery rested his hands on Valkyrie's shoulders. "Push me away," he said.

He moved in to hug her and Valkyrie turned so that he blocked her from the Torment's view, and she shoved him back and switched places with the reflection. She pressed herself against the wall of the building and didn't move, expecting to hear a shout of alarm. But no shout came. They hadn't noticed the switch.

Skulduggery and the reflection walked back around the corner, and Valkyrie made her way to the cover of the trees. She moved quietly, keeping low, and she didn't once peek. At first, she reasoned that she didn't want to risk being discovered, but she knew it wasn't that.

The truth was, she didn't want to see herself being killed.

She flinched when she heard the gunshot. Her skin was cold and she had goosebumps. She rubbed her arms through her coat.

A few minutes later she heard Skulduggery and Scapegrace approaching. She watched them go to the Bentley. Skulduggery placed the reflection's body in the trunk. It looked so *limp*. Valkyrie took a deep breath. Tearing up a photograph. That's all it was. That's all.

The Torment had disappeared back into the town, having

suddenly lost all interest. Scapegrace probably expected Skulduggery to rip him apart, but Skulduggery was too busy teasing Valkyrie. She came out from hiding and strolled over, her unease fading. If he was joking, that meant the plan had worked.

"She hardly ever shut up," Skulduggery was saying. "I pretended to be friends with her, but honestly, I just felt sorry for the poor girl. Not the brightest, you know?"

"You're such a goon," Valkyrie said, a grin forming, and Scapegrace turned and squealed. She ignored him. "Did we get what we need?"

"Bancrook," Skulduggery said. "Vengeous probably has Vile's armour by now, but the Grotesquery should still be in Bancrook. We got what we need."

"You're dead," Scapegrace said in a small voice. "You're... you're lying in the boot."

"Sorry to disappoint you, but my *reflection* is lying in the boot."

"No," Scapegrace said. "No, I've seen reflections, you can *tell* if something's a reflection..."

"Not this one," Skulduggery told him. "She uses it practically every day. Over the past year, it's kind of... grown, so if I were you, I wouldn't feel bad about being fooled. If I were you, there's a load of other things *I'd* choose to feel bad about."

"Like how you could have got away," Valkyrie said, "if you'd just kept walking, instead of coming over to gloat."

"I could have got away?"

"Free and clear."

"And... and now?"

"Now we're going to Bancrook," Skulduggery said, "and we're dropping you off at a holding cell along the way."

"I'm going back to jail?"

"Yes, you are."

Scapegrace sagged miserably. "But I don't like jail."

Skulduggery snapped the shackles into place around Scapegrace's wrists. "Today is not a good day to be a bad guy."

17

GRAVE ROBBING

he remains of Bancrook Castle stood on the top of a small hill. Valkyrie followed Skulduggery through the gaping hole in the wall that acted as its doorway. The castle was dark and quiet, and most of the roof had fallen in. Above them the sun was setting, and a startling orange had bled into the sky.

They hadn't had time to stop off at Haggard after depositing Scapegrace at the Sanctuary, so the body of the reflection was still in the Bentley. It was a creepy sensation, looking in at it, seeing it lying there, cold and unmoving. Valkyrie kept expecting to see it breathe, or to see some flutter of the eyelids, like it was only sleeping. But it just lay in the boot, a thing, a corpse with her face.

Skulduggery held up his hand and read the air, then nodded with satisfaction. "No one has been here for a long time. The Grotesquery must still be around here somewhere."

They walked deeper into the ruins, clicking their fingers and summoning flames into their hands. The light flickered off the moss-covered stones that made up the walls. They took the steps leading down, and passed beneath ground level. It was cold down here and damp. Valkyrie pulled her coat a little tighter around herself.

Skulduggery hunkered down, examining the ground, looking for any sign that the Grotesquery was buried underneath, and Valkyrie went up to a section of the wall and scraped away at a covering of moss.

"Anything suspicious?" Skulduggery asked.

"That depends. Are we treating ordinary walls as suspicious?"

"Not particularly."

"Then I got nothing."

She abandoned the moss-scraping and glanced at her watch. Dinner time at home. God, she was hungry. She thought of her reflection, about all the times it had sat at the table, pretending to be a part of the family, eating Valkyrie's dinner and speaking with Valkyrie's voice. She wondered if her parents were starting to love the reflection more than they loved her. She wondered if it would ever get to the point where she would be a stranger in her own home.

She shook her head. She didn't like thinking those thoughts. They came regularly, unwelcome visitors in her mind, they stayed far too long and they made too much mess. She focused on the positive. She was living a life of adventure. She was living the life she'd always wanted. It was perfectly understandable, every now and again, if she missed the simple little luxuries that she didn't have time for any more.

She frowned and turned to Skulduggery. "It's probably a bad sign when you start to think of your parents as mildly distracting luxuries, isn't it?"

"One would imagine so." He looked up at her. "Do you wish you could go to the family reunion?"

"What? No, no way."

"Have you been thinking about it?"

"I haven't really had time, what with the world being in danger and all."

"Somewhat understandable. But still, these things are

important. You should try to seize the opportunity to reconnect with the people who matter to you most."

Valkyrie nearly laughed. "Are we talking about the same family here?"

"Family's important," Skulduggery said.

"Tell me, and be honest, did you ever have an aunt as bad as Beryl?"

"Well, no. But I did have a cousin who was a cannibal."

"Really?"

"Oh, yes. When they caught him, he ate himself to hide the evidence."

"He couldn't have eaten himself, that's impossible."

"Well, he didn't eat *all* of himself, obviously. He left his mouth."

"Oh, my God, would you shut up, you're being— car."

"I'm being *car*?"

"No," she whispered, letting her flame go out. "There's a car coming." Skulduggery extinguished his own flame and grabbed her hand. They sprinted for the steps, ducking back as headlights swept by, and then ran on. There was another set of stairs leading up, through the caved-in roof, to the top of the ruins. The steps were covered in moss and slippery, but these things didn't seem to matter to Skulduggery.

They emerged into the gloom of the evening, as the sun was finally melting into the horizon. They pressed themselves to what was left of the castle's battlements, and peered over. The black jeep was parked directly beneath them. They watched a white van approach and stop. Seven people got out, wearing blood-splattered clothing. The Infected.

Baron Vengeous and Dusk got out of the jeep. Vengeous still had the cutlass in his belt, but if he had found Lord Vile's armour, he wasn't wearing it.

Dusk spoke with Vengeous, then issued orders to the Infected, and they took a long wooden crate from the white van. Everyone but Dusk followed Vengeous into the ruins.

Valkyrie switched positions and peered down the crumbling steps into the castle. Vengeous approached the only wall that was still intact and she heard his voice, though she couldn't make out the words. Dust started to rise from the wall and it began to shake. The topmost stone came loose and fell. Within moments the wall was tumbling down, the stones falling on each other and rolling into the shadows, and the small room behind it was revealed. Valkyrie was too high up to see into this room, but she knew what it contained. Vengeous sent the Infected in.

She peered over the battlement at Dusk, who was leaning

against the Jeep, keeping look-out, then she turned to Skulduggery. "Sanguine isn't here," she whispered.

"Not yet, no."

"*Please* tell me it's time to call for back-up."

"It's time to call for back-up."

"Oh, good."

She dug her phone out of her pocket, dialled and waited. When the Sanctuary's Administrator answered the phone, Valkyrie passed the information on in hushed tones. She hung up and nodded to Skulduggery, and held up both her hands with her fingers extended. Ten minutes until the Cleavers arrived.

The Infected re-emerged, carrying a figure between them. It looked like a mummy, all wrapped in dirty bandages, but it was huge, and judging by the difficulty with which the Infected were moving, it was heavy. They carried it towards the open crate. One of the Infected lost his grip and the body of the Grotesquery nearly fell. Vengeous flew into a rage, threw the offending Infected to the ground and glared, his eyes glowing yellow for a moment. The Infected tried getting up, but something was clearly wrong. His body started trembling, shaking uncontrollably. Even from here, Valkyrie could see the panic in his face.

And then he exploded in a mist of blood and fleshy chunks.

"Oh, my God," Valkyrie whispered.

"Stay here," Skulduggery said and started moving.

She frowned. "Where are you going?"

"I have to delay them until the Cleavers arrive. We can't afford to lose track of them – not now."

"Well, I'm going with you."

"No, you're not. You're important to Vengeous and we don't know why – until we do, you're staying out of sight."

"Then I'll stay up here and, I don't know, throw stones, and when you're finished I'll go down and help out."

He looked at her. "In order to finish, I'll have to have defeated six Infected, Dusk and Vengeous himself."

"Yeah. So?"

"The Infected I can manage."

She frowned. "And Vengeous? I mean, you *can* beat him, right?"

"Well," Skulduggery said, "I can certainly try. And trying is half the battle."

"What's the other half?"

He shrugged. "Hitting him more times than he hits me." He moved to the battlement. "If things go wrong, I'll lead them away. Once it's clear, get back to the car. If you don't see me in five minutes, then I've probably died a very brave and heroic death. Oh, and don't touch the radio – I've just got it tuned right where I want it and I don't want you messing that up."

And then Skulduggery placed his hand on the top of the battlement, vaulted over it and disappeared.

18

OLD ENEMIES

Valkyrie edged up to the battlement, peeking down as Skulduggery landed gently. Dusk turned his head like he had heard something, but then looked the other way. Skulduggery crept up behind him, wrapped an arm around his throat and hauled him back. Dusk struggled, tried to release the grip, but Skulduggery was cutting off the oxygen to his brain and Valkyrie knew it would be over in moments. Once Dusk had gone limp, Skulduggery laid him on the ground. The entire thing had been done in complete silence.

Skulduggery crept to the castle entrance and Valkyrie

moved to the very edge of the collapsed roof, lying flat and peering over. The Infected had managed to place the mummified figure into the crate without dropping it again. Valkyrie saw their eyes narrow when Skulduggery walked up. Vengeous still had his back to him.

"Hello, Baron," Skulduggery said. She saw Vengeous stiffen slightly, then turn.

"Of course," Vengeous said. "Who do they send to try and take me down? Not even a man. Not even a monster. They send *you*."

Skulduggery gave a little shrug. "How've you been, Baron?"

"You taint me," Vengeous said, disgust in his voice. "Even being in your presence, it taints me. I can feel it in the air. Even these Infected, these half-Undead, even they are more worthy of my time than you would ever be."

Skulduggery nodded. "So, you married or anything? Do I hear the pitter patter of tiny evil feet?"

"I will destroy you."

"You're still upset about that time I made you explode, aren't you? I can tell."

"You never stop talking, do you?"

"I don't *have* to talk," Skulduggery said. "I can be quiet." A moment passed. "So, who've you got in the crate? Is it the shrivelled, lifeless, patchwork corpse of the Grotesquery? Am I right? Because if it is, I'm afraid I can't let you take it. I could, you know, give you its big toe or something, as a keepsake, but that's about it."

"What you are saying, skeleton, is blasphemous."

"You're the one who dug up your own god."

Vengeous started forward, taking his cutlass from its sheath. "I wish I didn't have to kill you now. I wish I could see the fury it would wreak upon you for this blasphemy."

"You do realise I've got no skin to cut, right?"

Vengeous smiled again as he approached. "This sword is woven razor, the same process they use to make the Cleavers' scythes. It will shear through your bones."

"Ah," Skulduggery said, taking a step back.

Vengeous was almost upon him. "What's this? No jokes? No taunts? Let me see how confident you are now, you abomination."

Skulduggery's hand went into his jacket and came back out with his revolver. He aimed it squarely at Vengeous' face. Vengeous froze.

"As it turns out," Skulduggery said after a moment's consideration, "I'm still pretty confident."

"Are you going to shoot me?" Vengeous sneered. "I wouldn't

be surprised. What would a thing like you know about honour? Only a heathen would bring a gun to a swordfight."

"And only a moron would bring a sword to a gunfight."

Vengeous scowled. "As you can see," he said, "you are vastly outnumbered."

"I usually am."

"Your situation has become quite untenable."

"It usually does."

"You are within moments of being swarmed by these filthy creatures of Undeath and torn apart in a maelstrom of pain and fury."

Skulduggery paused. "OK, that's a new one on me."

"Kill him!" Vengeous barked.

The Infected started forward, Valkyrie saw Skulduggery wave his arm and a gust of wind raised a cloud of dust to obscure her view. She glimpsed Vengeous backing up, shielding his eyes. There were gunshots, flashes of fire, and gutteral snarls of anger, and the Infected flew backwards through the air. When the dust cleared, only Skulduggery and Vengeous were left standing.

"Six shots," Vengeous said. "I counted. Your gun is empty."

"You're assuming I didn't reload in all the confusion."

"And did you?"

Skulduggery hesitated. "No," he admitted and put the gun away.

Vengeous took a moment to look around. "The girl," he said. "Cain. Where is she?"

"She had to stay home unfortunately. It's a school night, so..."

"Pity. I would have liked her to see me kill you." Vengeous laid his cutlass on the ground. "And I won't be needing a sword to kill you." He strode towards Skulduggery, who raised his hand.

"Um, since you're not going to be using it, can I?"

Vengeous almost laughed. He punched and Skulduggery darted low and to the side, but Vengeous was expecting the manoeuvre and he brought his clenched fist down on Skulduggery's shoulder blade. Skulduggery tried to move in for a throw, but Vengeous shifted his weight slightly and stuck out his foot, and Skulduggery went tumbling. His leg hit the crate and he fell on to the Grotesquery.

Vengeous roared and reached in, grabbing Skulduggery and hauling him out. He sent out a right hook that cracked against the bone of Skulduggery's jaw. He followed it with a left cross, but Skulduggery managed to raise his arm in defence. The block turned to a strike to the throat, as sudden and savage as a snake.

Vengeous coughed and fell back, and Skulduggery kicked the inside of his leg.

Vengeous kept his guard close, protecting his head, but dropped it low when Skulduggery kicked for his ribs. The kick was a feint and turned to a step, and Skulduggery swung a punch, but Vengeous caught it, his left hand closing around the skeleton's right wrist. Vengeous surged upwards and in, his right elbow hitting Skulduggery's right shoulder like a bullet. Vengeous torqued his body and took Skulduggery off his feet and threw him to the ground, landing heavily on top of him.

Skulduggery's left hand came up to Vengeous's face, the fingers flexing, and Vengeous swatted the hand away before Skudluggery could push at the air. Vengeous punched, again and again, and grinned down at him.

"I'd hate to be you," Vengeous said. "A skeleton who feels pain. None of the advantages of a flesh and blood body, and all of its weaknesses. Whoever brought you back should have left you where you lay."

Skulduggery groaned. Some of the Infected were back on their feet and they looked at Skulduggery as he lay there. Vengeous stood and brushed the dust from his clothes. He picked up his cutlass.

"I'm going to cut you," Vengeous said, "into little tiny pieces.

I'm going to take a small part of your skull and turn it into some dice. Maybe I'll use the rest of you as keys on a piano. I wonder, skeleton, would you still be alive? Would you be conscious if you were dice, or keys on a piano?"

"Always wanted a life in music," Skulduggery mumbled.

Valkyrie couldn't watch any more. She got to her feet. "Hey!" Vengeous looked up to the collapsed roof and saw her.

"Heard you've been looking for me," she called out.

"Miss Cain," Vengeous said with a smile. "So you *are* here."

"That girl," Skulduggery muttered, "never does what she's bloody well told..."

"You want me, Baron?" Valkyrie shouted. "Come and get me!"

And then she stepped back and Vengeous started running up after her, and she went to the battlement and flung herself over.

19

ON THE RUN

This is so stupid, Valkyrie thought to herself as she ran. Her foot hit a rock and she almost fell. She didn't know where she was going or what she would do. She had no plan at all, whatsoever.

She ignored the trail and ran deeper into blackness. She could hear her pursuers now, the commands being shouted to the Infected. She could hear the van and when she looked over her shoulder she glimpsed its headlights, bobbing like crazy over the uneven ground.

Then the world left her and she was falling.

She hit the side of the hill and started to roll. The ground levelled off and she hit a patch of briars that tried to get in at her through her clothes. The headlights came around the bend and she flattened herself, the briars tearing at her hands and hair. She dragged herself through as the headlights hurtled towards her.

Missing her by a hand's breadth, the van roared by. Valkyrie stayed a moment to catch her breath then ripped the briars away and got up. There were shouts from all directions. The Infected almost had her surrounded, and the only reason she was still free was because they hadn't realised it yet. She set off, limping slightly. There was a road ahead. If she could get to the pitch blackness on the other side, she might have a chance at escape.

But now there was another set of headlights. The black jeep. She had to get across the road before she was cut off. And then there was somebody standing in her way.

Dusk grabbed her and she tried to hit him, but he threw her down. "Finally," he said, as though he was bored of a game. He was about to continue speaking, but she saw his face twitch and his hand went to his belly. His fingers dipped into his coat, brought out the syringe.

This was her chance and she couldn't afford to mess it up.

Forcing the fear and the panic from her mind, Valkyrie

splayed her fingers. The air shimmered and the syringe flew from his grasp, vanishing into the darkness. He cursed, tried to run after it, but lost his balance and stumbled. Valkyrie was up, already moving fast in the other direction.

"That was a mistake," she heard him mutter. "That serum was the only thing keeping me under control..."

She glanced back as Dusk took hold of his human form and tore it off, like a snake shucking its skin. The vampire beneath the flesh and clothes, the creature within the man, was bald and alabaster white, its eyes black and its fangs jagged. She knew Dusk hadn't been lying: that *had* been a mistake. Valkyrie sprinted, and the vampire bounded after her.

The Infected were all around her and the black jeep had picked her out with its headlights. Baron Vengeous could plainly see her, but she didn't care. Vengeous would keep her alive until he decided it was time to kill her. The vampire, on the other hand, would rip her to pieces right there and then.

It was bounding after her and gaining fast. One more leap and it would be on top of her. She couldn't afford to try anything, couldn't afford to use her powers. Adrenaline was pumping through her system. Her powers probably wouldn't even *work*.

She took Billy-Ray Sanguine's razor from her pocket,

unfolding it as she ran. Over the sound of the oncoming jeep, she heard Vengeous trying to call off the vampire, but she knew the beast wouldn't listen. A vampire, after it's shucked its skin, has no master. Skulduggery had called them the most efficient killers in the world. The only thing a vampire cared about was blood.

The bounding stopped and she felt it in the air, felt it descending, and Valkyrie turned and lashed out. The razor opened up the vampire's face as she fell backwards. The vampire that had once been Dusk roared in pain, hit the ground and came at her again before she even had time to roll to her feet.

The jeep was still approaching, and it wasn't slowing down. It swerved and swung around in a cloud of dust and smacked right into the vampire, flinging it back. The passenger door opened.

"In!" Skulduggery yelled. Valkyrie jumped in and the jeep shot off.

"Seatbelt," Skulduggery said. Valkyrie reached for it as he turned the wheel and her head hit the window.

"Ow!"

"Sorry. Wear your seatbelt."

The van was right behind them, filling the inside of the jeep with yellow light. Skulduggery braked and turned, gunning the engine, and the yellow light withdrew sharply as the van missed the hidden turn. They left the van in their dust and followed a trail through the hills.

Valkyrie grabbed the seatbelt and tugged it a few times before she got it to work. She settled into her seat and clicked it in, just as Skulduggery braked.

"OK," he said. "Out." He opened his door and got out, hurrying to the Bentley. Cursing his name, Valkyrie followed.

The silence of the night was eerie. And then the ground ahead of them cracked and crumbled, and Skulduggery pulled out his gun as Billy-Ray Sanguine rose to the surface.

"Well, I do declare," Sanguine said with a smile. "The great Skeleton Detective, in the flesh – figuratively speakin', of course."

Skulduggery regarded him warily. "Mr Sanguine, I've been hearing so much about you."

"That so?"

"You're quite the little psychopath, aren't you?"

"I try."

"So tell me something – why wait eighty years before you helped your old boss escape? Why didn't you just bust him out the day after he was caught?"

Sanguine shrugged. "I suppose I had what y'all might call a crisis of faith and my faith lost. These past eighty years, goin' it alone, it's been good, but somethin's been missing, y'know?"

"You're under arrest."

"Speakin' of which, and I don't mean to be rude, but I just popped by to pick up the li'l darlin' there. I'll be out of your hair in a moment – again, figuratively speakin'." He passed down into the ground with a smile on his face.

"Oh, hell," Valkyrie said and Skulduggery reached for her, but it was too late. The ground exploded and Sanguine grabbed her, and Valkyrie didn't even have time to cry out before he took her down into the ground with him.

20

UNDER THE GROUND

Valkyrie gasped for breath as she plunged down into the darkness. The earth shifted around her. It scraped into her back and crumbled at her feet. Dirt flew into her eyes and the sound of a rockslide roared in her ears. She clung on to Sanguine as they moved.

"Scared?" he said in her ear. "What if I were to just... let go?"

He was right in front of her – she could feel his breath on her cheek – but she couldn't see him. It was impossibly dark, whatever tunnel they were making filling up above them as they moved. Her gut twisted as real, raw terror spread through her.

"I'll burn you," she said, but the sound of rockslide drowned out her small voice. "*I'll burn you!*" she shouted. She heard him laugh.

"You burn me enough you might kill me and then what would you do? You'd be stuck here, buried alive under the ground with only my corpse for comfort."

They slowed, the rockslide lessened, and they came to a stop. Valkyrie was shaking. Sweat drenched her. Panic caught at her throat.

"I can see you, you know," he said. "My eyes were taken, but my sight remains. And here, in the dark? I can see best of all. I can see the fear on your face. You can't hide it from me. So here's what's gonna happen. I'm gonna put some dainty li'l shackles on those wrists of yours and then we're gonna go pay a visit to Baron Vengeous. That sound like a nice way to spend the rest of your life?"

Valkyrie tasted dirt in her mouth, but didn't answer. It was too dark. She could feel the rocks all around her. Despite her loathing, she realised she was clinging tightly to Sanguine, terrified he was going to let her go and leave her here. She felt him move, heard the earth shift, and felt something cold and metal close around her wrists.

"Oh, one other thing," he said. "My blade. Where is it?"

"Coat pocket," she whispered.

His hand dipped into the pocket, removing the straight razor.

"So good to have it back. It's like a part of me, y'know? Like a little piece of my soul..."

He could see in the dark, so she made sure he could see the contempt on her face. "Is there somewhere we need to go or are you going to keep us down here and bore me to death?"

He laughed, the rock shifted and they moved again, fast. She tried to work out how Sanguine did it, but it was as if the ground just parted for him then closed up when he'd passed. It was impossible to tell what direction they were going or even if they were headed up or down, and then suddenly the earth gave way and their momentum carried them through into the fresh air.

The moon, heavy and low in the dark sky. Trees and hedges and grass. Valkyrie fell to her knees, spitting dirt and sucking in air. The sweat that coated her body now chilled her, but the ground was solid and the roar was gone from her ears. She raised her head, looked back.

"Your chariot awaits, ma'am," Sanguine said, opening the door to the car that had been parked there. She tested the shackles, but they were on tight. She clicked her fingers, but no spark came. Her powers were bound.

Sanguine helped her to the car by gripping the back of her neck and forcing her in. Even if she managed to get away, there was nowhere to run. There were meadows in every direction. He closed the door, walked around the car and got in behind the wheel.

"Is it fun?" he asked suddenly. "Doin' all that detectin'? I always wanted to be a detective. I *was* one, for about a year. I liked the romance of it all. The suits, the hats, the dark alleys, the femme fatale, all that quick talkin'... But I couldn't stop *killin'* folk. I mean, they'd hire me, I'd try to solve their mystery, but halfway through I'd get bored and end up killin' them, and then the case'd be over and that'd be it. I solved one single murder that whole entire year, but I don't think that really counts, seein' as how I was the killer. I think that's kinda cheatin', in a way."

"Why are you doing this?" Valkyrie blurted out. "Why does he still want me? It's not like Skulduggery's going to back off just because I'm being held captive."

Sanguine stared. "Are you serious?" He laughed. "Li'l darlin', you ain't no *hostage*, you never were!"

"What?"

"This whole thing, everythin' that's happenin', it's *because* of you."

"What are you talking about?"

"You heard about the missin' ingredient, right? The one thing Vengeous couldn't get his hands on eighty years ago. You heard about that?"

"Of course. What's that got to do with me?"

"Sweetie, it *is* you. *You're* the missin' ingredient." She stared at him and his smile grew wider.

"You're a direct descendant of the Ancients, ain't you? What, you thought that little bit of information wouldn't get around? When I heard about that, I knew the time had come to set the Baron free."

"You're lying..."

"Scout's honour. The one thing he was missin' was blood with a certain type of power in it. Seein' as how he wasn't likely to get the blood of another Faceless One anytime soon, the next best thing is the blood of one of the guys who managed to *kill* a Faceless One. That was the last ingredient to the end-of–the-world-as-we-know-it cocktail he was brewin'. Must make you feel pretty special, huh?"

Valkyrie couldn't answer. She felt the colour drain from her face.

"This is good," Sanguine said, clearly delighted, as he started the engine. "This is *good*."

21

DONNING DARKNESS

It was time.

Vengeous felt its power, felt it pierce his skin and wrap itself around his insides. Even if he wanted to, even if he changed his mind about what he planned to do, it was too late now. It was pulling him forward. How could Vile ever have been beaten with power like this?

The Infected had laid out the armour on a table, in a small room at the rear of the church. From such humble beginnings, Vengeous thought to himself, and smiled.

He approached the table, reached out, but stopped, his hands hovering over the gauntlets. His fingers trailed in the air, moving over the chest-plate, the boots. *The first piece of armour he touched was the mask. He picked it up carefully, held it, felt it change and shift beneath his touch.*

The garments he wore — black and simple to the eye — were specially woven to ensure a successful binding. He would be wearing Lord Vile's armour — his body would need insulating against the raw power contained within, power that could sear his flesh and boil his blood.

By now, Billy-Ray Sanguine would have located the Cain girl and he would be bringing her to the church. The Baron himself had subdued Dusk, and injected him with the serum. By shedding his skin, Dusk had failed him, nearly cost him everything. But Vengeous would punish him later. For right now, all his dreams were about to come true.

As Baron Vengeous donned the armour, shadows rose from it like steam.

22

BLOOD AND SHADOWS

They drove deeper into the country, where the roads narrowed and twisted like snakes. Finally, they pulled up outside a dark old church and Sanguine got out, went around to Valkyrie's side and opened the door, then pulled her from the car. He took her arm and led her up the cracked, overgrown path. Vines clung to the crumbling walls and the small stained-glass windows were caked with grime and dust.

He pushed open the ancient double doors and guided her into the cold, dank church. There were still a few pews that hadn't rotted away, and there were hundreds of lit candles that sent the shadows dancing and pirouetting across the walls. The altar had been ransacked and cleared, replaced with a large slab, solid and proud, and upon that slab was the massive, bandaged body of the Grotesquery, covered in a sheet.

Baron Vengeous was waiting for them, clad in the black armour of Lord Vile. It was not what Valkyrie had expected. The armour did not clank or rattle, and it cast no sheen. It seemed to be alive, subtly moving and reshaping itself even as she watched.

There were others in the church, Infected men and women, the vampire virus working through their bodies, changing them every moment that passed. They stayed in the shadows as best they could.

She could see Dusk now. His human form had grown back, but it had kept the scar across his face. It was deep and ugly, and he was glaring at her with every ounce of hatred his blackened soul was capable of.

"Valkyrie Cain," Vengeous said, the mask distorting his voice into a rough whisper. "So nice of you to join us on this most auspicious of nights. The creature on this table will open the gateway for its brethren, and this world will be cleansed. The unworthy will be decimated and we will usher in a new paradise, and it's all thanks to you."

Sanguine took Valkyrie by the elbow and led her to the front pew, where he made her sit beside him, and they watched Vengeous lower his head, his hands raised above the body on the slab. Shadows started moving around Vengeous. The candles were flickering like a strong wind was blowing, but the inside of the church was deathly calm.

"The Grotesquery's gonna feed on you," Sanguine whispered, almost casual. "That good ole boy's been out for the count – he's gonna need your blood in his veins. Gonna have himself a slap up meal. You mind if I take pictures? Brought my own camera and everythin'."

"Knock yourself out."

"Thanks."

"No, really, run head first into the wall and knock yourself out because I'm telling you, you better be unconscious when Skulduggery gets here."

Sanguine grinned and sat back. "I can handle Mister Funnybones, don't you worry about that. Pay attention now, darlin', this is where it gets interestin'."

Valkyrie looked back at the altar just as the shadows bunched up behind Vengeous and descended on him like a shroud. He stiffened and his body jerked, as if he was being shot through with electric currents. The shadows started flowing out through his fingertips and down, passing through the sheet.

"Mr Sanguine," Vengeous whispered.

Sanguine pulled Valkyrie up and dragged her over to the slab. He grinned as he showed her his straight razor then grabbed her wrist. She tried to struggle but he was far too strong, and she cried out as he ran the cold blade across the palm of her right hand. But instead of running off her hand and dripping on to the sheet, her blood drifted to the shadow stream, mixing with it, twirling through it and around it, being fed into the body of the Grotesquery.

And that's when the double doors swung open and Skulduggery Pleasant strolled into the church.

The Infected snarled and Valkyrie pulled her hand from Sanguine's grip. Vengeous looked up from his dark work and his armour grew angry spikes, as Skulduggery walked up to the end of the aisle and sat in the front pew. He crossed his legs, settled into a comfortable position and waved his hand in the air.

"Don't let me interrupt," he said.

Valkyrie frowned. Not quite the rescue she was counting on.

The Infected moved into the light, closing in on Skulduggery, who was acting like he'd just popped by for a chat. Vengeous sent the last of the shadow stream into the Grotesquery and then stepped back. Valkyrie saw him sag slightly.

Vengeous brought his hands up to his head and undid the latches on the mask, lifting it off. His face was pale and shiny with sweat. His eyes were narrow and cold.

"Abomination," he said. "You came here alone? No Cleavers with you? Mr Bliss isn't by your side?"

"You know me, Baron, I like to take care of things myself. Also, when you beat me up, you broke my phone, so..."

A smile now, cracking across Vengeous's lips. "Did you come here to witness the beginning of your end?"

"No, not really. I just came here to do this."

Skulduggery reached into his jacket, pulled out a small black satchel and lobbed it on to the slab. It landed on the sheet, over the bandaged chest of the Grotesquery. Vengeous gazed at it, reached out...

"Wouldn't do that if I were you," Skulduggery said, holding up a small device. "One push of this button and this lovely little church is decorated with bits of your god."

"A bomb?" Vengeous said, anger rising in his voice. His armour swelled and thickened protectively. "You think explosives could harm a Faceless One?"

"But that's not a Faceless One, is it? At least not a *whole* one. I expect it's a tad fragile actually, after spending all that time locked away in a wall. And I'm betting all this has taken a lot out of *you* too. That one little bomb could take you both out at the same time. Well, I say little, but it's actually about fifteen times more powerful than the *last* one I threw at you, and you remember how sore *that* was."

Sanguine pushed Valkyrie closer to the slab. "You'll kill *her* right along with all of us."

"I don't have to," Skulduggery said patiently. "I either press this button and foil your insidious plot and kill my friend while I'm at it, or I don't, and we leave, and you just wait another three years for the next lunar eclipse. It's up to you, Baron."

Vengeous observed him. "Take her."

Dusk stepped forward. "The girl must die!"

"Silence!" Vengeous roared. He locked eyes with Dusk until the vampire backed down, the flickering candlelight playing on his scar.

Vengeous looked back at Skulduggery. "Take the girl," he sneered. "You won't get far."

"We'll get far enough. Valkyrie?" Valkyrie held her hands out to Sanguine.

He glared at her, then put his straight razor on the slab and muttered. He undid the shackles and stepped back. Valkyrie joined Skulduggery as he moved into the aisle, but not before she snatched up the razor.

"Hey!" Sanguine shouted.

"Be quiet," Vengeous snapped.

"She has my blade!"

"*I said be quiet!*"

Sanguine shut up. Valkyrie folded the blade into its handle and stuck it in her pocket. She moved backwards, at Skulduggery's side, and the Infected moved with them.

"You're only delaying the inevitable," Vengeous said. "With this armour, I am the most powerful living being in this world."

"But are you *happy?*" Skulduggery mused, clicking the fingers of his free hand and summoning a flame. He cast the fireball behind them, at the ground near the doorway. The Infected hissed at the flames. Vengeous still hadn't moved any nearer to the satchel of explosives.

"I will take you apart, abomination."

"So at least I have that to look forward to," Skulduggery said. "You won't want to make any sudden moves until we reach the road – I'll know if you crazy kids disturb the air around the nice bag of explosives."

"Blow it up," Valkyrie murmured out of the corner of her mouth.

"Can't do that," Skulduggery replied in a whisper. He

moved his hand and the flames parted in the doorway and they backed through them, out into the night air.

"Why not?"

"Not a bomb," he replied softly. "It's a bag with a collapsible jack, for changing tyres."

"What about the remote?"

"It opens my garage door. Don't tell them, but it doesn't even have any batteries in it." He waved his hand and the flames came together again to block off the exit. They kept walking backwards to the Bentley, keeping eye contact with the Infected through the flames, making sure no one cheated and rushed out too early.

"Do we have a plan?" she asked as they backed away from the church.

"We need to get the Grotesquery away from the bad guys," he said, "so we'll have to split up. I'm going to leave, you're going to hide under the van, wait until they load the Grotesquery in there, and then you're going to drive off, right out from under their noses."

"*What?*"

"It'll be really funny, trust me."

"Skulduggery, I'm thirteen. I can't drive."

He looked at her. "What do you mean you can't drive?"

"Am I talking in code? *I can't drive*, Skulduggery."

"But you've seen others drive, haven't you? You've seen *me* drive. I daresay you've seen your parents drive. So you know the fundamentals."

She stared at him. "I know the big round thing sticking out of the dashboard turns the wheels. That fundamental enough for you?"

"The van over there is an automatic. You put it in Drive – you go. You press one pedal – you go fast; you press another pedal – you stop. Easy."

She stared at him. "Oh, bloody hell," she muttered and darted for the van, sliding beneath it as Skulduggery jumped into the Bentley.

The Bentley's engine roared, the tyres spun and it sped away from the church as a wave of darkness erupted from the doorway, extinguishing the flames. Dusk led the Infected as they poured out into the night, followed by Baron Vengeous, tendrils of shadows wrapping and coiling around him like angry snakes. He hurled the satchel to the ground and the jack bounced into the long grass. He whipped the darkness against an Infected woman, who was blasted off her feet by the impact and went sailing high through the air.

Valkyrie stayed under the van and kept very, very quiet. She saw Billy-Ray Sanguine walk up.

"She took my blade," he said. "*Again.*"

"I don't care about your *blade*," Vengeous snapped. He turned to one of the Infected. "You. Move the Grotesquery into the van. This place will soon be teeming with Cleavers and I can't risk them damaging it."

The Infected hurried into the church then came back out, carrying the crate. Taking extra care, they loaded it into the van. They moved back towards the church, waiting for more orders, and Valkyrie slid herself from cover and got to her feet. She could hear Vengeous issuing commands from the other side of the van, and she took a deep breath and reached for the door.

It opened with a faint click and she got in slowly, keeping low. The key was in the ignition. She looked around to get her bearings, risked a glance out of the window at the bad guys and then turned the key. The engine came to life. Vengeous turned his head and frowned, moving to where he could see who was behind the wheel.

Valkyrie pulled the stick down to Drive and stamped her foot on the accelerator. She yelped as the van shot forward, fought to gain control of the steering. This was not fun. She wrenched the wheel to the right to avoid a tree, trying her best to keep the van on the narrow road. She saw the Infected running behind, but she couldn't afford to give them too much attention. It was seriously dark outside and she didn't know where the lights were.

She took one hand off the wheel long enough to flick a lever, and the wipers dragged themselves across the dry windshield. She went over a rock and bounced in her seat. She tried another lever and the indicator started blinking. Cursing Skulduggery, Valkyrie moved it up, down, to the side then tried twisting it, and the headlamps suddenly lit up the road ahead, just in time for her to cry out as the van swerved off the trail and hurtled over a hill.

Valkyrie was thrown around in her seat. Keeping one hand tight on the wheel, she clutched at the seatbelt, yanking it across her. She glanced down, trying to find the slot that the seatbelt clicked into. The bottom of the hill met up with the road again and she tried to steer on to it, but the van just kept going, and plunged down the next hill.

Valkyrie grabbed the seatbelt again, this time finding the slot, and the seatbelt clicked in and Valkyrie turned her full attention to driving, as the van hit a rocky outcrop, spun sideways and rolled. She smacked her head against the window as the world turned around her. She heard glass breaking and metal crunching. She protected her head as she pitched forward, and her arms slammed into the steering wheel, honking the horn. The van rolled on to another road and settled back on to its four wheels.

"Owww," Valkyrie moaned. She looked up to the cracked windscreen. Headlights. A car and a motorcycle were approaching, at speed.

Valkyrie pulled the door handle and had to hit the door with her shoulder to open it. She tried to get out, but the seatbelt wouldn't let her. She fumbled at the orange button and the belt retracted. Valkyrie stumbled out as Tanith's motorbike screeched to a halt.

The Bentley braked hard and Skulduggery jumped out, ran to her and caught her as her legs gave way. Words were exchanged, but Valkyrie couldn't make sense of most of them. There was a fuzz in her head as Skulduggery carried her to the Bentley. Her arm was hurting. She opened her eyes to see Tanith loading her bike into the back of the white van, beside the crate, then getting in behind the wheel.

Skulduggery said something in a faraway voice and Valkyrie tried to answer, but her tongue was too heavy and all the strength left her body.

23

ELEPHANTS AND BUNNIES

Kenspeckle poked her arm. "Does that hurt?"

"No," Valkyrie answered.

He nodded, scribbled something in his notebook. "Have you eaten?"

"One of your assistants brought me a burger for breakfast."

He sighed. "I meant, have you eaten *sensibly*?"

"I was very sensible while I was eating the burger. Didn't miss my mouth *once*."

He prodded her again. "What about that? Does that hurt?"

"Ow."

"I'll take that as a yes. Hopefully, the pain will teach you not to break yourself when your van crashes." Kenspeckle scribbled something else and Valkyrie looked around. There were no windows in here, but she could guess what kind of morning it was. Bright, blue skied, sunny and warm.

Kenspeckle closed his notebook and nodded. "You're making an excellent recovery," he said. "One more hour, the bone will be healed."

"Thanks, Kenspeckle."

"Think nothing of it."

"And, you know, sorry about what I said yesterday, about the salt water and the vampires..."

Kenspeckle chuckled. "Don't you worry about *me*, Valkyrie. I'm tougher than I look. Last night, when the nightmares came, they weren't so bad. I remember them being *awful*. Now, you just lie back there and let the muck do its work."

Feeling guiltier than ever, Valkyrie settled back on the bed. The mixture that coated her entire right arm was cold and slimy. It had to be reapplied every twenty minutes as its magical properties were absorbed through the skin.

She heard Skulduggery come into the medical bay. His fight with Vengeous had resulted in a fractured collarbone and a few cracked ribs. She looked over at him and laughed.

He stared at her. He was wearing a bright pink hospital gown, decorated with elephants and bunnies. It hung off him like a sheet on a hatstand.

"How come she gets the *blue* hospital gown?" he asked Kenspeckle.

"Hmm?" mumbled the professor.

Skulduggery's head tilted unhappily. "You said the only gowns you had left were these pink bunny ones, but Valkyrie is wearing a perfectly respectable *blue* one."

"Your point being?"

"Why am I wearing this ridiculous gown?"

"Because it amuses me."

Kenspeckle walked out and Skulduggery looked over at her. "The important thing," he said, "is that I can wear this gown and still maintain my dignity."

"Yes," she responded automatically. "Yes, you can."

"You can stop grinning any time now."

"I am so trying, I swear."

He walked over and when he spoke his voice had changed slightly, tinged with concern. "Feeling OK?"

"Yes."

"Are you sure?"

"Yes. No. I don't know. Whatever happens with the Grotesquery, it's my fault."

"Nonsense."

"But I'm the missing ingredient."

"That doesn't make it your fault, Valkyrie. However, if you insist on taking responsibility for something you never had any control over, you can use that to make you stronger. You're going to need all the strength you can muster, especially when Dusk catches up to you."

She frowned. "Why Dusk?"

"Oh, yes, something I should maybe mention. Dusk will be wanting to kill you. He has a history of vendettas. He holds a grudge and he doesn't let it go until he's spilled blood."

"And because I cut his face...?"

"You cut his face with Sanguine's blade, the scars from which do not heal."

"Ah. That'd... that'd make him pretty mad, wouldn't it?"

"I just thought you'd like to know."

"So what are we going to do about Guild? Since he's working with the bad guys and everything...?"

"Now, we don't know that. It's not fact. Not yet." Skulduggery was quiet for a moment. "Even so, it would be foolish not to take precautions. We will report back to Guild if and when we have to. At no time will we tell him what we're planning, where we're going or who we're hoping to punch next. Agreed?"

"Agreed. So he doesn't know we have the Grotesquery?"

"I may have forgotten to tell him. I *did* remember to tell Mr Bliss though, so he has organised three Cleavers to provide security. Any more than that, unfortunately, and it would come to the attention of the Grand Mage."

"I just hope you realise, after Sagacious Tome and now Guild, that I'm never going to be able to trust anyone in a position of authority ever again."

Skulduggery's head tilted. "You don't view *me* as an authority figure?"

She laughed. Then stopped. "Oh. I'm sorry. You were serious?"

"That's lovely, that is," he said as Kenspeckle wandered in.

"Detective, you will no doubt be happy to know that my assistants are moving the Grotesquery into my brand-new private Morgue, where it will clutter up the place just when I've finally managed to get everything in order."

Valkyrie frowned. "What would you need a private morgue for?"

"Experiments," Kenspeckle said. "Experiments so bizarre and unnatural they would surely make you vomit."

"Professor Grouse," Skulduggery said, "we brought the Grotesquery here not only because your facility is more advanced than the Sanctuary's, but also because you are the leading expert in science magic."

"Mm," Kenspeckle said gruffly. "It is. And I am."

"We need your help. We have a chance to dismantle the Grotesquery and hide the pieces all over the world so it can never be put back together, and we need you to do it."

"Fine," Kenspeckle said gruffly. "But you, Valkyrie, must rest. And you, Detective, must not place her in any danger for the next, oh, let's say an hour. Do we have a deal?"

"I can rest," Valkyrie said.

"And I can manage an hour," Skulduggery said.

"All right then," said Kenspeckle. "If you'll excuse me, I have a monster to take apart."

24

ARGUS

The old hospital was steeped in dead terror and stale tears. How many people had breathed their last while lying on those small beds? How many had spent their final nights in those tiny rooms, sleeping fitfully while their nightmares rampaged across the landscape of their minds? When Baron Vengeous walked these halls he fancied he could count every single one of them.

The psychiatric ward was the best. Here, even without the sensitivities brought on by his new armour, he could sense the echoes of fear, madness and desperation. But with the armour, these echoes soaked into him, making him stronger. He felt his armour flourish after all those years of neglect in that cavern.

This would be the perfect place for the Grotesquery to break down the borders between realities, open the portal and invite the Faceless Ones to return. Now all he needed was the Grotesquery itself – but that wasn't going to be a problem. For all his flashes of rage and his fearsome temper, Vengeous was a military man first and foremost. True, he had suffered a setback, but he had already initiated a plan to rectify the situation.

One of the Infected was standing further along the corridor and it opened the door as he approached. He could tell by its eyes that it was close to becoming a true vampire. He had already ordered Dusk to kill them all before that happened. Dusk, because of the serums he used, controlled the vampire part of himself, but the Infected would be far too unpredictable to keep around.

Vengeous focused on the armour, drawing it back in. He had been letting it writhe and revel in the collected anguish of the old building, but now it was time for business.

Billy-Ray Sanguine was waiting for him. There was a man shackled to an operating table, and when Vengeous walked into the room, the man's eyes widened.

"Impossible," he breathed. "You're dead. You're... it can't be you, you're dead!" Vengeous realised that with the helmet obscuring his face, the man thought Venguous was Lord Vile, risen from the grave to exact a terrible revenge. He said nothing.

"This is a trick!" the man said, straining against his shackles. "I don't know what you think you're doing, but you've made a huge mistake! Do you even know who I am?"

"Sure we do," Sanguine drawled. "You're a lily-livered sorcerer who's managed to stay alive by runnin' from every conceivable fight. Why do you think we chose you?"

"Chose me?" the man repeated. "Chose me for what?"

"For a quick answer," Vengeous said, aware that the helmet even made him sound like Vile.

The man paled. He was sweating already. "What... what do you want to know?"

"As you can probably tell," Sanguine said, "I ain't from around these parts. And the gentleman who is makin' you mess your britches right now... well, he's been away for a time. So we need you, chuckles, to tell us where someone might go with the inanimate corpse of a half-god in order to, oh, I dunno, destroy it."

The man licked his lips. "And... and then you'll let me go?"

"Yeah, why not?"

Vengeous felt his armour coil. This man's fear was too potent to ignore. Vengeous narrowed his eyes, controlling the armour through sheer force of will.

"They'd go to the Sanctuary," the man said.

"That ain't what we're lookin' for," Sanguine responded. "We got people keepin' an eye on the Sanctuary and they ain't turned up there.

We're lookin' for somethin' a little more specialist, y'know?"

The man frowned. "Then... then maybe they've gone to Grouse."

"Kenspeckle Grouse?" Vengeous said.

"Uh, yeah. He does work for the Sanctuary. They'd bring anything weird to him."

"Where?"

"An old cinema, closed down now, the Hibernian. Are you going to let me go now?" Sanguine looked at Vengeous, and Vengeous looked at their captive.

"What did you do during the war?" Vengeous asked.

"Uh... well... not much."

"I know you, Argus."

"No. I mean no, sir, we've never met. I did some work for Baron Vengeous, but..."

"You supplied Baron Vengeous with the location of a safehouse, when he needed somewhere to lie low for a few days."

"I... yes... but how would you—?"

"Skulduggery Pleasant tracked him to that safehouse, Argus. The information you supplied led directly to his capture."

"That's not my fault. That's... it wasn't my fault."

"The safehouse was known to our enemies, but in your stupidity, you hadn't realised that."

"OK," Argus said quickly, "OK, I made a mistake and Vengeous got arrested. But, Lord Vile, what's it got to do with you?"

"I am not Lord Vile," Vengeous said. He reached up and removed the helmet, and it melted into his gloves and flowed into the rest of the armour.

"Oh no," Argus whispered when he saw Vengeous' face. "Oh, please, no."

Vengeous glared and Argus shook uncontrollably, and then it was as if his body forgot everything it had ever learned about how to stay in one piece. His torso exploded outwards and his limbs were flung to the corners of the room. His head popped open and his insides dripped from the walls.

Vengeous turned to Sanguine. "The Hibernian Cinema. We're leaving immediately."

The Texan brushed a piece of Argus' brain from his jacket. "And if we happen to encounter any dark-haired young girls along the way?"

"You have my permission to kill whomever you deem fit."

Billy-Ray Sanguine smiled. "Yes, sir. Thank you, sir."

25

A SMATTERING
OF SLAUGHTERING

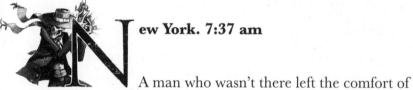**N**ew York. 7:37 am

A man who wasn't there left the comfort of the shadows and strode after the three businessmen. He crossed Bleecker Street, followed them up Hudson, three steps behind them the whole way, and they never even sensed him. They were talking about Sanctuary business, slipping into code words whenever a civilian passed within earshot. They were sorcerers, these businessmen, and important ones at that.

The man who wasn't there followed them to the parking lot off West 13th Street, to their car, and when he judged the moment was right, he struck. The businessmen, the sorcerers, saw the air part and a figure blur, but it was too late to raise the alarm, and far too late to defend themselves.

Bologna. 10:51 am

Five of them: young, powerful and eager to prove themselves. They wore black clothes, leather coats and sunglasses. Their hair was spiked and their skin was pierced. They liked to think of themselves as goth-punks. No one argued. No one argued and *lived* anyway.

Italy in April. It was warm and sunny. The goth-punks waited around the statue of Poseidon, fighting off boredom by scaring the occasional passer-by.

One of them, a girl with no hair and wild eyes, spotted their target as he crossed the square. They moved towards him as a pack, grinning in anticipation.

He saw them and frowned, his step faltering. He started to back away. He worked with the Sanctuary in Venice – they knew he wouldn't be willing to use his powers out here, in full view of the public.

He started to run. They gave chase, the thrill of the hunt making them laugh.

Tokyo. 7:18 pm

The woman in the pinstriped suit sat in the hotel lobby and read the newspaper. The suit was deep navy, the skirt stopped just past her knees, and beneath the jacket she wore an off-white blouse. Her shoes matched her suit. Her nail varnish matched her lipstick. She was a very elegant, very precise woman.

Her phone, impossibly sleek and thin, beeped once, alerting her to the time. She folded the newspaper and placed it on the seat as she stood.

Two men, one old, one young, entered the hotel lobby. The woman appreciated punctuality.

She joined them at the elevator. The men didn't speak to each other. While they waited for the elevator to arrive, a young foreign couple walked up, in Japan for a holiday perhaps. The woman didn't mind. It didn't alter her plan one bit.

The elevator arrived, the doors slid open and they all stepped in. The young couple pressed the button for the eighth floor. The old man pressed the button for the penthouse. The woman didn't press any button.

The doors closed, the elevator started moving, and the woman's nails grew long and her teeth grew sharp. She killed everyone and painted the elevator walls with their blood.

London. 9:56 am

Springheeled Jack looked down at the man he was about to kill, and for the first time in his life he wondered *why*.

He wasn't suddenly struck by his own sins. He wasn't having an attack of conscience or anything pedestrian like that. He wasn't having one of those *epiphany* things. It was just a voice, that was all, just a voice in the back of his mind telling him to ask something. But ask what? He'd never had the urge to ask any of his victims *anything* before. He didn't know where to start. Did he just strike up a conversation?

"Hello," he said, as nicely as he could.

The man was a sorcerer, but not a very good fighter. He lay crumpled in the alleyway and had a scared look in his eyes. Jack felt uncomfortable. This was a new situation, and he didn't like new situations. He liked to kill people. Taunt them, sure. Maybe make a witty remark. But not... not *talk* to them. Not *ask* them something.

He blamed Billy-Ray Sanguine. Sanguine had taken Jack

out of his cell, taken him through the wall, through the ground and out into fresh air. He had talked a little, mentioned a hospital in Ireland called Clearwater, something like that, and then he had looked like maybe he'd said too much, so he'd shut up. Jack hadn't cared at the time. He'd been freed, after all, and all he had to do in return was kill someone. But the thought was nagging at him – *why*? Why had Sanguine wanted this bloke dead?

Jack tried to sound casual. "If someone wanted you dead, hypothetically, what do you think their reasons would be?"

"Please don't kill me," the man whispered.

"I'm not gonna kill you," Jack lied and gave a reassuring laugh. "Why would you think I was gonna kill you?"

"You attacked me," the man said. "And you dragged me into this alley. And, and you *told* me you were going to kill me." Jack cursed under his breath. This guy had a good memory.

"Forget about all that," he said. "Someone wants you dead. I'm curious as to why that may be. Who are you?"

"My name is—"

"I know your bloody name, pally. What do you do? Why are you so important?"

"I'm not important, not at all. I work for the Council of Elders here in London. I'm just, I help co-ordinate things."

"Like what? What are you co-ordinating now, for example?"

"We're... sending help to Ireland. Baron Vengeous has escaped from—"

"Damn it!"

The man shrieked and recoiled, but Jack was too busy being angry to bother attacking him. So Sanguine was working with that nutter Vengeous again, carrying out his orders as usual. Only this time, he'd tried to get Jack to do some of the dirty work.

"I been hoodwinked," he said. He looked down at the man. "If Vengeous is involved, that means all this is about the Faceless Ones, right?"

"Y-yes."

"I been hoodwinked. That's... unprofessional, that is."

"So are you going to let me go? You don't want to help the Faceless Ones, right? So are you going to let me go?"

Jack hunkered down. "I'd love to, pally. I really would. But see, I was sprung from jail an' I always repay my debts."

"But... but by killing me, you'll be helping them!"

"I'll just have to find some other way to get back at 'em, then. No hard feelings."

The conversation came to its natural conclusion with a bit more begging and then Jack killed the guy, so that stopped too.

Jack straightened his top hat and walked away. He still had a few friends, friends who could transport him where he wanted to go.

And it was such a long time since he'd been to Ireland.

26

MURDER IN THE NEW MORGUE

tentor and Civet struggled to move the Grotesquery off the stretcher and on to the operating table. The Grotesquery was big and heavy and awkward, but most of all it was big and heavy. They had just managed to drag the top half over when the stretcher squeaked and moved, and the Grotesquery started to fall. Civet tried to grab it, but he went under and the Grotesquery dropped, very slowly, on top of him.

"Help!" Civet cried.

Professor Grouse stormed in. "What on earth are you playing at?"

"It, it fell," Stentor said, standing to attention.

"I can see that!" Grouse barked. "That specimen is a rare opportunity to study a hybrid form, you imbecile. I don't want it damaged."

"Yes, Professor. Sorry."

"Why were you trying to move it by yourself? Where's Civet?"

Civet managed to raise a hand. "Here I am, Professor."

"What on earth are you doing down there, Civet?"

"Trying to breathe, sir."

"Well, get up!"

"I would, sir, but it's very heavy. If you could maybe grab an arm or something..."

"I'm an old man, you fool. You expect me to lift that monstrosity off you?"

"Not by yourself, but maybe if Stentor were to help, then I could wriggle out. It really is getting difficult to breathe under here. I think my lung is collapsing."

Grouse gestured. "Stentor, help me lift."

"Yes, Professor."

Together, they pulled the Grotesquery back far enough to enable Civet to squirm out.

"I've never dropped a specimen," Grouse said as they

grunted and heaved. "I was never pinned by a corpse either, Civet. You remember that."

"Yes, sir," said Civet, as he finally managed to extricate himself.

Grouse hunkered down beside the Grotesquery, then took a pair of scissors and carefully snipped a few bandages away, revealing the scarred flesh beneath. "Astonishing," he murmured. "So many parts from different creatures, all merged into the one being. A being borne of impossible horrors."

Stentor nodded. "It'd be even more impressive if it *worked* though."

"Less talking," Grouse snapped, "more lifting. Lift it on to the table. And no more damage to it, you hear? I swear, you're lucky I'm so easy-going. Stentor. Bend your knees when you lift, you idiot."

"Sorry sir."

They strained and lifted, and suddenly Civet let go and jumped back. Stentor clung on, holding the Grotesquery half on, half off the table.

"What's wrong now?" Grouse demanded.

"Professor," Civet said nervously, "are you sure this thing is dead?"

"It's not a thing, it's a specimen."

"Sorry, sir. Are you sure this specimen is dead? I... I think it moved."

"Of course it moved. You moved it."

"No, sir. I mean, I think it moved on its own."

"Well, I don't see how that could be. The ritual to bring it to life was interrupted – only a small portion of Valkyrie Cain's blood was transfused."

Civet hesitated then grabbed a massive arm and helped Stentor slide it further on to the table.

He leaped away. "OK!" he said loudly. "OK, that time I *definitely* felt it move!"

"A lot of energy was passed into it," Grouse said, frowning. "It may just be a residual spasm. The muscles may simply be reacting to stimuli."

"It wasn't a spasm," Civet said. "I swear."

Grouse looked at the bandage-wrapped body. It was big and cold and unmoving. "Very well," he said. "How many Cleavers are stationed here?"

"Three."

"OK, then. Boys, I want you both to go upstairs, tell the Cleavers to come down here, tell them we may have a—"

And then the Grotesquery sat up and Civet yelled and jumped back, but Stentor was too slow and it grabbed his head in its big hand and crushed it like a freshly laid egg.

27

RISE OF THE GROTESQUERY

Valkyrie opened her eyes. Was that a scream? She sat up and looked out into the corridor. The lights were flickering. She heard running footsteps. Then nothing. Something was wrong. Something was very wrong.

She got out of bed, her limbs protesting, her arm aching. Her bare feet touched the cold floor. She padded to the small wardrobe built into the wall, where she found her socks and boots. She pulled them on quickly in the darkened room, and she was just shrugging into her coat when she heard someone crying for help. Then a *thud* and the crying stopped.

Valkyrie poked her head out the door, looked up towards the morgue, and saw the figure moving through the dim corridor like some kind of puppet with half its strings cut. It moved in a jerky manner, stiff and uncoordinated, but even as she watched, it seemed to move a little more smoothly, like it was getting used to its own body. It stepped into a pool of light.

The Grotesquery. It was alive.

She saw the bandages – so old they might have turned to dust under her gaze – that had been used to keep it in one piece. She saw flesh between the bandages, and scars, and stitching. Its ribcage looked like it had been cracked and pulled open, so that now each rib punctured through its torso.

It had something that looked like a massive boil growing on the top of its left wrist and on the underside there was a thick ridge of flesh. Its right arm was huge, the muscles curling impossibly around one another, all the way down to its massive hand. Its fingers were thick, each tipped with a talon. The bandages covered its face completely, not even a gap for the eyes. Here and there black blood had soaked through.

Why was there no alarm? The Grotesquery was alive, but there was no alarm. Valkyrie stepped back, grabbed a chair and stood on it. She clicked her fingers but nothing happened. Her eyes narrowed. She focused, clicked her fingers again until she made a spark, cultivated it into a flame and held it up to the smoke detectors. After a moment the sprinkler system activated and the alarm pierced the silence.

She hurried back to the door as three Cleavers ran by. It was only when they got close to it that she realised how big the Grotesquery truly was. It towered above the tallest of them. They were used to dealing with serious threats. But they had never seen anything like this.

The Grotesquery batted away the swipe of a scythe and grabbed the first Cleaver by the throat. It lifted him high overhead as it swatted the second Cleaver into the wall. The third Cleaver swung his scythe and the Grotesquery swung his colleague's body into him. Valkyrie heard bones break.

Three seconds. The Grotesquery had killed three Cleavers in three seconds.

Valkyrie stepped back inside her room. The sprinklers were drenching her. She could run for it. Step out of the doorway, turn right, sprint the length of the corridor to the Research Area, then get to the stairs. She'd pass through the screen and be running from the cinema before the Grotesquery even saw her. It was still slow, it wouldn't even be able to catch her if it *did* see her. She could do it. So why wasn't she running?

Valkyrie backed away. She could see the shadow on the wall

outside her open door, getting closer. Her legs were unsteady and her arm still hurt. Fear coiled and thrashed in her belly. She felt the wall behind her and pressed herself to it. The darkness of the room didn't seem dark enough. It would see her. No, it didn't need to see her. It had no eyes.

And then it was too late to run, because the Grotesquery was passing the doorway, water running down its body. She could smell it now – it smelled of formaldehyde and mould. She held her breath and didn't move.

The Grotesquery stopped. Valkyrie readied herself. If it turned to her she'd launch herself forward, hit it with everything she had, hurl enough fireballs to send those bandages up in flames. Like that would be enough to stop it. Like that would be enough to save her.

Its head turned slightly, but not in her direction, as if the Grotesquery was listening for something, beyond the alarm. She suddenly thought of a radar that it could use to sense her, but a radar that had been unused for so long it wasn't as sharp as it could be.

She felt her muscles weaken and a coldness swept into her mind. Terror was robbing her of her strength. The thought that she'd be unable to move seeped in, grew and festered. The things she had learned meant nothing. The skills, the powers, the magic – to the Grotesquery she'd be even more ineffectual than the Cleavers it had just killed. Something less than a threat. Something less than an insect.

But it moved. It took another step, and another, and soon it was out of sight, moving on down the corridor. Valkyrie felt tears mix with the water that was running down her face. She blinked them back. She wasn't going to die. Not today.

She pushed away from the wall, balanced herself on shaky legs. She waited a few moments, then made her way to the door, her feet splashing slightly as she moved. She got to the door and peeked out, and fingers closed around her throat. She was yanked out into the corridor, her feet off the ground, gagging and spitting and trying to breathe.

The Grotesquery had its head raised, looking up at her with no eyes, examining her. Her hands were at its massive wrist, at those fingers, trying to pry them loose.

Something less than an insect.

She kicked, her boots slamming into the thing. She pelted her fists down on its forearm. It didn't make one bit of difference. Her heartbeat thundered in her ears. Darkness crept into her vision. She couldn't breathe. She needed to breathe. She was going to die.

She clicked her fingers, managed to summon a flame then

pressed her hand to the Grotesquery's bandages. The bandages instantly caught fire and then instantly snuffed out. No more tricks. She was done.

Then there was movement behind the Grotesquery – Skulduggery and Tanith, sprinting. The Grotesquery didn't need to turn. When they were right behind, it swung its left fist back. Skulduggery dodged under it and Tanith leaped to the ceiling, her sword flashing and now Valkyrie was dropping. Skulduggery swooped in, snatched her up and kept running, Tanith beside them.

The Grotesquery regarded its injured hand with something approaching curiosity. They stopped and looked back, as the flesh closed over and healed.

There was movement at the doorway beside them and Kenspeckle limped into the corridor.

"Stay behind us," Skulduggery ordered.

Kenspeckle grunted. "I plan to."

They felt the air pressure change and Valkyrie's ears popped. "What's happening?" she called out over the alarm.

"Its power is returning," Kenspeckle said grimly.

Skulduggery took his gun from his jacket. "This is our only chance to stop it before it becomes too strong."

He walked up to the Grotesquery, firing six times as he went, and six small explosions of black blood erupted against the Grotesquery's chest, barely making it stagger. Skulduggery put the gun away, clicked his fingers and unleashed two continuous streams of fire, turning the space between them to steam. The flames hit the Grotesquery but didn't catch.

Skulduggery pushed at the air with both hands and the air rippled. The Grotesquery was forced backwards. Skulduggery did it again and the Grotesquery fought to resist. Skulduggery went to do it a third time, and the Grotesquery reached out with its huge right arm and the arm unravelled. Long strips of flesh, each tipped with a talon, lacerated the air around Skulduggery. He cried out and fell back and the strips returned, wrapped around each other and reformed the arm. The Grotesquery smacked Skulduggery and he hurtled backwards through the air.

Tanith ran up, her hair plastered to her scalp and her sword darting out. The Grotesquery tried grabbing her, but she was too fast. She rolled and cut its leg then leaped up and slashed its arm. Both wounds closed over.

Its right arm unravelled again and she ducked and dodged, then jumped and flipped, and now she was upside down on the ceiling. She advanced, but the Grotesquery kept its distance. It raised its left arm.

Kenspeckle shouted a warning, but the fire alarm drowned

him out. The growth on top of the Grotesquery's left wrist, what Valkyrie had thought was a massive boil, suddenly contracted and a yellow liquid shot out. Tanith had to fling herself sideways to avoid it and she crashed to the ground. The liquid hit the ceiling and ate through it in an instant, leaving a gaping hole.

Skulduggery ran to join her and Tanith got to her feet, and even though the boil was now empty, the Grotesquery was still holding out its left arm. Skulduggery reached for Tanith, but he was a second too late.

A thin spike emerged from the ridge on the underside of the Grotesquery's wrist and jabbed into Tanith's side. She cried out and the spike retracted, returning to its sheath. Skulduggery caught Tanith as she collapsed. He backed away.

The Grotesquery looked at its hands and flexed its fingers, as if it was discovering what it could do with each passing moment.

Valkyrie and Kenspeckle ran up. Tanith was unconscious. Her veins were visible through her skin and they were a sickly green colour.

"She's been infected," Kenspeckle said. "Helaquin poison. She has maybe twenty minutes before she dies."

"How do we cure it?" Skulduggery asked.

The alarm whined and went silent, and the sprinklers cut off.

"I haven't seen this poison for fifty years," Kenspeckle said. "I don't have an antidote here. There is some at the Sanctuary if we can get there in time."

"I'll lead the Grotesquery away," Valkyrie said. "Meet you at the car."

Skulduggery looked up sharply. "What? No! You take Tanith—"

"Don't tell her this," Valkyrie said, "but she's too heavy for me to carry." And she ran before Skulduggery could stop her.

"Valkyrie!" he roared.

Her boots splashed as she sprinted. The Grotesquery held its arms wide, welcoming her. There was no way past it on either side and she didn't have Tanith's ceiling-running skills, so when the Grotesquery reached for her, Valkyrie dropped, sliding on the wet floor, between its legs. Once she was clear she scrambled up and ran on. She glanced back. The Grotesquery was turning, following her.

So that worked, Valkyrie thought to herself. *Now what the hell am I going to do?*

Just as she turned the corner, Skulduggery shouted something, something like *the vanity light*. She kept running. She passed the elevators, shut down because of the fire alert, and headed for the back stairs. The Grotesquery hadn't even reached the corner yet. She slowed, catching her breath, keeping her eyes on the corner. The vanity light. What had Skulduggery meant?

The Grotesquery came around the corner. The back stairs, the ones that joined up with the main stairs behind the screen, were right behind her and she readied herself to sprint if the patchwork monstrosity came up with any more surprises.

And then it disappeared, like it had been swallowed by the empty space around it. Valkyrie blinked. Another of its hybrid abilities, like the stinger and the acid and the unravelling arm. Teleportation.

Skulduggery hadn't said *the vanity light*, he had said *The Vanishing Night*. *The Vanishing Night* had been one of Gordon's earliest bestsellers. It had dealt with a creature, a Shibbach, that could appear anywhere, commit a very messy and overly-detailed murder then vanish and reappear a hundred kilometres away. She remembered Gordon now, the Gordon in the Echo Stone, telling her about the pieces of a Shibbach that Vengeous had grafted on.

Valkyrie didn't even have to look around to know the Grotesquery was behind her. She tried to run but her boot slipped on the wet ground, just as its right hand snatched at her. She fell sideways, glimpsed the Grotesquery's bandaged head and tumbled down the stairs. She sprawled to a painful stop, grabbed the banister and hauled herself to her feet. She was at the main stairs now, and she took them two at a time, going dangerously fast.

She reached the ground and sprinted for the screen, passed through and leaped off the stage. She ran for the exit, crashed through the door and the midday sunlight struck her like a fist.

"Valkyrie!" Skulduggery shouted. The Bentley was ahead, engine running, and beyond it Baron Vengeous was striding through the lane towards them, followed by Sanguine and Dusk and his pack of Infected.

The Grotesquery stepped out of thin air with a soft *whump*. Valkyrie dodged it and ran as the Bentley started moving. She jumped for the open window and Kenspeckle grabbed her and dragged her in as Skulduggery floored it. Tanith was in the backseat, still unconscious, and when Valkyrie righted herself she looked back and saw Baron Vengeous approaching the Grotesquery.

The Grotesquery turned its head, keeping its eyeless gaze fixed on the car.

"Seatbelt," Skulduggery said.

28

GOOD GUYS CONVENE

Bliss, flanked by Cleavers, was waiting at the rear of the Sanctuary. The Bentley pulled up sharply and Bliss yanked the door open, then lifted Tanith out. Her veins were sickly yellow spiderwebs that spread beneath her waxy skin, and she was barely breathing.

"Out of my way, out of my way," Kenspeckle muttered, shoving people aside. Bliss laid Tanith on the ground and handed Kenspeckle three different coloured leaves. He wrapped them around each other, tightly, then held them between his clasped hands and closed his eyes. A light shone from within, bright enough to almost turn his hands translucent. Valkyrie could see the bones of his fingers.

The light faded. Bliss took a clear tube and held it out, and Kenspeckle opened his hands slightly. He let a fine, multicoloured dust – the remains of the leaves – sift gently into the tube. Bliss added a few drops of a deep red liquid that smelled vaguely of sulphur, and Kenspeckle took the tube and shook it, mixing the contents. Bliss handed him a syringe gun and Kenspeckle loaded the tube into it.

"Hold her," Kenspeckle said.

Bliss placed his hands on Tanith's shoulders, Skulduggery held down one arm and Valkyrie pinned the other. The Cleavers secured her legs. Kenspeckle pressed the syringe gun to Tanith's neck and the gun hissed with compressed air. The concoction emptied into her bloodstream.

Tanith thrashed and Valkyrie lost her grip on her arm. She grabbed it again, struggled to press it to the ground, and eventually had to kneel on it to keep it in place. Tanith bucked and writhed as the antidote worked through her. The yellow veins surged red, and her muscles knotted and strained.

"Try to make sure she doesn't swallow her tongue," Kenspeckle said.

And then Tanith went limp and the veins were no longer

visible. Colour returned to her face.

"Will she be all right?" Valkyrie asked.

Kenspeckle raised an eyebrow. "Am I a magic-scientific genius or am I not?"

"You are."

"Then of course she'll be all right," he said. "Which is more than I can say for my assistants. Do you know how hard it is to get good assistants these days? Granted, neither of them were actually any good, but..." He brushed his hands off and shook his head. "They were fine lads. They didn't deserve to die like that." He looked at Skulduggery. "You'll stop it then?"

"We'll stop it."

"Fair enough." Kenspeckle stood up. "Let's get her inside."

Valkyrie was sore. Her arm was stiffening up and her body was covered in bruises. She had cut her lip without realising it and for some reason had a black eye, presumably the result of crashing the van or the tumble she took down the stairs.

Tanith was sitting beside her and she was sulking. Tanith always sulked when she lost a fight. After she had fought the White Cleaver last year she had spent most of her recovery time staring out the window, scowling.

The antidote had neutralised the effects of the Helaquin

poison, and the wound the stinger had made was already stitched up and healing. The moment she was able, Tanith had gone off and sharpened her sword. It lay on the table before them in its black scabbard.

They were in the Sanctuary meeting room. Mr Bliss was seated at the far end of the table and Skulduggery was standing against the wall, arms crossed and unmoving. The doors opened. Guild stalked in.

"Who do I blame?" he thundered. "Tell me, who? We had the Grotesquery in *custody*? We had it and I wasn't *informed*?"

"I take full responsibility," Skulduggery said.

"You do, do you? That would be quite noble if I wasn't blaming you *anyway*! You went behind my back, Detective. You requested the services of three Cleavers for guard duty and you didn't follow procedure. Where are those Cleavers now?"

Skulduggery hesitated. "They were killed."

"Well, that's marvellous news, isn't it?" Guild snapped. "Tell me, is there any part of this operation that you didn't botch?"

"Operation's not over yet."

Guild glared. "You're lucky I even let you in here, Detective. I don't know how Eachan Meritorious handled things, but your reckless behaviour will not be tolerated by the new Council!"

"Council of one," Tanith murmured.

Guild whirled. "I'm sorry? I didn't quite catch that. Could you repeat what you said so we can all hear it?"

Tanith looked at him. "Sure. I said 'council of one', referring to the fact that the Council is not the Council until it has all three members."

The Elder Mage bristled. "Your opinion is of little consequence in *this* country, Miss Low. You work for the Sanctuary in London, you shouldn't even *be* here."

"Actually I'm freelance," Tanith responded.

"And I requested her help," Skulduggery said. "It seems we could use it. Didn't you say we would be getting reinforcements?" Guild's face went red, but Bliss spoke before he could start shouting again.

"All the offers of international aid have been withdrawn. In the past few hours there have been attacks on personnel connected to practically every Sanctuary around the world."

"Distractions," Skulduggery said, "to keep everyone else busy. We've been isolated."

"Indeed we have."

"But who would be powerful enough to organise all this?" Valkyrie asked. "Vengeous?"

"This has taken a lot of planning," Skulduggery said. "Vengeous wouldn't have had the time."

"That's not what we should be concentrating on," Guild snapped. "We have to find the Grotesquery and stop it. *That* is our one and only concern."

"The lunar eclipse will take place at ten minutes past midnight tonight," Bliss said. "That leaves us with nine hours until the Grotesquery is strong enough to open the portal."

Guild laid both hands flat on the table. "So what are we doing about it? Please tell me we're not all sitting around just *waiting* for something to happen!"

"We have all the sensitives on alert," Skulduggery said. "Every psychic and seer we know is reaching out."

"And if they don't find anything, skeleton?"

Skulduggery, who was still leaning against the wall with his arms crossed, tilted his head as he looked back at Guild. "Then I recommend we work the case."

"What does that even mean?" Guild raged. "We are facing a global catastrophe that could mean the end of everything, and you're talking about *working the case*?"

"I'm a detective," Skulduggery said. "It's what I do."

"Well, you haven't been doing a very good job of it, have you?"

Skulduggery stood up straight now, hands down by his sides. "Working backwards," he said calmly. "Person or persons unknown have arranged to isolate us just when we need reinforcements to stop the Grotesquery. The Grotesquery is up and about because Vengeous finally got the missing ingredients he needed. Vengeous is out of his secret prison because Billy-Ray Sanguine broke in and freed him. Billy-Ray Sanguine knew where this secret prison was located because somebody in a position of power divulged this information."

"You're getting off topic again," Guild scowled.

"Somebody in a position of power," Skulduggery continued, "divulged this information, presumably for a big reward. Now, here's where I start speculating. It's possible that this same somebody only rose to this position of power because he promised that once he was there, he would find the location of the secret prison and pass it on. He would have made a deal with a powerful person or persons unknown, very possibly the same powerful person or persons unknown who have isolated us from the international community, but, very likely, he wouldn't have known who these mysterious benefactors planned to break out of that secret prison or, indeed, why."

Guild narrowed his eyes. "You better not be implying what I think you're implying."

Skulduggery nodded to a slim file on the table. "That file is a record of the meetings you've had with other councils across the world since you were elected Grand Mage. You have had approximately twice the number of meetings with the Russian Council as you have had with anyone else."

"These are official Sanctuary matters and are *none* of your business," Guild said, the veins in his neck standing out.

"Three of those meetings were about security concerns in the wake of Serpine's activities, where you would have been privy to confidential information including, but not restricted to, the location of various secret prisons in Russian territories."

Guild stalked up to Skulduggery and for a moment Valkyrie thought he might hit him. Skulduggery didn't move a fraction.

"You are accusing me of aiding a prison break?"

"Like I said, I'm speculating. But if I were to accuse you of anything, it would probably be more along the lines of treason."

"You're fired," Guild said.

Skulduggery tilted his head. "You can't afford to lose me."

"Oh, we can," Guild snarled, walking for the door.

"I have a job to do," Skulduggery said, "and I intend to do it. You may be a traitor, Guild, but you don't want the Faceless Ones back any more than I do."

Guild reached the door and turned, his lip curled. "Then do

it, skeleton. Stop the Grotesquery. Do your job. And once you're done, never set foot in here again." He left and nobody spoke for a while. Then Skulduggery nodded.

"I really think he's starting to like me."

29

PICKING UP A TAIL

They left the Sanctuary and drove through the narrower streets of Dublin. Skulduggery parked the Bentley once they reached the Temple Bar area, and they walked the rest of the way. Even though he was wearing his disguise, he was drawing all the usual looks from passers-by, who sifted in and out of the many pubs and restaurants.

They crossed the square, navigated between the hundred or so students who lounged around on the steps. Valkyrie liked Temple Bar. It was vibrant and packed, and there was music and laughter and chat everywhere. But if they failed to stop the Grotesquery, when this night was over, it could all be nothing but dust and rubble and screaming.

They reached a shop with a brightly coloured mural on its wall, and Skulduggery knocked on the door. From somewhere inside there came voices, and a few moments later the door rattled as it was unlocked. A man in his early twenties opened it. His eyebrows, nose, ears, lips and tongue were pierced, and he was wearing old jeans, a Thin Lizzy T-shirt and a dog collar.

"Hello Finbar," Skulduggery said. "I'm here to collect my belongings."

"Skul-man?" Finbar said, in such a way that suggested that befuddlement was his natural state of being. "Is that you? What's up with that hair and those gigantic sunglasses, man?"

"It's a disguise."

"Oh. Yeah, I get it. Nice. So hey, wow. How long's it been?"

"Since we last spoke?"

"Yeah. Must be years, yeah?"

"Last month, Finbar."

"Hmm? Oh, right. OK. And who's this you have with you?"

"I'm Valkyrie Cain," Valkyrie said, shaking his hand. He wore many rings.

"Valkyrie Cain," Finbar said, rolling the name around in his mouth. "Nice one. My name's Finbar Wrong. I'm an old friend of the Skul-man's, isn't that right, Skul-man?"

"Not really."

Finbar shook his head. "Nope, wouldn't call us *friends*, exactly. Associates, or... or... not colleagues, but... I mean, we know each other, like, but..."

"I'm going to have to hurry you along," Skulduggery said. "I gave you a small case to keep for me and I need it back."

"A case?"

"A black case. I told you I needed somewhere to keep some supplies, in case of emergencies."

"Is there an emergency?"

"I'm afraid so."

Finbar's eyes widened and his piercings glittered in the sunlight. "Oh, man. I'm not gonna die, am I?"

"I hope not."

"Me too, man. Me too. I got so much to live for, y'know? Hey, did I tell you me and Sharon are getting married? Finally, yeah?"

"Finbar, I don't know who Sharon is and I really need that case."

"All right, man," Finbar said, nodding. "I'm going to see if I can find it. It's got to be somewhere, right?"

"So suggest the laws of probability." Finbar wandered back into the shop and Valkyrie looked at Skulduggery.

"What's in the case?" she asked.

"My other gun, a few bullets, various bits and pieces, a spike bomb, an old paperback I've never read, a pack of cards—"

"Spike bomb?"

"Mm? Yes."

"What's a spike bomb?"

"It's a bomb with a spike in it."

"You gave a bomb to *that* guy? Is it safe?"

"It's a bomb, Valkyrie. Of course it's not safe. The case, however, is *very* safe. Whether he's been using it as a coffee table, a footstool or if he's simply spent the last few years throwing it down a flight of stairs, its contents will be in no way damaged. Providing he can *find* the thing."

Finbar reappeared. "I'm getting warmer, man, I know it. It's not in the front, so I'm thinking it's in the back, yeah? So I'm going to check out the back right now. You guys want to come in?"

"We're good out here," Valkyrie said politely.

"OK, cool. You sure? Skul-man? Sharon's in there, man. Why don't you say hi?"

"Because I don't know her, Finbar."

"Right, yeah, OK." Finbar wandered off again.

Valkyrie checked the clock on her phone. If she was home right now, living a normal life, she'd probably be figuring out what to wear to the reunion. Not that it would take long. She had one dress in her entire wardrobe, which she wore rarely, and with great reluctance. She figured that the Toxic Twins would have already started their beauty regime by this stage, applying eighty-four layers of makeup and figuring out which colour lipstick made them look the most trashy. Valkyrie was glad she had a reflection to go instead of her.

"Oh, hell," she said suddenly.

"What's wrong?"

"The reflection. It's still in the back of the Bentley."

Skulduggery's head tilted. "Oh. Oh, we seem to have forgotten about that."

Valkyrie closed her eyes. "If I don't go to the reunion, Mum'll go mental."

"Look on the bright side. If the world ends, none of that will matter."

She waited a moment without speaking, then he nodded. "That's probably not a great consolation," he admitted.

Finbar wandered back, holding a black case. "Found it,

man. Reason I couldn't see it, it was on the floor and there was someone sleeping on it. Y'know, for a pillow. It's good though. So, here."

Skulduggery took the case. "Thank you very much, Finbar."

"Absolutely no problemo, man. Hey, this emergency thing – it's serious?"

"Yes, it is."

"You need some help? It's been a while since I was, y'know, in the field or even out the door, but I still got it."

"I'm sure you do, but we can handle it."

"Oh, right. OK. Probably a good thing. I don't know if I got it any more, y'know? Don't know if I ever did, but... What were we saying?"

"We were saying congratulations on your upcoming wedding to Sharon."

"Oh, thanks, Skul-man."

"I'm sure you'll be very happy together."

"Yeah, me too. I mean, I've only known her three days, but sometimes you just gotta... get married... to someone..." He trailed off and looked puzzled. "I think."

"Well," Skulduggery said, "thank you for keeping this for me. Stay out of trouble."

"You got it. Hey, who's that with you?"

Skulduggery tilted his head. "This is Valkyrie. She introduced herself."

"Naw, man, not her. The guy in black." Valkyrie stiffened and fought the urge to look round.

"Where is he?" Skulduggery asked.

"Across the street, doing a pretty good job of keeping out of sight, but you know me, Skul-man. Eyes like a feathery thing. Whatchmacallit. Hawk."

"And he's watching us?"

"Yep. Wait, no. Not watching you. Watching *her*."

"What does he look like?" Valkyrie asked.

"Black hair, pretty pale. Ugly scar on his face. Looks like a vamp."

"You should get back inside," Skulduggery said. "Lock the doors."

"You got it, kemo sabe. I'll keep my crucifix close."

"Vampires aren't scared of a crucifix, Finbar."

"I don't plan to wave it at him, I plan to hit him with it. It's really heavy. I figure I can do some considerable damage to his head." He stepped back and closed the door.

Skulduggery and Valkyrie walked back through Temple Bar to the Bentley.

"Is Dusk still following us?" Valkyrie asked, keeping her voice low.

"I think so," Skulduggery answered. "This is the break we've been looking for. Dusk has a grudge against you. We're quite lucky in fact."

"Very lucky," Valkyrie agreed dryly. "Very lucky that a vampire wants to kill me. Are we going to lure him into a trap?"

"Indeed we are. But not here. He won't get close enough. He has to believe you're alone."

Valkyrie narrowed her eyes. "That sounds suspiciously like a suggestion that I should act as bait..."

"You have to go to the reunion."

"No no no..."

"You can't be around me, or Tanith, or any sorcerer. Dusk wouldn't risk it. He'll only strike when he thinks you're alone. That way he can take his time when he kills you."

"You're not making me feel any better about this."

"You're going to the reunion."

Valkyrie sagged.

"Tanith and I will wait nearby. The moment Dusk tries anything, we'll step in."

"But my family. My aunts and uncles and cousins and second cousins and..."

"We'll protect them."

"What? No, I mean my family is really, *really* annoying. When they're drunk, they all start dancing and that's just... that's just *wrong*."

"You'll have a wonderful time."

"I hate you."

"I know."

30

FIGHT

Springheeled Jack stood on the roof of Clearwater Hospital and looked down at the creature, admiring the beauty and the savagery, the sheer power he could feel, even from where he was standing.

"Quite a thing, ain't it?"

Jack wiped any hint of admiration from his face and turned as Sanguine strolled towards him.

"You lied to me," he said.

Sanguine nodded. "That I did. How'd you find us?"

"You told me where you were stayin', remember?"

"I did? Me an' my big mouth, I swear... So, you seen the critter down there. 'What do you think?"

"This all has to do with the Faceless Ones," Jack said and hit Sanguine. The Texan stumbled back, and he was straightening up when Jack kicked him off the edge of the building. Jack jumped, flipped and landed on the ground beside Sanguine.

"Ow," Sanguine said, flat on his back. His sunglasses had come off and Jack looked at the holes where his eyes should have been.

"I don't like being used," Jack said.

"If I'd apologised before, would you still have kicked me off the roof?"

"Probably."

"Figured as much."

Sanguine struck out with his leg, his boot cracking into Jack's knee. He rolled up and launched himself forward, forced Jack against the wall, driving in punches. Jack's hat fell.

Sanguine punched and Jack ducked. Sanguine's knuckles hit the wall and he howled. Jack shoved him away, giving himself enough room to manoeuvre, and he jumped and kicked, and Sanguine went sprawling.

"You can't beat me, Yank," Jack snarled.

"Yanks are from the North," Sanguine muttered, getting up.

"I'm a Southern boy." He came forward again and Jack ducked and dodged, flipping himself sideways. Sanguine growled in frustration. Jack smacked him and gave him another kick in the head, and once more Sanguine hit the ground.

Jack looked down at him. "So where is he? Where's Vengeous?"

"Ain't here right now," Sanguine said, not trying to get up.

"It's just you and him, is it? You and him and that thing?"

"We got vamps too. You know Dusk?"

"Met him in London once. He didn't realise the rooftops was *my* patch. We got into a bit of a scuffle, you might say."

Sanguine sat up and groaned. "Well, I'd love to watch you two kill each other, but he ain't around either. He's off on one of his vendettas, goin' after a girl in Haggard."

"You used me, Sanguine."

Slowly, Sanguine reached out, picked up his sunglasses and got to his feet. "You came all the way to Ireland to berate me, that what you did?"

"I came here to find out what you're up to."

"And then what?"

"If I don't like it? I'll stop it."

Sanguine's sunglasses were back on and he laughed. "That critter out there, *that's* what we're up to. You wanna stop that?

You go right ahead, my ugly little friend." The ground at Sanguine's feet started to crumble. "Go back to London, Jack. You can't do anythin' to hurt us here. We're too strong, buddy. What could you possible do to upset our plans?"

Sanguine grinned, and he lowered into the ground and disappeared.

31

THE EDGLEY FAMILY
REUNION THING

Valkyrie checked that her parents had gone to the reunion and the house was empty, then she walked outside and waved. The Bentley drove up, Skulduggery got out, and together they lifted the reflection's body out of the boot and carried it into the house and up the stairs.

They positioned the reflection in front of the mirror and then let it drop gently forward. It passed through the glass, slumping to the mirrored room within. After a moment, the reflection stirred and stood up. It turned to them, its face placid and blank. Valkyrie fought down an irrational feeling of guilt for what they had put the reflection through. She started to imagine that it had a reproachful look in its eyes. She reached out, touched the glass and the reflection's memories swarmed into her mind.

She clutched her chest and took a step back. "Oh God."

Skulduggery steadied her. "Are you OK?"

"I just remembered what it was like to be shot."

"Was it fun?"

"Amazingly, no."

She stood up straighter. The reflection in the mirror was normal now. "I'm all right. I'm good."

"Then I shall leave you. You're going to have to walk to the golf club, I'm afraid. But don't worry, we'll be watching."

"What if I go to the reunion and Dusk doesn't fall for the trap? Then we're all just wasting our time."

"This is the only option we have, Valkyrie. Are you going to wear a dress?"

"Are you sure I can't go like this?"

"He'll be cautious enough as it is. You have to appear completely unaware."

"Fine," she growled. "A dress."

"I'm sure you'll look lovely," Skulduggery said as he left the room.

She called after him. "If anyone starts a sing-song at this thing, the world can fend for itself, all right?"

She heard his voice as he walked down the stairs. "That's fair."

Her eyes narrowed. The reflection's memories had mixed with her own, sidled into position like they always did, but there was something else now. A feeling. She shook her head. The reflection was incapable of feelings. It was a receptacle, a thing that absorbed experiences, ready to be downloaded. There were never any feelings, any emotions. Valkyrie wasn't even sure if this new thing *was* an emotion. It hovered in her mind just beyond her reach. Whenever she focused on it, it scattered.

No, it wasn't an emotion, but it *was* something. Something she couldn't pin down. A black spot in her memory. Her reflection had hidden something from her.

This, Valkyrie thought to herself, *is probably not a good sign.*

There were more here than she had expected. They filled the function room almost to capacity – people talking and laughing and shaking hands and hugging. Aunts and uncles and cousins of every degree, adding to the cacophony of chatter that came at Valkyrie like a wall of sound, slamming into her the moment she opened the door.

Most of these people she didn't know – she'd never seen them before, and would never see them again. It didn't exactly fill her with regret. She doubted she was missing out on anything spectacular.

Her dress looked nice, she had to admit. It was black and pretty, but she couldn't get comfortable. If Dusk *did* fall into the trap and try to attack, she'd regret not wearing trousers and boots, she knew she would.

"Stephanie?" She turned. The man was in his forties. His comb-over was neither subtle nor successful.

"It is Stephanie, isn't it? Desmond's daughter?"

Valkyrie drew a smile on to her face. "Yep," she said. "It's me."

"Ah! Wonderful!" the man said, grabbing her into a hug that lasted two uncomfortable seconds. He released her and stepped back. The sudden movement had dislodged his comb-over. Valkyrie thought it polite not to mention it.

"Last time I saw you, you were knee-high to a grasshopper! You must have been, I don't know, four? You were tiny! Now look at you! You're beautiful! I can't get over how much you've grown!"

"Yeah, nine years'll do that."

"Bet you don't remember me," he said, wagging his finger for some unknown reason.

"You're right," she said.

"Go on, have a guess."

"I have no idea."

"Go on, rack your brains, try to remember!"

"I don't know," she said, speaking slowly and taking extra care with the words in case he had missed her meaning.

"I'll give you a clue," he said, missing the point entirely. "Your grandfather and my father were brothers."

"You're my dad's cousin."

"Yes!" he said – almost cheered in fact. "Now do you remember?"

She looked at him and thought how amazing it was that he, like most of the people here, was the direct descendant of a race of super-magical Ancients, and yet it looked like he would have difficulty crossing the street without assistance.

"I have to go," she said, motioning over his left shoulder. He turned to look and she moved off to his right.

Valkyrie checked the time on her phone and found herself hoping that she'd get attacked by a pack of vampires sooner rather than later. This was a cruel and unusual ordeal she was going through, and if this turned out to be her last night alive, well then that just wasn't fair. She nodded to people she vaguely recognised, but walked right by before they had a chance to tell her how small she once was.

And then the Toxic Twins were blocking her way. Crystal's bottle-blonde hair was so straight it looked like it'd been ironed, and Carol's hair was hanging in ringlets that looked like a pack of worms trying to squirm to freedom.

"Thought you'd be here," Crystal said with much disgust.

"The family part of family reunion gave it away, huh?"

"Glad to see you didn't spend too long getting dressed up," Carol said and they both sniggered.

"Why are you even here?" Crystal asked. "It's not like we have any other rich uncles for you to suck up to before they kick the bucket."

"Oh, good, it's nice to know that you're finally over that."

The twins stepped in close and tried their best to loom over her. Not an easy task when they were both four centimetres shorter.

"You cheated us out of our rightful inheritance," Carol said, her lips curling unattractively. "That house Gordon left you should have been ours. Your parents had already been left the villa in France so *we* should have got the house."

"That would have been fair," Crystal snarled. "But he left it to *you*. You got everything. Do you expect us to just forget that?"

"Look at you," Carol said, flicking Valkyrie's shoulder with a finger. "You're a child, for God's sake. What do you need a house for? We're sixteen; do you know what we could do if we had that house? The parties we would have? Do you know how cool we'd be?"

"Do you even know how much that place is worth? We'd sell it and we'd be rich!"

"But we didn't get it, did we? You got it because you sucked up and you pretended to be the perfect little niece, and now you think you're so great."

"You're not great, you stupid little kid. You don't know anything, no one likes you, and look at you, you're not even that pretty!"

Valkyrie looked at them both. "You know," she said, "I'm trying to remember if there was ever a time when the rotten things you said actually affected me. I'm trying to remember if your amateur bullying ever actually worked, and you know what? I don't think it did."

Carol tried to laugh scornfully.

"Do you know why? Because I really and truly do not care. I don't have any feelings towards you at all, good or bad. To me, you're simply... *not there*. You know?"

They glared at her and Valkyrie smiled graciously. "Have a great night, OK?" And she left them there.

She moved through the crowd as best she could, squeezing

between tables and avoiding throngs wherever possible. She saw her mother and managed to get to her without someone trying to hug her.

"Steph," her mother said, smiling brightly. "You're here! Finally! How was last night?"

"It was good," Valkyrie lied. "Me and Hannah, you know, just stayed up chatting. Gossiping about, like, boys, and stuff." She faltered, suddenly realising she had no idea what girls her age talked about.

"And you wore the dress," her mother said. "It looks lovely."

"Lovely won't do me much good if there's a riot."

Her mother looked at her. "You are so odd sometimes. So when did you get here?"

"A few minutes ago. Where's Dad?"

"Oh, he's around here somewhere. You know what Edgleys are like. Any excuse to talk about themselves and they grab it with both hands. Having fun?"

Valkyrie shrugged. "Ah, it's OK. Don't know many people. What about you? Are you having a good time?"

Her mother laughed and leaned in close. "Get me out of here," she said with a brilliant smile.

Valkyrie blinked. "I'm sorry?"

Her mother nodded like she was agreeing enthusiastically. "I can't stay here one minute longer. I'm going to explode."

"You want to leave?"

Her mother waved to someone and looked at Valkyrie and kept the brilliant smile. "More then anything in the world. You see that lady over there?"

"The one with the strange-shaped head?"

"She'll talk about her dogs. All night. She has three. They're all small. What is it with small dogs? What's wrong with big dogs? I like big dogs."

"Are we getting a dog?"

"What? No. My point is, we should make up an excuse and leave early."

With Dusk and his Infected minions out there? Not bloody likely.

"We're here for Dad," Valkyrie said. "We've got to stay here and support him. He'd stay for *your* family reunion."

"I suppose..."

"It's only one night, Mum. After tonight you'll never have to see them again."

"I thought you'd be the first one bolting for the door."

Valkyrie shrugged. "I don't know. Sometimes I think I don't spend enough time with you guys."

Her mother looked at her and her tone softened. "You're

just growing up. I mean, yes, it would be fantastic if we could spend time together like we used to, but you need your space and your privacy. I understand that, love. Really."

"Do you miss the way it used to be?"

"I'd be lying if I said no. But I'll take what I can get. You spend a lot of time in your room and that's, you know, that's fine. You're distant sometimes, but that's fine too."

Valkyrie couldn't meet her eyes. "I don't mean to be distant," she said.

Her mother wrapped an arm around her shoulders. "I know you don't. And you're not *always* distant. At times like these, it's like nothing has changed. You're the same old Steph."

"But other times... I'm not, right?"

"Maybe, but I still love you no matter what. And your dad and me, we're just thankful that you're keeping safe. Other kids your age, they're out there getting into trouble, getting hurt, doing God knows what. At least *we* know where you are."

"In my room," Valkyrie said, trying a smile. She thought of the reflection, sitting on the sofa while her dad told a bad joke, or standing in the kitchen while her mother told it about her day. It made her feel rotten inside, all twisty, so she stopped.

After all, she had other things to be worrying about tonight.

32

SHADOW SHARDS

China walked quickly through the underground car park, her bodyguards on either side. It was quiet here and vast, and their footsteps echoed loudly.

One of her bodyguards, a man named Sev, stopped suddenly and looked back the way they had come. His eyes narrowed. "Something's wrong." His associate, a petite woman called Zephyr, took a gun from beneath her jacket.

"Miss Sorrows," she said softly, "please get behind me."

China did as she asked. The bodyguards were training their guns on a seemingly empty part of the car park. As far as China could see, there was absolutely nothing there that could pose any threat – but that was why she had hired them. They were good. They were the best.

Baron Vengeous stepped into the light. The armour looked to be part of him. Small trails of shadows danced at the seams, like they were still getting used to their new host. Vengeous wasn't wearing the helmet and his smile was cold. His cutlass hung from his waist.

Sev and Zephyr moved as one. The years they had spent fighting alongside each other had honed their skills, and when they were together there was no one who could stand in their way.

Until tonight.

Zephyr went to fire, but a shadow rose up. It struck her in the chest and she flew backwards, the breath rushing out of her. Sev got a shot off, and then the darkness sliced through him and he stiffened and fell. He was dead before he hit the hard ground.

Vengeous looked at China. "I *said* I'd be back for you. But tell me, before I have to hurt you, have you reconsidered your position?"

China's shoulders straightened and her voice became light, and she was suddenly as self-assured as always.

"You mean have I decided to come back into the fold?" she

said. "I'm afraid not. My reasons are both complex and varied, but can actually be reduced to something quite simple. I realised that you were all insane and highly irritating. You, in particular, annoyed me."

"You are a brave woman to be taunting me."

"I'm not taunting you, sweetie. I'm just really bored of this conversation."

The shadows moved at Vengeous's command and China twisted out of the way, the shadows skimming past and slashing into the car behind her.

Her laugh was birdsong. "If you want my advice, give it up. Lay down that ridiculous armour, put that Grotesquery thing out of its misery and walk back into that nice little cell they're keeping for you."

"I'm disappointed in you, China. The Faceless Ones are about to return and you could have been by their side."

Zephyr held out her hand and her gun flew into her grip and she fired, aiming for the head. The shadows became a cloud that covered Vengeous's face, soaking up the bullets and spitting them out again. When the gun clicked empty, the shadows settled.

"Please," Vengeous said, "tell me you have something more to offer."

Zephyr jumped up and clicked her fingers and a fireball rocketed across the space between them, but a wave of darkness reared up and swallowed it. Vengeous gestured and the wave smacked into her and she stumbled. She tried to push at the air, but a shadow closed around her wrist and yanked her off her feet. She slammed into a nearby car and the shadow flicked her, she hit the pillar and crumpled to the ground.

Vengeous turned back to China as if Zephyr had been nothing more than a pesky fly he'd had to swat. "Do you remember the stories we heard as children, about what the dark gods did to traitors? All of those stories will come true for you, betrayer. You will be my gift to them. You will have the honour of being the first life they consume."

China slipped off her jacket and let it fall. She breathed out and markings of the deepest black started carving through her skin. They spread over her bare arms, across her shoulders and neck, ran down her chest and trailed beneath her clothes. They carved into her face, twisting and settling into symbols, and she looked at Vengeous with those blue eyes, with those magnificent tattoos etched all over her body, and she smiled. Baron Vengeous smiled back.

China crossed her arms and tapped the matching symbols on her triceps. They glowed as she flung her arms out and a blue pulse shot at Vengeous, who deflected it with a shield of shadow. The shield turned sharp and it moved like a shark fin along the ground, and China intertwined her fingers and thrust out both palms. The symbols on her palms mingled and became a beam of dazzling light that burst through the fin, scattering bits of shadow.

Vengeous reached out with the darkness at his fingertips, wrapped them around a car. He stepped back and thrust his arms out and the car lifted into the air. China threw herself to one side. The car missed her by centimetres.

She moved forward, using the symbols on her body to hurl one attack after another, but Vengeous batted them all aside. Not once, but twice did he send a sneaky tendril of shadow to sweep her feet from under her, and each time she fell, he laughed. When he was close enough, Vengeous sent a slab of solid darkness smashing into her jaw. He grinned. He used the shadows to hit her again, and again she stumbled. The armour shifted, changed according to Vengeous's needs and intentions.

China's hair was a mess. Her make-up was smeared with blood and grime and her clothes were torn and dirty. Vengeous grabbed her and threw her, face first, into a pillar. She hit it and spun, dropping to the ground painfully.

Vengeous walked over, hunkered down, prodded China with

a finger. Her eyes flickered open, in time to see Zephyr rise up behind the Baron. The way she was holding her side, China knew the bodyguard's ribs were broken. But still she didn't give up. China allowed herself to admire her determination, as foolhardy as it was.

Zephyr charged at Vengeous, but the shadows turned sharp, and even as she was leaping they pierced her body from all sides.

She came to a sudden stop, suspended in the air by these shards of darkness that emanated from Vengeous' armour. China watched her try to take a breath, but her lungs were punctured, sliced through. Zephyr gagged on her own blood.

"No challenge," the Baron said. "No challenge at all."

The darkness convulsed and Zephyr's body tore apart.

33

THE CALM BEFORE
THE STORM

p on the dance floor, a portly man was throwing his wife around with gay abandon, twirling and twisting and having a ball, while his wife spent her time looking terrified. When she finally broke free she slapped his arm and went to storm off, but dizziness overtook her and she wobbled sideways and collided with another dancer, and it was like a glorious domino effect in slow motion, with extra squealing.

Something for Valkyrie to grin at, at least.

The band announced, in a loud muffle that was completely

distorted by the feedback on the microphone, that they were going to slow things down now. The band consisted of two gents in black slacks and blue sparkly jackets. One of them played saxophone, and he wasn't much good, and the other wore sunglasses and sang and played keyboard, and he didn't do any of those particularly well. That is to say, he didn't sing or play the keyboard particularly well – he wore sunglasses as competently as anyone who chose to wear sunglasses at night. None of this seemed to matter to a room full of drunken people who would dance to anything as long as they thought they recognised the tune.

There was a doorway leading to another room, presumably where all the tables and chairs were stored between functions. It was dark in here and Valkyrie didn't turn on the light. She put her coat on the remaining table and took a long box from its pocket. She laid the box next to the coat and opened it. She had asked Skulduggery to stop by Gordon's house on the way back. She'd told him there was something she had to pick up, and he hadn't inquired as to what that may have been. She was glad he hadn't asked. The Echo Stone glowed and Echo-Gordon faded up.

"Are we here?" he whispered excitedly.

"Be careful now," Valkyrie warned. "If anyone sees you..."

"I know, I know," Echo-Gordon said, inching towards the door. He peeked out. "Look at them all. It's been years since I've seen these people. I don't even know half of them." She stood beside him. He pointed.

"There's your mum. My, she looks beautiful. Will you tell her that?"

"Sure."

"And there's Fergus. And there's your dad. Oh, and Beryl. What's she doing? Her face looks strained. Is she having a stroke?"

"I think she's smiling."

He shook his head sadly. "Not a good look for her. And good God, where is that music coming from?" He moved slightly so he could see the stage and the two morons in blue. "Well, that's just... terrible. And there are actually people dancing? Horrific. I wouldn't be caught dead up there." He paused, thought about what he'd said and grinned.

Valkyrie moved to the window and glanced out, but it was too dark to see anything.

"Scared?" Echo-Gordon asked, his tone a little softer now.

She shrugged. "I don't like being bait for a vampire."

"There's a shocking piece of news," he said, smiling. "If you were to change your mind, Skulduggery would understand, you know. There's no shame in fear." She nodded, but didn't answer.

"I know him," Echo-Gordon continued. "He doesn't want to see you hurt, and I *certainly* don't want to see you hurt. Stephanie, or Valkyrie, or whatever name you go by. You are still my favourite niece and I am still your wise uncle."

She smiled. "You're wise?"

He pretended to be insulted. "So says the girl who's acting as vampire bait."

"Point taken."

She saw movement outside the door, someone coming in. She pointed and Echo-Gordon panicked, looked around for somewhere to hide and darted behind the door.

Carol and Crystal barged in, knocking the door open wider. It swung all the way until it was flat against the wall, having passed through Echo-Gordon completely. He now stood there in plain view, with his eyes closed. If Carol and Crystal were to look around, they'd see their dead uncle standing right behind them.

"Oh," Carol said, looking at Valkyrie. "It's you."

"Yes," Valkyrie said stiffly. "It is."

"Here with all your friends, are you?" Crystal said and the twins laughed.

Behind them, Echo-Gordon opened one eye, realised he

wasn't hiding behind the door any more and started to panic again.

"I'm just getting a break from everyone," Valkyrie said. "What brings you two in here?"

Echo-Gordon got on his hands and knees and crawled under the table, passing through the long tablecloth without disturbing it.

Carol regarded Valkyrie with half-closed eyelids, in what was presumably meant to indicate scorn. "We're looking for somewhere to light up," she said, producing the cigarette from her frightfully gaudy purse.

"You smoke?" Crystal asked.

"No," Valkyrie said. "Never really saw the point."

"Typical," Carol muttered and Crystal made a show of trying not to laugh. "We're going somewhere else then. Oh, and you better not tell on us, all right? You better keep your mouth shut."

"You got it."

The twins looked at each other triumphantly and walked out without another word.

Echo-Gordon stood up through the table and stepped out of it. "Ah, the twins. I'll never forget the day they were born," and his smile dipped as he added, "no matter how hard I try..." He noticed Valkyrie looking out of the window again.

He spoke kindly. "Fear is a good thing, you know."

"It doesn't feel good."

"But it keeps you alive. Bravery, after all, isn't the *absence* of fear. Bravery is the acknowledgement and the *conquering* of fear."

She smiled. "I think I read that on the back of a cornflakes packet."

Echo-Gordon nodded. "Understandable. That's where I get all my wisdom."

Valkyrie left the window, looked out of the door at her relations as they laughed and talked and drank and danced.

"I *am* scared," she said. "I'm scared of being hurt and I'm scared of dying. But mostly I'm scared of letting down my parents. Other kids my age, I can see it, they're embarrassed by their folks. Maybe the mother won't stop fussing or the father thinks he's funny when he's not. But I love my parents because they're good people. If we fail in this, if we don't stop Vengeous and the Grotesquery, then my parents—" and suddenly, unexpectedly, her voice cracked, "—will die."

The image of her uncle looked at her and didn't say anything.

"I can't let that happen," she said.

Echo-Gordon looked at her and she saw it all in his eyes, and he didn't need to say anything. He just nodded and murmured, "Well, all right then."

He looked back at the party, his broad smile returning, and he nodded. "It's time to put me back in the box, I'm afraid. You have things to do, don't you?"

"Yes, I do." She picked up the stone, placed it in the box.

"Thank you for this," Echo-Gordon said. "It was nice being around the family again. Reminds me just how much I don't miss them." Valkyrie laughed and closed the box.

"Be careful," he said and faded away.

She walked out to the function room. She saw her father talking with Fergus and another man. Her mother was sitting at a table, pretending to be asleep. Beryl stood alone, looking around like a startled heron. She spied someone she hadn't gossiped with and descended with alarming zeal. Carol and Crystal entered from another room. Carol was looking a little green and Crystal was red-faced with a coughing fit.

Valkyrie stepped through the glass doors, on to the small balcony, felt the fresh breeze and looked out over the dark golf course. Beyond the course were the dunes, and the beach, and the sea. Both hands resting on the balcony railing, Valkyrie took a deep, calming breath.

Something moved over the dark golf course. She blinked.

For a moment it had looked like a person, running and keeping low, but now there was no one there. Were this any other night, she might have been inclined to believe it was merely her mind playing tricks on her. But this wasn't any other night.

The vampire was coming.

34

UNFINISHED BUSINESS

Tanith sat in the Bentley and tried not to fidget. Her body wasn't used to sitting still and not doing anything. Skulduggery, sitting beside her, was a model of stillness and everlasting patience. She tried to relax, but every so often a shot of adrenaline would pump through her and her right leg would kick out involuntarily. It was very embarrassing.

They were parked on a slight bluff overlooking the putting green. From here they could see the golf clubhouse, but they were far enough away so that Dusk wouldn't recognise the car.

Once they saw anything suspicious, the Bentley would be able to speed down the narrow road and they'd be able to intercept the vampire before he even got *close* to the reunion. It was a good plan.

The moon was full and bright. Tanith checked her watch. The lunar eclipse was three hours away. Plenty of time to get what they needed to get and do what they needed to do. Hopefully.

Something hit the Bentley and the car shook. Tanith grabbed her sword and leaped out. Skulduggery was out the other side, gun in hand. An old man stood in the silver moonlight and looked at them. Tanith had never seen him before. He didn't look like one of the Infected. She started to relax.

"You lied to me," the old man said.

"You wanted to see the girl die," Skulduggery responded. "You got what you wanted." He wasn't putting his gun away. Tanith knew who it was now. She gripped her sword tighter.

The Torment's eyes were fierce. "It was a sham. I knew there was something wrong, but I had been in that cellar for so long I couldn't see it. It was a reflection, wasn't it? You did something to a reflection, improved it, so that it would fool me. You cheated."

"We don't have time for this. We've got a busy night ahead of us."

"Oh, yes," the Torment said with a smile. "You do."

He opened his mouth wide and a jet of black hit Skulduggery and knocked him back. Tanith tried to move away, but he turned to her and the stream of darkness struck her with such force it knocked her off her feet. She rolled, keeping her mouth and eyes shut. She heard the black stuff, whatever it was, splatter on the ground beside her. It was inky and foul-smelling, but it had substance and when she pulled it off her it came away in thick strips.

She opened her eyes, saw the Torment wipe his mouth and grin. She pulled away another strip of black, threw it down, where it joined the pool. And then the pool started to shift. It moved in on itself, bunched up and thickened and grew legs.

Lots of legs.

"Oh, hell," Tanith muttered as the black stuff formed into spiders and the spiders clacked.

Skulduggery clicked his fingers and hurled twin fireballs into the lake of scuttling blackness that was filling the ground before them.

Tanith's sword was out, slicing at the spiders as they leaped for her. The blade cut through their hard bodies and dark green blood splashed on to her tunic. She felt something on her leg and swatted at it, and another spider leaped on to her shoulder. She slammed the sword hilt into it and stepped back, stood on another spider that squished underfoot and she slipped. The ground went away and she was falling then she hit something solid and flipped over as she tumbled down the bluff.

Tanith rolled through long grass, burst through it to level ground, realised she was on the putting green. A few spiders had joined her for the trip and she looked up as they leaped for her. She fell back again, flicking her wrist, the sword-blade catching the moonlight. One of the spiders squealed. Tanith grunted with satisfaction.

She looked up at the bluff, to where the Bentley was parked, saw a wave of darkness blacker than the night spilling over and coming down towards her. Hundreds of spider legs clacking against stone and earth.

"I've got this," Skulduggery said from beside her right shoulder. She hadn't even heard him join her.

He stepped forward and raised his arms, like he was welcoming the wave of eight-legged killers. Tanith watched his fingers curl slightly as he took hold of some invisible thing, and then, ever so slowly, he moved his hands clockwise. The long grass swayed in the sudden breeze.

And then Skulduggery struck, his fingers tightening, his hands moving over each other in wide circles, and the spiders were lifted high off the ground. They spun in a whirlwind, more and more of them getting sucked in.

Tanith's sword dealt with the few that the whirlwind didn't trap, and then she stepped back and marvelled at Skulduggery's control. His hands moved faster and faster, in tighter and tighter circles, and the whirlwind narrowed and became a mass of churning black bodies. Then Skulduggery twisted his hands and the whirlwind folded in on itself, and the night was filled with terrible cracking sounds. Green blood, thick and heavy, spurted into the warm air.

Skulduggery dropped his hands and the mangled bodies of the spiders fell to the putting green.

"We have to get to Valkyrie," he said, turning towards the golf club. Tanith went to follow him, but stopped when he stopped.

The Torment was standing between them and the clubhouse, and the inky substance filled his eyes and rolled down his cheeks like tears. It ran from his nostrils and his ears and his mouth, and spread over his skin, in through his hair and his beard, covering his clothes and spreading further. His arms jerked, his hands becoming talons, and his shoes split as his legs grew and the blackness covered him completely. He arched his back and lifted his arms, and two pairs of giant spider legs burst from his torso, flexed and touched down. His limbs kept growing, and his body lifted off the ground as a third eye opened on his forehead and blinked.

He stopped growing. His eight legs clacked and his mouth was open wide and showing teeth. The Torment-spider looked down at them and chattered.

35

ATTACK OF THE VAMPIRES

Valkyrie walked from the party and went downstairs, passed the trophy cabinet and the golfing Wall of Fame, and as she approached the doors she saw someone standing just outside. The doors were glass, with stainless-steel handles, and the car park outside was supposed to be lit up – but right now it was in darkness. The lights must have shorted out.

The man wasn't moving. She could see his outline but not his features.

Valkyrie slowed. She could feel his eyes on her. The closer

she got, the more she could see. There were others out there with him, just standing there in the gloom. She stopped, looked at him through the glass.

The man reached for the handle and rattled the door, but it wouldn't open. This time of night, it was controlled by the door release button on the inside. If someone wanted to get in, they had to talk into the intercom, get a member of staff to come down and open the door. Dusk pressed his face against the glass door and looked at her. She could see his scar quite clearly.

She heard a window break somewhere else on the ground floor and she turned and ran back to the stairs, taking them three at a time. She burst into the function room, assailed by the music and the noise. She looked around for some way to secure the door, but there was nothing. There was no lock. She could barricade it, but how long would that last? And what would she tell everyone in here? What would she tell her parents? And where the hell was Skulduggery?

There had to be a way. Valkyrie needed to stop people from getting hurt, and she needed to do so without alerting anyone to the fact that they were in danger. She opened the door a crack.

The lights were out and the Infected were climbing the stairs. It was her they wanted. They'd ignore everyone else if they thought they could get her.

Valkyrie slipped out, making sure the door closed behind her and the people on the stairs saw her then bolted for the staircase, heading up to the top floor. Footsteps behind her, running, and she reached the top floor and glanced around quickly, getting her bearings.

Her adrenaline was pumping. The air shifted and she felt someone almost upon her. She ducked down and spun, bringing her right arm around in a wide arc to slam into the Infected man's back and send him flipping over her straightened leg. Another grabbed at her, and she batted the arms away and snapped her elbow into his chest. Her attacker crashed back. The others tumbled over him and snarled.

She sprinted down the corridor and barged into a dark room, almost tripping over a chair. The patio stood out against the darkness along the far wall and she made for that, the Infected right behind her. She pulled open the balcony doors and she ran out and leaped over the railing.

Wind rushed in her ears.

Directly below her, the Infected stood outside the glass doors, waiting for their Undead comrades to flush her out. They looked up in surprise, and saw her flying over them.

And then the tarmac-covered driveway was coming at her and she used both hands, trying to manipulate the air. She did her best to cushion her fall but this wasn't the easy drop from her bedroom window, this was much higher, it was at an angle, and she hadn't taken into account the sheer velocity...

She landed and cried out in pain as she rolled, knees and elbows striking the driveway, her hip scraping as she tumbled, her skin torn and bleeding. She knew she should have worn trousers.

The world rocked to a stop, balanced itself out and she opened her eyes. The Infected were standing looking at her, and Dusk strode through them, his eyes narrowed and his lips curled in hatred. And then Valkyrie was up and running.

She was sore, she felt blood on her legs and arms, but she ignored the pain. She looked back, saw the mass of Infected surge after her.

She passed the club gates and took the first road to her left, losing a shoe in the process and cursing herself for not wearing boots. It was narrow, and dark, with fields on one side and a row of back gardens on the other. She came to a junction. Up one way she could see headlights, so she turned down the other, leading the Infected away from any bystanders. She darted in off the road, running behind the Pizza Palace and the video store, realising her mistake when she heard the voices around the next corner. The pub had a back door that smokers used.

She veered off to her right, ran for the garden wall and leaped over it. She stayed low, and wondered for a moment if she'd managed to lose the Infected so easily. Dusk dropped on to her from above and she cried out. He sent her reeling.

"I'm not following the rules any more," he said. She looked at him, saw him shaking. He took a syringe from his coat and let it drop. "No more rules. No more serum. This time, there'll be nothing to stop me tearing you limb from limb." He grunted as the pain hit.

"I'm sorry I cut you," Valkyrie tried, backing away.

"Too late. You can run if you want. Adrenaline makes the blood taste sweeter." He smiled and she saw the fangs start to protrude through his gums.

He brought his hands to his shirt, and then, like Superman, he ripped the shirt open. Unlike Superman, however, he took his flesh with it, revealing the chalk-white skin of the creature underneath.

Valkyrie darted towards him and his eyes widened in surprise. She dived, snatched the syringe from the ground and plunged it into his leg.

Dusk roared, kicked her on to her back, his transformation interrupted. He tried to rip off the rest of his humanity, but his human skin tore at the neck. This wasn't the smooth shucking she'd seen the previous night. This was messy and painful.

Valkyrie scrambled up. The Infected had heard Dusk's anguished cries, and they were closing in.

36

GIANT SPIDER MADNESS

The Edgley family reunion was taking up the main function hall, at the front of the building, leaving the rear of the golf club in darkness. That was probably a good thing, Tanith reflected, as she watched Skulduggery fly backwards through the air.

The Torment-spider turned to her and she dodged a slash from one of his talons. She turned and ran, but he was much faster. Tanith jumped for the side of the building and ran upwards, a ploy that had got her out of a lot of trouble in the past, but then, she had never faced a giant spider before.

His talons clacked as he followed her up, chattering as he came. She stepped over the ledge, on to the rooftop, then turned and waited for him to follow. The spider legs appeared over the edge first, then the head and the torso, and Tanith lunged. Her sword flashed, but hit one of the armour plates that protected the Torment-spider's underside. His leg swept in and crashed against her, and Tanith lost the blade, hit the rooftop and rolled. She reached for her sword, but a talon stepped on it.

Tanith backed away. The Torment-spider chattered once more then went quiet. His three eyes, devoid of any recognisable human trait, observed her. She knew he could strike and she'd never see it coming.

"Excuse me," she said as politely as she could, "I believe you're standing on my sword." The Torment-spider didn't answer. She briefly wondered if he *could* answer, if there was any kind of rational being left in there.

"I don't think this is entirely fair," she continued. "You're angry with Skulduggery because he didn't kill Valkyrie, but you and me, we've never even met. I mean, you have no *reason* to attack me. You don't even *know* me. If you got to know me, if you took the time, I'm sure you'd really like me. I'm a likeable girl. Everyone says so." The Torment-spider chattered in a short burst.

"Did you know, and this is a fact here, did you know that most spiders are really, really ugly? It's true. The women spiders have a really hard time of it. I saw it in a documentary. Why do you think the black widow kills the guys she mates with? Shame, that's why. I'm not saying *you're* ugly. Who am I to judge? I've only got two legs, right?" The Torment-spider advanced. Tanith took another step back.

"I didn't mean to insult you. Did I insult you? I didn't mean to. I'm sure, for a giant spider person, you're quite the catch. And, hey, looks aren't everything, yeah? You know what us girls really go for? A sense of humour. And you look like a guy who is ready to laugh. Am I right?" The Torment-spider chattered angrily.

"I thought so. So now that we've had this little talk, what do you say we stop beating around the bush, and you come and have a go?"

The Torment-spider went quiet again and Tanith smiled up at him.

"If you think you're hard enough."

A moment passed then the Torment-spider reared up, ready to strike, and Tanith sprinted towards him, dived between the legs that were still supporting his weight and snatched up her sword.

The giant spider scuttled around and Tanith slashed

upwards. Her sword raked across the armour until it found the space between the plates. The Torment-spider squealed and thrashed, and Tanith threw herself out from under him to avoid being crushed.

She felt a gust of wind and Skulduggery dropped on to the rooftop. He splayed his hands and the air pulsed, catching the Torment-spider on its underside and flipping him over. He landed on his back, his eight legs kicking and flailing. Tanith leaped in, landed on the spider's belly and stuck the tip of her blade in between the armour plates.

The Torment-spider stopped flailing instantly.

"Good boy," Tanith said.

Skulduggery walked around so he could see the Torment-spider's eyes. "I'm assuming, because you know when to stop struggling, that you're still capable of logical thought, so I'm only going to say this once. You either get in line or you get out of our way. We have a job to do tonight, and right now my partner is in danger and I have run out of patience. So what do you want to do – continue fighting or make a deal?"

For a second, Tanith didn't think Skulduggery would get an answer, but then that mouth opened and an old man's voice croaked from between those teeth.

"I'm listening."

37

TOOTH AND CLAW

Valkyrie sprinted for the next wall and leaped over it, into the garden. There was a higher wall ahead and she ran and snapped her hands out. The air rippled and she was propelled upwards, grabbing the top of the wall and hauling herself over. When she landed the garden was dark, the wall casting a deep shadow over the grass. She ran up by the side of the house and beyond.

She was on a narrow road now and turned left, her lungs burning with a fierceness she liked, the kind of fierceness she felt when she was swimming. She knew she could run forever with that fire inside her. She veered off on to an even narrower road, more like a lane than anything else. She could hear them behind her. The pack of Infected was more dispersed now, but the faster ones were steadily gaining. She passed her house.

The pier was just ahead and Valkyrie sprinted for it. The sea was rough tonight, she could hear its strength, and she knew this wasn't going to be easy, but she didn't have a choice. They were right behind her.

Did they know? Had Dusk told them about their vulnerability to salt water? A thought flashed into her mind. These weren't full vampires, they were only Infected. Would the water still have the fatal affect? She didn't have time to second-guess herself. This was the only plan she had and the only chance she had left.

Valkyrie ran to the edge of the pier and jumped, just like she had done on countless occasions when she was a child. She hit the water and it clutched at her and swallowed her completely. She kicked and shot back to the surface. She lost her other shoe. It was too dark for the Infected to see what was below them and they had no idea there was only one safe way to make that jump. Valkyrie heard sudden cries of pain mixed with sickening thuds as they landed, just like J. J. Pearl, smashing their bones on the rocks.

She'd never swum here at this time of night, however, and the waters were strong and strange to her. They pulled and pushed and threatened to drag her down, or away from the shore, but she fought them. More of the Infected came, splashing into the water all around her, and immediately they began to panic. She heard their cries, choked off by their rapidly constricting windpipes. One of them reached out in desperation, grabbing her and pulling her down.

Valkyrie's head went under and she twisted, prying the fingers from her arm and kicking the Infected person away from her. She lost sight of him in the cold blackness, but she was too far down and the water was too rough. She was going to drown.

An image flashed into her mind – the previous year, Skulduggery rising from the sea and walking across its surface. Her training. She needed to use her training. Skulduggery had taught her what she needed to know. She just had to calm down and focus.

Ignoring the pain in her lungs, Valkyrie brought her hands in close. She felt the current that was trying to drag her downwards, felt its strength and speed, but stopped fighting and let it take her, surrendering herself until she was a part of it. She hooked her fingers and for the first time became aware of the water as a mass of conflicting and opposing forces. She could feel these forces beneath her, above her and around her. She hooked into them and then she turned.

The current twisted behind her and now she was swimming, buffeted by the water. She passed the Infected as they flailed and she broke the surface, taking a deep breath. She thrust her arms out and caught the current again, went under, and for a terrible second thought she had misjudged this whole thing, but she regained her control, and guided the current as best she could towards the beach. She let go and the water around her turned gentle – relatively gentle – and she swam on until she could stand.

Gulping in lungfuls of air, Valkyrie looked back at the pier. It was hard to see because of the lights that faced her making everything before her one solid black mass. She dragged herself out of the sea. The tide was in so there wasn't much beach for her to stagger on to, but she managed to stumble on to the shore that remained. And then something came out of the shadows and struck her and she hit the sand.

She struggled and twisted, but someone else was there and a fist hit her face. The shape of a man, standing above her, crouching slightly.

Dusk.

The human flesh he had tried to remove still clung in places to his vampire skin, and it looked raw and red and painful. His right hand was tipped with talons, but his left was human and still had a watch strapped to its wrist. His face was the face of a man, a handsome man who now had a scar, but the fangs of a vampire had split his gums and torn his lips.

Valkyrie flexed her fingers, waited until her head was clear. Dusk wasn't moving. She thrust her hand out and now he did move, grabbing her wrist before she had the chance to push at the air. He hauled her up and spun her around, grabbed her from behind and exposed her throat. Valkyrie froze.

The vampire's laugh was guttural. "I'm not going to kill you. I'm going to turn you. You will be like I am."

She tried to speak, tried to say something, but her words had been taken from her. She felt his breath on her skin.

"Do you know who you're going to kill first, Cain?" he asked. "Do you know who you are going to rip apart, because the bloodlust will be the only thing that matters? Your parents."

"No," she breathed.

"For what you've done to me, for the scar you've inflicted and the pain you're causing me right *now*, I'm going to make sure that when the time comes, you'll be *begging* me to let you kill your own parents."

And then a voice. "Dusk."

The vampire turned and there was someone there, in the dark, leaping at them. Valkyrie felt an impact and fell forward. She heard the vampire hit the sand and snarl. She looked back as the two figures clashed.

The one who had saved her – she had thought it was Skulduggery, but saw now that it was not – was fast, as fast as Dusk. He wore a ragged old suit and a battered top hat.

Dusk swiped and the figure in the top hat ducked, his own fingernails raking across the vampire's belly, drawing blood. Dusk roared in anger and the figure flipped, driving a foot into his face. Dusk dropped back then suddenly lunged. He caught the newcomer in mid-leap, taking them both into the surf. Claws slashed and the man in the top hat cried out.

Valkyrie grabbed a stone, flat but thick and heavy. Dusk was on his feet, above the newcomer, and Valkyrie ran at him, slamming the stone on to the back of his head. Dusk dropped slightly and the newcomer kicked up, catching Dusk full in the face.

Valkyrie felt the air between them and she splayed both of her hands, hitting Dusk in the back and taking him off his feet. He splashed into the waves. The newcomer was on his feet, and suddenly sprang straight up, disappearing into the dark.

Dusk was rising out of the water, his human face contorted

with hatred. His mouth, which had been tightly closed against the salt water, opened in a snarl. He couldn't see the man in the top hat, but he glared at Valkyrie and moved towards her. At the last moment he looked up, in time to see the newcomer dropping down on top of him. The newcomer's heels slammed into Dusk's upturned face and the vampire crumpled into the wet sand.

Valkyrie watched the man in the top hat examine his wounds and mutter.

"Is he dead?" she asked.

"Naw," he answered, a little out of breath. "Just sleepin'." He spoke with a thick London accent. "Savin' people ain't normally my thing, but I figure since he was after you, you've got somethin' to do with Vengeous, am I right?"

"Well... I'm trying to stop him, yes."

"Good enough. See, they roped me into doin' 'em a favour. Didn't appreciate that. So here I am, doin' *you* a favour. That big guy, the ugly one? They're keepin' him at Clearwater Hospital. Don't know what you can do with that information, but if it messes up Sanguine's plans then I'm happy." He doffed his hat to her and started to walk off. She frowned.

"You're Springheeled Jack."

He stopped and turned. "Yes, I am, love."

"You're a bad guy."

His smile was unpleasant. "Right again."

She stepped back. "You're meant to be in prison. Tanith put you there."

Jack frowned. "You know Tanith Low?"

"Of course."

"She's... she's close?"

"She's somewhere around here, yes. She's with Skulduggery."

"Oh, bloody 'ell," Jack said, looking around nervously. "Oh, that's not good. 'Ave I just helped 'em?"

"I'm afraid you have."

"Oh, for... oh, for 'eaven's sake. Well that's just... That's just typical, that is. Don't tell either of 'em I was here, right? I saved your neck. Literally, your neck I saved. Promise me."

"Are you going to leave the country?"

"I'm leavin' now."

"Then I'll tell them tomorrow. If any of us are still alive."

"You're a right lady, you are. G'night now. And good luck."

And with a leap and a bound, Springheeled Jack was gone.

38

THOSE ABOUT TO DIE...

The earth's shadow was starting to creep across the face of the full moon. The convoy stopped on a quiet road. Engines were cut and headlights snapped off. The Cleavers jumped from the back of the trucks, making not one sound as they lined up and waited for instructions.

Valkyrie swung her leg off Tanith's bike and took off the helmet. She was nervous. Her palms were sweating and her teeth wouldn't stop chattering.

"Feeling OK?" Tanith asked, keeping her voice low.

"I'm good," Valkyrie lied. "I'm grand. We're just, you know, we're about to fight a *god*, like."

"Part of a god," Tanith corrected. "Parts of other things too."

Valkyrie looked at her and shook her head in wonder. "You're actually looking forward to this, aren't you?"

"Hell, yeah. I mean, fighting a *god*, part of a god, hybrid god, whatever. As you say, this is big. This is *major*. I've fought all kinds over the years, but... a god. Assuming I survive this, where do I go from here? What would top fighting a god?"

"I don't know," Valkyrie said. "Fighting two gods?"

The Bentley pulled up and Skulduggery and Mr. Bliss got out. Skulduggery took off his coat and scarf and left them in the car. He and Bliss approached and the Cleavers stood to attention. Valkyrie had to fight down the irrational urge to salute.

"Billy-Ray Sanguine and the Grotesquery are in a derelict hospital just north of here," Bliss said, addressing them all. "The vampire known as Dusk is currently in our custody, but the whereabouts of Baron Vengeous are still unknown. We can assume that he is on his way. He wouldn't want to miss the return of the Faceless Ones."

"I want you all to know," Skulduggery said, "that we are the first line of defence. In fact, we're practically the *only* line of defence. If we fail, there won't be a whole lot anyone else will be able to do. What I'm trying to say is that failure at this point isn't really the smart move to make. We are *not* to fail, do I make myself absolutely clear? Failure is bad, it won't help us in the short term and certainly won't do us any favours in the long run, and I think I've lost track of this speech, and I'm not too sure where it's headed. But I know where it started and that's what you've got to keep in mind. Has anyone seen my hat?"

"You put it on the roof of the car when you were taking off your coat," Valkyrie said.

"Did I? I did, excellent."

"We will attack in two waves," Bliss said, steering the briefing back into the realms of relevance. "The first wave will consist of Tanith Low, Valkyrie Cain, Skulduggery Pleasant and myself. The second wave will be you Cleavers."

"We're seizing our chance *now*," Skulduggery said, "before Vengeous returns and we have a battle on two fronts. The first wave will weaken the Grotesquery. We're going to hit it with everything we've got, and not give it any time to teleport away or to heal. Once we know that it is damaged, we'll call in the second wave. Does anyone have any questions? No? No one? No questions? You sure?"

Bliss turned to him. "There do not seem to be any questions."

Skulduggery nodded. "They're a fine lot."

Bliss gestured and the Cleavers divided into groups, and Valkyrie and Skulduggery strode away.

"I used to be so good at that kind of thing," Skulduggery said quietly.

"Well, my morale is certainly boosted," Valkyrie informed him.

"Really?"

"God, no. That was *terrible*."

Tanith and Bliss joined them and they stepped into the trees. Valkyrie moved as stealthily as she could, but the others were moving in complete silence. She glimpsed Cleavers all around, their grey uniforms mixing with the gloom and the darkness until they became mere hints of people.

They stopped just inside the treeline. Ahead of them, past an old metal fence, was the main hospital building. The black jeep was parked outside and Sanguine emerged from the hospital doors, holding a phone to his ear.

"OK," Sanguine said, his voice clear in the quiet night, "I can hear you better now, go ahead."

As Sanguine listened to whatever was being said on the

other end of the phone, Valkyrie glanced at her companions, suddenly realising that Skulduggery was no longer with them. She looked back at Sanguine.

"So that's it then?" he was saying. "I just leave? Naw, that ugly critter is back there, standin' around and not doin' a whole lot."

Valkyrie narrowed her eyes, squinting into the darkness behind Sanguine. She saw something move. Skulduggery.

Sanguine continued talking, totally unaware of the Skeleton Detective sneaking up behind him. "I'm pretty sure the vampire's taken care of, we don't have to worry about him any more. And what about our friend the Baron?"

Valkyrie frowned. *Who* was Sanguine talking to?

"You sure?" he was saying. "You don't want me to...? No, no, I ain't questionin' you, I just... Yeah, I know who's payin' my salary. Hey, no skin off my chin, if that's the way you want it. I'm walkin' away now." He put the phone in his pocket and smirked.

"Have a nice life, Baron," he said softly, then turned and walked straight into Skulduggery's fist.

He staggered and went for his knife, but Skulduggery chopped at his wrist and his fingers sprang open, sending the knife flying. He swung a punch and Skulduggery caught him and smacked his head off the jeep. Sanguine slumped to the ground. Skulduggery picked up the knife and flung it away, then motioned for the others to join him.

They broke from the treeline. The large gate had already been blasted open and they moved through it, up to Skulduggery. He had Sanguine's phone in his hand and he was checking through it.

"Whoever that was," he said, "their number is blocked."

"Sanguine's been taking orders from someone else the whole time," Tanith said. "The persons in power you were talking about earlier, the ones who got Guild on to the council, the ones who took away all our support. He's working for *them*."

"And Vengeous doesn't know about it," Valkyrie said.

Skulduggery put the phone away. "That's a mystery for tomorrow," he said. "Providing there *is* a tomorrow."

He turned to Bliss and nodded. Bliss took a little run and then leaped, caught the edge of the roof and effortlessly pulled himself up. Tanith adjusted her centre of gravity and walked up the wall after him. Skulduggery held Valkyrie around the waist and the air shimmered as they shot upwards, gently touching down on the roof. Keeping very quiet, they crossed the rooftop.

There were four big, sturdy old buildings surrounding a large concrete courtyard. The courtyard had a small island of green where a spindly tree tried to grow.

The Grotesquery stood in the exact centre, unmoving. It was wearing a garment of sorts, made of thick, black leather that hung from its waist and gathered on the ground behind it.

Out here in the moonlight, the Grotesquery seemed even more wrong. Nothing this horrible should be allowed to exist on a night so beautiful. Its right arm glistened and the sac on its left wrist bulged with yellow acid. The silver light displayed its cracked and splintered ribcage in sickening detail, and black blood soaked the bandages covering its face.

Valkyrie and her companions crouched. The Cleavers took up positions all the way along the rooftop, surrounding the courtyard. Valkyrie's stomach churned. Her fingertips tingled. She needed to do something and soon. The anticipation, the excitement and the dread and the fear, were overpowering. Their first encounter with the Grotesquery had not ended well, but there were more of them now. They were stronger – but it was stronger too. She wondered if they were strong enough to kill it.

It was like Skulduggery was reading her mind. "This thing," he said softly, "the part of it that is a Faceless One, it died once. It can do so again." She nodded, but didn't speak. She didn't trust her voice.

Skulduggery looked over at Mr Bliss and he nodded, and then Mr Bliss stood, stepped off the edge of the roof and dropped all the way to the ground. Tanith ran down the side of the building, sliding the sword from its scabbard. Skulduggery and Valkyrie jumped, displacing the air beneath them to ease their descent. Valkyrie landed heavily, but managed not to stumble.

"I thought we were going to use the element of surprise," she said as they strode towards their target.

"We never had it," Skulduggery said calmly. "It knew we were here all along. It just doesn't care."

All four of them moved apart, coming at the Grotesquery from different angles.

Bliss didn't waste time with words, threats, vows or demands. He just walked right up to it and threw a punch. Valkyrie felt the concussion of the blow as it landed. The Grotesquery didn't even stagger. Instead it looked at Bliss through its filthy bandages, drew back its right fist and hit him. Bliss was launched backwards and crashed through the wall of the old building.

Skulduggery moved in and Tanith leaped, her sword flashing in the moonlight. The Grotesquery's right arm unravelled and its talons sliced towards Skulduggery. They cut his jacket then wrapped around him. He was picked up and swung towards Tanith. She twisted in mid-air and sprang off Skulduggery's shoulder, flipping over the Grotesquery's head. Skulduggery broke free and the Grotesquery reformed its arm and swung its massive fist. Skulduggery drew in the air to block it and Tanith slashed at the arm, which healed instantly.

Valkyrie clicked her fingers, turned the sparks to fireballs and threw them. The first missed, but the second exploded against the Grotesquery's side. Its stinger darted and Tanith ducked then lunged, her sword piercing its chest, but the Grotesquery smashed down on her arm and the bone snapped. Tanith cried out and was shoved away. The Grotesquery removed the sword and dropped it, and the wound healed.

Bliss extricated himself from the hole he had made in the side of the building. He dusted himself off, like being thrown through a wall was a mere minor inconvenience, but the first step he took was unsteady. He'd been hurt.

Skulduggery reached into his jacket, pulled out his revolver. Then he reached in with the other hand, to the other side, and pulled out an identical revolver. He thumbed back both hammers and fired. Twelve shots, hitting the Grotesquery with unerring accuracy, and then he dropped the guns and ran forward. Valkyrie saw something in his hand, a metal cylinder attached to a metal spike.

Skulduggery jumped, stabbing the spike into the area he'd been shooting. The Grotesquery took hold of him and flung him back, but the cylinder had a red light on top and it was flashing. The explosion sent Valkyrie to her knees, her ears ringing, spots dancing before her eyes. She looked back, hopeful, but the Grotesquery was standing there as if nothing had happened. A wound on its arm opened for a split second, enough for a drop of black blood to leak out, but then it closed. Was it weakening?

Tanith gathered her strength and sprang, but the Grotesquery batted her away. Her body twisted as she fell and when she hit the ground, she tried to get up again but couldn't.

The Grotesquery raised its left arm and Valkyrie dived. She held both hands out towards Tanith, felt the spaces between them, felt how they linked together, and when the stinger darted out she pushed and the air rippled. Tanith was sent skidding along the ground and the stinger missed. Valkyrie looked up, realising that she was now the Grotesquery's main focus of attention.

"The Cleavers," Valkyrie whispered. "Somebody signal the Cleavers..."

And then Bliss was there, standing between Valkyrie and the approaching Grotesquery. Instead of striking, Bliss pressed both hands to its chest and started to push. The creature kept walking. Bliss locked his body, but he was being driven slowly back. Valkyrie could hear him straining. Not even Bliss's legendary strength could stop it.

And then, amazingly, it faltered. Bliss gave another heave and the Grotesquery was actually forced to take a step back.

Tanith made herself get up on one knee and finally stand. The Grotesquery had stopped walking altogether and now seemed to be examining Bliss. It held up its left hand close to him.

"Tanith?" Bliss said through gritted teeth. His face was drenched with sweat. "If you wouldn't mind..."

Tanith looked quickly to Valkyrie. "Sword."

Valkyrie reached out, felt the air around them, used the air to close around the fallen sword and then she twisted her wrist and the sword flew from the ground into Tanith's left hand. Tanith was already swinging when the stinger darted, her blade intercepting it before it could reach Bliss.

The tip of the stinger fell to the ground. Valkyrie and Tanith stared down at it.

"I hurt it," Tanith said in disbelief.

"About time," Bliss muttered, drew back his right hand and let loose with an almighty punch that sent the Grotesquery reeling.

"Cleavers!" Bliss roared. "Attack!"

39

FACING VENGEOUS

The Grotesquery flailed and struck out and three Cleavers were flung away, but there were more to take their place.

Skulduggery and Valkyrie stood together. Tanith cradled her broken arm. Bliss had taken a step back to catch his breath. They watched the Cleavers attack and it was a sight to behold. They moved as a perfect team, silently and without the need for orders. They knew what they had to do, and they backed each other up, compensated for injuries, reinforced and provided distraction. The Grotesquery was not granted a single moment to recover.

Valkyrie saw the growth on its left wrist contract, spitting acid. It caught a Cleaver full in the chest and he went down, trying to tear his coat off, but dying before he was able. The Grotesquery's right arm unravelled again, and all five talons plunged into another Cleaver and then tore out. The Cleaver was thrown through the air like a rag doll.

A slice across the Grotesquery's tendon made it stagger. Another slice, across its back, splattered the ground with black blood. It lashed out wildly, struck nothing but air and stumbled to one knee. The Cleavers swarmed over it as it tried to heal itself.

And just when things were going right, everything went wrong. There came a voice from behind them – "*Heathens!*" – and they looked around. Baron Vengeous had returned.

He stood on the same rooftop they themselves had stood on, and the shadows whipped around him angrily. His armour shifted, became sharp, and when he walked forward, the shadows snaked over the edge and down to the ground. He strode on darkness and the darkness lowered him to the courtyard.

The Cleavers broke off their attack. The Grotesquery was on its knees. Its body was trying to mend the wounds it had suffered. It didn't get up.

"How dare you!" Vengeous thundered as he stalked towards them. "How dare you attack a *living god!*"

"It's not a god," Skulduggery said. "And it won't be living for much longer."

Valkyrie looked closer at the shadows around Vengeous. There seemed to be a clump of darkness trailing after him. Suddenly the darkness unwrapped and let its captive go and China Sorrows tumbled to the ground. Vengeous left her in his wake.

Bliss went to meet him. "You will go no further," he said.

"Then stop me," Vengeous snarled.

"That is my intention," Bliss said and punched.

Vengeous held up a hand, collecting shadows to form a barrier. Bliss hit the barrier and they all heard his knuckles break.

The armour shifted, reinforcing Vengeous's fist, and he smiled as he delivered a punch of his own. The blow caught Bliss beneath the chin, lifting him and sending him hurtling back.

Skulduggery lifted his gun and fired, aiming for the head. The shadows became a cloud that covered Vengeous' face, soaking up the bullets and spitting them out again. When the gun clicked empty, the shadows settled.

"Well, that didn't work," Skulduggery muttered.

"Cleavers," Tanith said, gripping her sword, "we have a new target." She ran forward and the Cleavers sprang. Vengeous held his arm out straight.

"Oh, damn it," was all Skulduggery had time to say before a wave of darkness erupted from Vengeous's hand and slammed into Tanith and the Cleavers. Skulduggery grabbed Valkyrie and dragged her down, the darkness passing above them. She glimpsed everyone else slump to the ground, unconscious.

There was a moment of stillness and then Vengeous reached out his arm, and a streak of shadow wrapped around Skulduggery and pulled him closer. Valkyrie felt something tighten around her ankle and then she was skidding along the ground, into the middle of the courtyard. The shadow released her and she rolled to a stop beside Skulduggery. Vengeous looked down at them.

"I am almost impressed. You actually managed to hurt the Grotesquery. I didn't think you'd be capable of such a feat."

"We're full of surprises," Skulduggery said and sprang. A sliver of shadows smacked him down. He groaned and rolled over. "That obviously wasn't one of them."

"None of you understands yet, do you?" Vengeous said. "You are no longer a threat. I am the most powerful sorcerer on this planet. When the Faceless Ones return, I will rule by their side. What hope do you have against me?"

Skulduggery stood and Valkyrie got to her feet by his side.

"Baron Vengeous," Skulduggery said, "I'm placing you under arrest."

Vengeous laughed. Valkyrie looked beyond him, at China, who was moving slightly. Her white trousers were slashed and torn, and her waistcoat was dirty and bloodied.

"Here we are at the end," Vengeous said, "and I'm wondering, have you, unlike China, learned your lesson? Are you ready to accept that the world belongs to the Faceless Ones? Are you ready to praise their name?"

"They're not here yet, Baron," Skulduggery said.

"But they're coming. You must realise that. The Grotesquery will call them and they will know the way back. And correct me if I'm wrong, but you seem to be out of reinforcements."

"Who says we need them?" Skulduggery asked and snapped his hand out. The air rippled and Vengeous stepped aside and flung back his arm. A wave of blackness hit Skulduggery and took him off his feet.

Valkyrie ducked under a return swipe and scooped up two small pieces of rubble. She brought her hands together, acting on pure instinct, and felt the air around them and *pushed*, the pieces of rubble shot at Vengeous like bullets. He sent shadows to intercept them and they exploded in dry clouds of dust. He pointed at Valkyrie and the shadow slammed into her.

"So, so easy," he laughed.

The shadows were on her again, wrapping around her, picking her up and moving her back, slamming her against the wall. She felt the cold darkness seep through her clothes and tried to move, but couldn't.

Skulduggery hit the wall beside her, the shadows pinning him. "You're nothing without that armour," he said.

Vengeous smiled at his prisoners as he walked over. "Is this the part where you goad me? Where you insult my honour? This armour is a weapon, abomination. I'm hardly going to abandon my weapon right before the killing stroke, just so I can give my opponent a sporting chance. If my enemy is weakened then my enemy will be destroyed. Such is the way of the dark gods."

"Please don't kill me!" Valkyrie blurted.

"Valkyrie," Skulduggery said. "Don't worry, I'll get us out of this."

"He won't get you out of anything," Vengeous said. "You seem to have chosen the wrong side, my dear."

"Then I'll *change* sides!"

Vengeous smiled, amused. "Do you hear that, abomination?

Faced with the reality of the situation, your protégé has abandoned you."

Skulduggery shook his head. "Valkyrie, listen to me..."

"What?" Valkyrie snapped. "Are you going to tell me it'll be all right? Are you going to tell me to be brave? He's going to kill us! Baron, please, I don't want to die! Let me prove myself! Let me kill him for you!"

"You'd do that?" Vengeous asked. "Kill your mentor? Murder him in cold blood?"

"It's not murder if he's already dead."

Vengeous considered the proposal. "I suppose there is a certain poetry to it. Very well, Miss Cain. You get to be the one to kill him."

The shadows withdrew and Valkyrie dropped to the ground. She wiped her eyes with her sleeve and looked at Skulduggery, who was now hanging there quite limply.

"How do you intend to kill him?" Vengeous asked.

"I think I know how," she answered. "Something he said a while ago. Something about his weakness."

Vengeous motioned for her to come forward and she moved unsteadily to his side. She faced Skulduggery and raised her arms. "I'm sorry," she said.

Valkyrie closed her eyes, drew her hands into claws and

pulled her arms in close to her body, making the air shimmer around her, and then she twisted to Vengeous, but he smacked her arms away and grabbed her by the throat and lifted her off her feet.

"Did you really think I was that naïve?" he laughed as she kicked at the armour. "Such a clumsy attempt. If this is the best the abomination has taught you, you really should have asked for a better teacher."

Her hands closed around his wrist and she lifted herself, easing the pressure off her throat for a moment. "You're a military man," she managed to say. "You should recognise a feint when you see it."

"Oh, is *that* what this is? You distracted me long enough to get into the perfect position, is that it?"

"Precisely," she answered. "And now comes the moment when I launch the attack and beat you down."

He laughed again. "Well, pardon the expression, Miss Cain – but you and what army?"

Valkyrie gave him a smile, took one hand away from his wrist and pointed over his shoulder.

"That one," she said. He looked around as China Sorrows stepped up behind him.

40

FIGHT TO THE DEATH

China's whole body was covered in swirling black tattoos. Vengeous threw Valkyrie down and she watched China dodge an attack, tapping matching tattoos on her legs. They glowed green beneath her torn trousers and now she was a blur, weaving her way past Vengeous's shadows.

He snarled in annoyance and lashed out, but she was too fast, and now she was in close. Some of the tattoos glowed red, she grabbed him and punched and Vengeous was taken off his feet.

His shadows curled around him and let him down gently then they shot at China. She clapped her hands together and the tattoos on her palms touched and mingled and a yellow barrier went up. The shadows struck the barrier and China grunted, but the barrier held.

The shadows around Skulduggery started to fade, as Vengeous' attention was focused elsewhere. Skulduggery broke free and dropped to the ground. He moved to Valkyrie, grabbing her arm.

"We have to get out of here," he said urgently.

"But we can help—"

"We can't stop him, he's too powerful."

"We're just going to retreat?"

"We're not retreating, we're advancing in reverse. Stick with me and stay low."

They sprinted for the main hospital building. Valkyrie looked over at the battle, saw a trail of shadows sneak around behind China, attack the barrier from there. The barrier was weakening. China dropped to one knee, her hands still flat against each other.

Valkyrie held on to Skulduggery, the air rippled and they shot up to the rooftop.

"We can't just leave her!" Valkyrie said as they ran.

"Agreed," Skulduggery said. "But we can't beat him when he's wearing that armour, that much we know. We need to find a way to get that armour off."

"What? But the only way we could do that is by getting in close, and we can't get past those shadows!"

"Exactly. So we need to cheat."

They jumped down the other side, landing beside the jeep, and found what Skulduggery was looking for.

"Ah," Valkyrie said. "Clever."

"Naturally."

Valkyrie crept across the rooftop. The battle was over. Unconscious Cleavers lay all around, the Grotesquery was still trying to heal itself, and China was hurt and on her knees. Baron Vengeous was standing behind her, gazing at his armoured hands.

"I can see why someone would choose necromancy," Vengeous was saying. "It has its limitations of course, but for the sheer *thrill* of using it against one's enemies... It's hard to beat.

"I fought alongside Vile during the war. I never liked him. He was... different. He had secrets. But I knew he was powerful. I just never realised *how* powerful. Nothing compared to the

Faceless Ones obviously, but still... potent. And now, that power is mine."

"You're not..." China muttered.

"I'm sorry? I didn't quite catch that."

Valkyrie stayed low and kept moving, getting closer.

"You're not in his league," China said, finding the strength to speak. "Vile... was extraordinary... You just wear his clothes."

"I wield his power," Vengeous said. "I wield the power of necromancy."

"It isn't yours," China said, and she laughed and it sounded brittle and painful. "You're right. Vile *was* different. He could have used his power to... to change the world... but you, Baron? You wouldn't know where to begin."

The victorious smile had drifted from the Baron's face. He gathered darkness in his hands. "I should have killed you years ago," he said.

The darkness hit China and flipped her over and then Billy-Ray Sanguine erupted from the ground behind Vengeous with Skulduggery Pleasant clinging to his back and holding a gun to his head.

Skulduggery threw Sanguine away and dropped his gun, grabbing Vengeous in a chokehold before he could even turn. Valkyrie leaped off the roof and displaced the air beneath her as Sanguine straightened up. She landed and focused, splayed her hand and he shot back off his feet.

Vengeous twisted violently, but Skulduggery held on. Valkyrie heard a small click amid all the curses and and she saw the armour's chest-plate open and a mist of darkness burst forth.

Vengeous screamed in rage and tried to pull away, but Skulduggery had a good grip on the chest plate. He threw it to the ground and Vengeous stumbled forward. Darkness leaked from the armour and dissipated in the night air.

Vengeous extended a hand and the shadows whipped for Skulduggery, but they were frail and slight. Skulduggery broke them and moved in, hitting Vengeous in the sternum with the heel of his palm. Vengeous gasped and staggered, tried again, but the shadows missed Skulduggery entirely this time, and the detective went low and to the side, raking an elbow across Vengeous's ribs and then driving it back and down into his kidney. Vengeous's knees buckled and he hissed in pain.

Something moved in the corner of Valkyrie's eye and she turned just as Sanguine rammed into her. He took her off her feet and she hit the floor. He was standing right over her, reaching down, and she punched the side of his knee. It hurt her fist, but hurt him more, and she rolled and got up, but he grabbed her again, hands on her throat.

She punched him in the gut, in the jaw, but he shook it off and grinned, fingers tightening. She punched him square on the nose and he howled and she grabbed his little finger and wrenched. He howled again and let go. She booted him in the groin and he gasped and reached for her then doubled over as the pain hit.

Vengeous got Skulduggery in some kind of lock that would have torn the muscles and sinew of a man with muscles and sinew. Skulduggery wriggled out of it and went to work with his elbows, slamming them like bullets into Vengeous's face and body.

Sanguine moaned in pain and went to get up, and Valkyrie grabbed him from behind, pressing his own straight razor against his throat.

"So that's where it is," he said, trying to pull back from the blade, but Valkyrie held him tight.

"Don't even try to do your disappearing act here," she warned him. "The moment I see the ground start to crack, you're dead."

The laugh that escaped his lips was dry. "You can't kill me, darlin'. You're one of the good guys. That'd be murder."

She pressed the blade in deeper. "See if I care."

She looked around as Vengeous snatched up his cutlass. The

blade flashed as Skulduggery held up his right hand to protect himself, and it sliced through his upper arm. He cried out and fell back, his severed arm falling to the ground, still wrapped in its sleeve. Vengeous kicked and Skulduggery went down, and Vengeous stood over him, cutlass raised.

"Baron!" Valkyrie shouted. He looked over, cutlass frozen in mid-swing. "Put the sword down."

Vengeous laughed. "Or what? You'll cut Sanguine's throat? Go ahead."

"I'm not kidding. I'll do it."

"I believe you."

"I'll do anythin'," Sanguine pleaded. "I'll go away, I'll never come back, I'll never see you again, I swear."

Vengeous looked faintly disgusted. "Try dying with some dignity, you godless wretch."

"Shut up, old man!" Sanguine shouted.

Vengeous laughed. "Look up, girl. It's almost time."

Valkyrie looked up at the clear night, at the full moon. The Earth's shadow had almost covered it.

"Can you feel it?" Vengeous asked. "The world is about to change."

Valkyrie felt a hand close over her own and suddenly Sanguine was twisting and she went right over his shoulder, landing in a tumble, the straight razor gone from her grip. She turned, ready to defend herself, but Sanguine took a look at the situation and then looked back at her, folded the razor into his pocket and sank through the ground.

Vengeous smiled at her then looked down at Skulduggery. "The eclipse is almost upon us, abomination. The Faceless Ones are coming. Everything I have planned, everything I have dreamed of, is being realised. You have failed."

"Not yet I haven't," Skulduggery muttered.

"What are you going to do?" Vengeous mocked. "Have you a clever surprise in store for me, up your sleeve? Be careful now, you only have one left."

"Then for my next trick," Skulduggery said and then faltered. "Ah, sod it, I couldn't be bothered thinking up something smart to say. Valkyrie."

Valkyrie clicked her fingers and hurled a fireball. It struck Vengeous in the chest, and the clothes he wore under the armour were set alight. Vengeous cursed and used the shadows to douse the flames. The revolver skimmed across the ground into Skulduggery's left hand and he fired.

The cutlass fell. Blood started to trickle from Vengeous's burnt chest. Vengeous could only stare down into Skulduggery's empty eye-sockets.

"But... but this isn't how I'm supposed to die," he said weakly. "Not... like this. Not by your hand. You're... you're an abomination."

"I'm a lot of things," Skulduggery said and dropped his gun.

Vengeous staggered back. He saw Valkyrie, reached for her. There was no strength in his grip. She pushed him and he fell.

Vengeous crawled to the Grotesquery. "Tell them I'm sorry," he whispered. "I've failed them..."

The Grotesquery moved its hand so that it touched Vengeous's face. It looked almost tender, until the hand gripped and wrenched and the Baron's head snapped to one side. The Grotesquery let go and the body crumpled.

The Grotesquery struggled to its feet. The last of the moon's brightness slipped into shadow. The Grotesquery stood, and although it looked unsteady, it didn't fall.

Skulduggery tried to rise, but couldn't. He snapped his fingers but no spark came. "Fireball," he said to Valkyrie. His voice was strained, sounded weak. "Shoot a fireball into the sky. It's our last chance."

She frowned, not understanding the request, but obeying nonetheless. Her thumb pressed to her index finger and they slid off each other with a *click*. The friction made a spark, she caught the spark in the palm of her hand and then it was a flame. She poured her energy into it, made the flame bigger, dipped her shoulder for the wind up and then threw. The fireball went straight up into the night, burning brightest at its peak, and then faded to nothing. She looked back at Skulduggery.

"That should do it," he mumbled and let himself collapse.

"What do I do now?" she asked, but he didn't answer.

She picked up Tanith's sword and looked over at the Grotesquery.

"Hey," she said. It turned to her and her mouth went dry. Everyone else had fallen. She was on her own.

"I overestimated you," a voice said and Valkyrie turned. The Torment approached, stepping over the prone bodies of the Cleavers. "I overestimated all of you. I thought you'd be able to manage this on your own."

The fireball. It must have been a signal, calling upon the last piece of back-up they had. Valkyrie briefly wondered what Skulduggery had had to agree to in order to enlist the Torment's services. She was pretty sure it wasn't anything cheerful.

"Leave," the old man said. "I don't like being this close to you. Leave me to take care of this creature."

"I'm not going anywhere," Valkyrie said, her words scraping from her throat.

"Then stand aside," he snapped, "and allow me to clean up your mess."

"*My* mess?"

"This monstrosity would not be alive if it wasn't for you and the blood that is in your veins. Your very existence is a threat to every living thing on this world."

It was an argument she didn't have the time nor the inclination to win, so Valkyrie backed off. She watched as the inky liquid leaked from the old man's eyes and ears and nose and mouth. She watched his arms and legs turn black and grow long, and the spider legs burst through his already-ripped shirt. She watched an eye open in the middle of his forehead and his torso lift off the ground, and she watched the Torment-spider look down at the Grotesquery with a pitiless gaze.

"Hello, monster," he said and vomited blackness.

The blackness hit the Grotesquery and it stumbled as the blackness grew and became spiders. The Grotesquery reeled, spiders all over its body, attacking as one.

The Grotesquery caught one of the spiders in its massive right hand and squeezed, the spider burst. The Torment-spider scuttled after it, swiping with his front leg, catching the Grotesquery across the back. The Grotesquery hit the ground, bursting the spiders beneath it, and the Torment-spider stabbed downwards. The tips of two legs pierced the Grotesquery, pinning it where it lay.

And then it vanished and the air above the Torment-spider opened up. The Grotesquery dropped on to the Torment-spider's back. The Torment-spider reared up, trying to dislodge his attacker, but the Grotesquery had him in its grip now. Valkyrie saw the stinger dart out, but its point had been severed and it rebounded uselessly off the Torment-spider's armour plates.

The Torment-spider was cursing, the panic turning the curses into shrieks. The Grotesquery's right arm unravelled, the strands wrapping around his throat, pulling him back, making him rear up higher. The Torment-spider stumbled over the bodies of the Cleavers and the Grotesquery yanked back hard, and he tipped over. He landed on his back, his eight legs kicking in the air. The Grotesquery was slow to get up, but it was getting up nevertheless. The Torment-spider, however, was unable to roll on to its side.

"Help me!" the Torment-spider screeched.

Valkyrie felt the sword in her hand. If she could get to the Grotesquery before it stood, she might have a chance. But her legs wouldn't move.

The Torment was shrinking. His spider legs were retracting into his body, his own arms and legs reforming, the blackness absorbed through the pores of his skin. Valkyrie watched the race between the Torment, trying to reassert his human guise in order to get up, and the Grotesquery, who was now on one knee and struggling to stand.

The Grotesquery won the race by three seconds. It looked down at the Torment, now a pale and weak old man, helpless at its feet. Its huge right hand reached down, picked the old man up by his long hair, held him off the ground. The Torment moaned in pain.

Valkyrie looked down at her leg and willed it to move. One step. All she needed was to take one step, the first step, and the rest would take of itself.

Her leg moved. She took the step. The Grotesquery swung its arm and Valkyrie heard a tearing noise and the Torment was flung away.

The Grotesquery dropped the piece of scalp in its hand, turning to Valkyrie as she lunged, swinging the sword and cutting into its left arm. It grabbed for her but she ducked under and spun, using the sword the way Tanith had shown her, and the blade found the Grotesquery's side and opened it up.

Valkyrie skipped back, holding the sword in both hands, her eyes on the wound she'd just inflicted. She watched the parted skin try to reform, try to heal, then stop altogether.

The Grotesquery growled. Its right arm unravelled and came at her. One of the strips wrapped itself around her ankle and yanked her off her feet. She fell and the other strips darted at her. A talon ripped open her cheek and she felt her own warm blood splash across her face.

She reached forward and the sword sheared through the strip around her ankle. The Grotesquery recoiled, the strips snapping back, trying to reform the arm. The middle finger was missing.

Valkyrie jumped up, swinging the sword diagonally across the Grotesquery's chest, lopping off sections of splayed ribcage. Another swipe took the Grotesquery's left hand. It fell to the ground.

The Grotesquery backed off, flailing at her to keep her away. She waited for her chance and dived. The sword slid between the damaged ribcage and the Grotesquery stiffened. Valkyrie gripped the hilt with both hands and angled it downwards, towards its heart, and she rammed it in deeper and twisted. The Grotesquery screamed.

The scream hit her like a fist and darkness poured from the Grotesquery's injuries. It slipped into her and her legs gave out and she collapsed. She felt the darkness move within her, racking her body with pain. Her spine arched. Images flashed into her head, images of the last time she had felt such agony. Serpine, pointing at her, his green eyes starting to fade, his body turning to dust.

Her muscles started to spasm and she retched and gagged and tried to cry. And then the darkness left her and she opened her eyes, tears blurring her vision, watching the darkness rise from her, rise into the air and dissipate. She gulped in a breath.

"Are you OK?" she heard Skulduggery ask from somewhere far in the distance.

She raised her head. The Grotesquery was on the ground, unmoving. Little pieces of darkness still drifted from its body. She rolled over, up on to her elbow. "Ow," she groaned. "That was sore."

Skulduggery walked over slowly. He had picked up his severed arm and was now holding it out to her.

"Here," he said. "Let me give you a hand."

She decided not to respond to his terrible, terrible joke, and allowed herself to be helped to her feet. She touched a hand to her face, felt the blood that was still running from the wound. Her cheek was numb, but she knew that wouldn't last. The pain was about to hit.

"We didn't die," she said.

"Of course not. I'm too clever to die and you're too pretty."

"I *am* pretty," Valkyrie said, managing a grin.

"My, my," said a familiar voice from behind them. They turned.

"Look at what you've done," Sanguine said, shaking his head with mock severity. "You have foiled our insidious little plot. You have emerged triumphant and victorious. Curse you, do-gooders. Curse you."

"You don't seem too upset that you've lost," Valkyrie said.

He laughed and took off his sunglasses. He started to clean them with a handkerchief. "What, you think this is over? You actually think this is finished? Li'l darlin', it's only just *begun*. But don't fret, I'll see you both again real soon. Y'all take care now, y'hear?"

He put the sunglasses back on as the ground beneath his feet started to crack, and as he sank down into it, he blew Valkyrie a kiss.

After a few moments, when they were sure he wasn't going to pop back up, Skulduggery looked at her.

"So that plan worked out well," he said.

"Skulduggery, your entire plan consisted of, and I quote, '*let's get up close and then see what happens*'."

"All the same," he said, "I think the whole thing worked out rather beautifully."

41

BILLY-RAY SANGUINE'S ERSTWHILE EMPLOYER

illy-Ray Sanguine sat in the shade and watched the pretty girls walk by. The square was alive with people, with chatter, with the glorious aroma of food. It was a beautiful day and he was halfway up the mountains in the walled town of San Gimignano, enjoying a fine cappuccino.

A pair of stunning Italian girls walked by, looked at him and giggled to each other. He smiled and they giggled again.

"Behave yourself," said the man sitting beside him.

Sanguine grinned. "Just admirin' the scenery."

The man put a thin envelope on the table, placed one manicured fingertip on top of it and slid it across.

"Your payment," he said, "for a job well done."

Sanguine looked inside the envelope and, quite unconsciously, he licked his bottom lip. He put the envelope in his jacket.

"It worked then?"

The man nodded. "Did Vengeous suspect?"

"He hadn't a clue," Sanguine sneered. "Guy was so caught up in himself he never imagined he was bein' played. Not for a moment."

"He used to be a fine ally," the man said sadly.

"Yet you had no hesitation in lettin' him take the fall for you and your little group."

The man raised his eyes and Sanguine forced himself to not look away. "The Diablerie needed to remain unseen," the man said. "We have too much at stake to risk being uncovered so soon. However, now that the Grotesquery has fulfilled its purpose, that need is coming to an end."

"You knew Vengeous wouldn't succeed, didn't you?"

"Not at all and we did everything in our power to help him."

"I don't understand," Sanguine said, leaning forward slightly. "The Grotesquery didn't open no portal. It never got the chance to bring the Faceless Ones back. I mean... didn't your plan fail?"

"The Baron's plan failed. Our plan is quite intact."

"I don't... how?"

The man smiled. "It called to them. Its death-scream called to the

Faceless Ones. Our gods have been lost for millennia, barricaded outside our reality, unable to find their way back. Now they know where we are." The man stood, and buttoned his jacket. "They're coming, Billy-Ray. Our gods are coming back. All we have to do is be ready to open the door."

The man walked from the table and the crowd swallowed him. A few moments later, through a brief gap, Sanguine saw him standing with a woman, and the gap closed over and they vanished.

Sanguine let his cappuccino go cold. Once, he had worshipped the Faceless Ones, but eighty years ago he'd realised that if they returned and took over he wouldn't particularly enjoy it. Still, a job was a job, and he didn't let his own political or religious beliefs interfere, and besides, the Diablerie was a group who paid well. His hand drifted to his jacket pocket, to the slim envelope secreted there, and all misgivings fled from his mind. He stood and left the table, walking in the direction of the two pretty Italian girls who had passed him.

43

BAD THINGS

The heat broke and the rain came with the night. Valkyrie sat down by the pier, her coat slick and wet. It wasn't the black coat, the one that kept saving her life. This one was deep blue and it had a hood that she wore up. Her jeans were soaked. She didn't care.

It had been two days since they'd faced Baron Vengeous and the Grotesquery at Clearwater Hospital, and despite Kenspeckle's science magic, Valkyrie still ached. The gash on her cheek had healed up without even a scar, and all the other cuts and bruises had faded away to nothing, but her body was stiff and tired. She was alive though, so whenever something hurt, she didn't complain – she just felt glad that she was able to feel *anything*.

Haggard was quiet and sleeping. The sea came in against the pier and bucked against it, like it was trying to dislodge it, maybe grab it and pull it down into its depths. The air was fresh and she breathed it in, deep and slow and long. She didn't close her eyes. She kept her gaze on the water until she heard the car.

The Bentley stopped and its headlights cut off. Skulduggery got out, walked over to her, his coat flapping in the breeze. The rain spilled over the brim of his hat and dripped to his shoulders.

"Still keeping watch?" he asked.

Valkyrie shrugged. "Not all of Dusk's vampires were infected at the same time. There may have been one or two, freshly infected, that the water didn't kill. If nothing pops out at me by tomorrow night then I'll believe that they're all dead."

"And then you'll sleep?"

"I promise." She looked up at him. "How's your arm?"

He showed her his right hand and wriggled his gloved fingers. "Reattached and getting back to normal, thanks to Kenspeckle. We've had a rough few days."

"Yes we have."

"Did Tanith come and see you?"

Valkyrie nodded. "Came by earlier on her way to the airport. She told me Mr Bliss was taking care of the Grotesquery, taking it apart and stuff."

"Taking it apart, separating it into all its original components then chopping it up, cremating and scattering the remains. It's safe to say that the Grotesquery won't be returning. Or if it does, it'll be in really, *really* small pieces."

"And Vile's armour?"

Skulduggery hesitated. "Thurid Guild has it. Apparently, he plans to hide it away where no one can ever use it for evil again."

"Do you believe him?"

"I believe he plans to hide it away until he has a use for it."

Valkyrie got up so that she was standing beside him. "Are you still fired?"

"I am."

"But don't they see that it was *his* greed and *his* stupidity that helped Vengeous escape in the first place?"

Skulduggery's head tilted. "Who are *they*? There *is* no *they*. Guild is the Grand Mage, *he's* the one in charge. There is no one to watch the watchmen, Valkyrie."

"There's us."

He laughed. "I suppose there is."

There was a gust of wind that blew her hood down. She didn't fix it. "So what are you going to do?"

"I'm going to do what I've always done – solve crimes and save the world, usually with mere seconds to spare. Although granted, this time it was *you* who saved the world. Well done, by the way."

"Thanks."

"We'll get by. It won't be easy, operating without the Sanctuary's resources, but we'll manage. There is something larger at work here. It isn't over."

Valkyrie's hair was plastered to her scalp, and the rainwater ran in sheets down her face. "Sanguine's mysterious bosses."

"Indeed. Someone is working behind the scenes, keeping out of the spotlight as much as possible. But I fear that time is coming to an end, and we need to be ready for whatever happens next." He looked at her. "Bad things are coming for us, Valkyrie."

"That seems to be what bad things do, all right."

With the wind and the rain, she almost didn't feel it, but she saw the way Skulduggery tilted his head and so she examined the sensations that the air brought to her skin. The air currents twisted and writhed, but there was a space behind them that the air buffeted, in the same way that the sea buffeted the pier.

They turned slowly and saw the vampire. Its arms were sinewy and veins stood out against its wet, white skin. It was hungry, yet to feed, and it was having difficulty breathing. But it had survived and now it was looking for its first prey. It bared its fangs and its black eyes narrowed. Muscles coiled.

It came at them through the rain and Skulduggery was moving, taking his gun from his coat, and Valkyrie summoned a flame into her hand and prepared, once again, to fight.